Fanny N. D Murfree

Felicia

A novel

Fanny N. D Murfree

Felicia
A novel

ISBN/EAN: 9783337027315

Printed in Europe, USA, Canada, Australia, Japan

Cover: Foto ©Andreas Hilbeck / pixelio.de

More available books at **www.hansebooks.com**

FELICIA

A NOVEL

BY

FANNY N. D. MURFREE

BOSTON AND NEW YORK
HOUGHTON, MIFFLIN AND COMPANY
The Riverside Press, Cambridge
1893

FOURTH EDITION.

The Riverside Press, Cambridge, Mass., U. S. A.
Electrotyped and Printed by H. O. Houghton & Co.

FELICIA.

I.

THE Reverend Robert Raymond prided himself, in a seemly and clerical fashion, on his tact. So innocent and candid was this endowment as he possessed it that it was distinctly apparent, and the disaffected of the congregation construed him as a scheming man, unduly versed in the ways of the world for a clergyman. Among the persons who interpreted him more justly was a young girl, who sat near him, one summer morning, in a large parlor on the shady side of the house. The welcome watering-carts rumbled up and down the street, giving to the air the taste of sudden. showers; the breeze waved the curtains, stirred the plants in the balcony, and wafted freshly into the room the odors of heliotrope and geranium.

Mr. Raymond looked with some admiration at the brilliant face, with its background of fluttering lace and flowers. He was one of those men whose attitude toward women is something of the paternal, at once protective and indulgent; he found a certain charm in their caprices, and just now the evident petulance of his wife's young cousin induced not so much tolerance as approval.

"Oh, it's all very well for you to preach, cousin Robert" — she cried.

"So some people think," he interpolated, with a laugh.

— "about duty and obedience, and all that; but what is *my* duty? — that's what I want to know."

If he had told her the exact truth, he would have said that in his opinion it was her duty to be charming, like the blue sky, the sunshine, the tints on that rosebud against the gray stone there. But it will not do even for a clergyman to always speak his whole mind, so he sedately replied that her duties would probably define themselves distinctly enough as the years went by, and he did not doubt she would be very faithful in their performance.

"I do hope I shall know what they are," she declared, with animation. "Now, what am I to do? Nothing pleases papa. He was determined, he said, that his only daughter should have all the advantages that money could command, and he gave them to me, and I fully availed myself of them. Now," culminatively, "he is not satisfied."

The Reverend Robert Raymond said to himself that the old Judge must be hard to please if he were indeed dissatisfied with the result of his investment. To speak disrespectfully of the Chancellor behind his back was a privilege claimed by many people besides the lawyers whom a hard fate compelled to practice in his court. A notable metropolitan school, the regimen of regular hours, diet, and exercise, and a carefully devised curriculum had returned to him, as a finished product of feminine education, this young woman of twenty-two, of fine mind, manners, health, and morals, sufficiently well grounded in useful branches, moderately accomplished in the modern languages, music, and painting, with an exceedingly lively and cultivated imagination, and with keen appreciation and consummate tact in all matters pertaining to dress and personal adornment. The possession of this last talent was manifest in her fresh and well-chosen morning toilette, — white, sparsely trimmed with delicately fine embroideries and a few knots of purple ribbon. There was a distinct arrogation of simplicity, but the minuteness and perfection of detail showed that a taste for the ornate in decoration was only held in subjection by the laws of the appropriate. She was very pretty. A flush on her face accented the fairness of her complexion; her eyes, so deeply blue that they were almost purple, were downcast and shaded by dark lashes; her parted lips — the upper one particularly delicate, sensitive, and well cut, curving downward — showed a line of small white teeth; her nose was straight and noticeably narrow from the point to the line of the nostril, —· this, with the oval of her face, gave her a look of much refinement; her hair, a red-brown, almost auburn, was brushed back, but close about her brow the heat had curled sundry tendrils that had a tinge of gold; when she looked up and laughed, dimples were apparent in the soft rose of each cheek.

"I am growing very cynical," she cried. "I am sour and disappointed." Then she looked down again and pouted. She understood human nature well enough to know that she might pout as much as she chose in cousin Robert's presence.

"In what, may I ask, are you disappointed?" he demanded, with due gravity.

"In life," replied Miss Felicia Hamilton, sententiously.

"That's sad," said cousin Robert.

"In life," she repeated, this time vivaciously. "It promises one thing, and it offers another. I am educated to one set of views, and when I have developed what mind I have according to them, suddenly I am expected to conform to another set, entirely different. This was the way of it, cousin Robert." She bent upon him a smile calculated to win to partisanship a more obdurate heart than his, and continued with a delightful show of confidence: —

"You see, when I was young — quite young, I mean, ten years ago — I was a little bookworm; very intellectual, I assure you, though you might not think it now. I read everything; I was very precocious. I cared nothing for the other young girls and their amusements, or pretty things to wear, or music, — only for books, books. Papa said that was all wrong. He did not want me to grow up shy, and absorbed, and awkward. He wanted me to shine in society, to be elaborately educated, and have fine manners. So he sent me to Madame Sevier, and there I remained ten years, even during the vacations. She and the rest of them did their duty, and I tried to do mine. Now, what do you think papa says? That I am frivolous and spoiled; that I care too much for dress and society, and am not domestic *at all!*" — with much exclamatory emphasis of pretty eyes and lips, — "and don't love home. Frivolous, — that's what he calls me!"

Two tears rose to the violet eyes that rested on cousin Robert's face, and his heart was hot within him against the absent Judge.

"Your father expects you to be 'domestic' after ten years with Madame Sevier?" sarcastically commented this wise clerical confidant and spiritual pastor.

"And we saw a great deal of very fashionable society with Madame Sevier," resumed the young lady suddenly, and with much vivacity. "And in summer she had directions to take me to the mountains and the seashore, — Newport, Saratoga, the White Mountains. We went — everywhere. She knew — everybody; that is, everybody worth knowing. Now, is that the kind of training to fit a girl for a sleepy little Southern country town like Blankburg?"

"Any young men?" inquired cousin Robert, demurely.

She looked at him expressively.

"Such sticks!" she said, concisely.

Cousin Robert's face betrayed no amusement. It was a long, thin face, with bright gray eyes, a hooked nose, some premature wrinkles, a straggling mustache, fine teeth, a large mouth, and occasionally a brilliant smile. His lank figure was disposed in a comfortable attitude in an easy-chair, and his white hands, with their slim, nervous fingers, rested on its arms. His hat and cane ornamented a table near by, and his wife's parasol was on the sofa. This was not a pastoral call, merely a prolonged cousinly visit.

"Why are they sticks?" he asked.

"Divinity students," she replied, with a certain scorn. Then, with an abrupt resumption of her smooth manner, "Don't you think, cousin Robert, that such men are very young? I don't mean in years, — some of them are not very young in years, — but in experience. They are rather — well, raw, you know, or perhaps crude."

"I think 'raw' is the word you want," he said. "They are apt to be raw till some such young lady as you takes them in hand, when they generally get done very brown indeed."

She did not reply directly to this. Men like cousin Robert have only themselves to thank if their feminine acquaintance regard them as chiefly useful in preventing conversation from degenerating into monologue.

" Papa considers it very unseemly that I do not rate those young men more highly. He says they are well read, and cultivated, and all that. Of course they are. It is their *métier* to be cultivated. But they know books, and nothing else. They don't know life ; they don't know human nature. Those young men talk books until I am ready to perish : Herbert Spencer, and systems, and refutations, and everything in books, from Pliny up and down. Now, I am tired of Pliny. I have heard all I want to hear about Pliny ; I used to read about Pliny myself, a long time ago, — when I was young. Papa can't understand all that. He thinks a town with a flourishing theological school is the very place to please a young woman with a cultivated understanding. And among them all I find it dull in Blankburg, — dull as the grave."

" I hope you do not find society in this city so dull as in Blankburg," said cousin Robert, sympathetically.

" So far as I can judge, being a stranger," she replied, demurely, her manner conveying an intimation that a visitor's verdict must of necessity be favorable, " society here may be very pleasant. Now, you must understand, cousin Robert," she added, with a sudden return of liveliness, and bending upon him convincing eyes, " I am not a missish young woman, eager to meet an Adonis with a dark mustache. I don't want to fall in love, and I don't want to marry any one " —

" Very, very magnanimous," murmured cousin Robert.

— " but I want to see some interesting people; men who know life, and politics, and the world, and society." She seemed conscious of a little vagueness, for she added, after a moment's reflection, "I can't explain exactly what I mean. I think I mean men who are intellectual and not eager to display the fact, and polished but not priggish, and who observe instead of expecting others to observe them. I don't care if they are young or old, married or single, American or foreign. I only want them to be interesting. That doesn't seem too much to ask of human nature, does it ? "

Cousin Robert admitted that it did not, and added that if the congregation of St. Paul's offered any of the material she approved as entertainment, he might venture to promise that it was at her disposal.

She glanced at him archly.

" Will you warrant them ignorant of Pliny ? " she asked, mischievously. Then she turned again to the window.

Her companion had observed that her attention had very slightly wandered during the last few seconds, as her eyes had rested on some object apparently advancing down the sidewalk. He leaned forward, looked out, and suddenly drew back, with palpable annoyance expressed on his face.

Two ladies, who had been discussing 🐖 the back parlor a supposed cabal of the disaffected against the Reverend Robert's tenure of office, — their conference gaining much of confidential effect from the employment of a mysterious undertone and acquiescent nods when words failed, — now entered the front room. Mrs. John Hamilton, a plump little lady, with a brilliant complexion and round, intent eyes, might have seemed always listening, so serious was her expression and so marked her general air of attention and responsibility. Mrs. Raymond, on the contrary, seemed irresponsible, inattentive, and inconsequent. She was much younger than her husband, was fair-haired, blue-eyed, and childish and indefinite in manner. She looked about vaguely for her parasol, and when she had secured it strolled to her husband's armchair, and leaned against it, with her elbows on its back.

"Is n't it time for us to go home, dear?" she suggested.

And now came the emergency which drew on cousin Robert's store of tact.

Her attitude gave her a glimpse of the street, and of a gentleman at this moment traversing the crossing.

"Why, Robert, there is Hugh Kennett!" she exclaimed, suddenly.

The gentleman on the crossing raised his eyes; they gravely met those of Miss Hamilton; in another instant he had passed out of sight, and she looked back into the room. Mr. Raymond had at length relinquished the armchair, and was standing with his back to the window, in such a position that, as he rose to his feet, he must have prevented the passer from recognizing either him or his wife. This fact, his neglect of Mrs. Raymond's question, and the swift, significant glance that he gave her did not escape the attention of our observant young lady; she recognized cousin Robert's adroitness. She speculated a little on the subject. "Did he want me not to see that they know that gentleman?" she said to herself. Cousin Robert was not the sort of man to manœuvre causelessly in trifling social emergencies; yet he had clumsily attempted to ignore the existence of his friend. "That was an odd thing," thought Felicia, puzzled.

Shortly after this the visitors took their departure, and as they walked up the street Mr. Raymond gave his wife a little warning.

"Amy, be careful how you mention Kennett before your cousin. She is very young and impressionable, and it is undesirable that she should become interested in him. She knows very few pleasant people here, and he is an extremely agreeable sort of fellow, and " —

"That is an excellent reason why he should be mentioned," said little Mrs. Amy, with the air of seeing both sides of a question.

"Oh, good gracious!" ejaculated the Reverend Robert Raymond, like any other exclamatory miserable sinner, "think of the old Judge."

"I forgot the Judge," said Amy, quickly and apprehensively. "I will be careful."

People thus unexpectedly reminded of the Judge were apt to hurriedly concede the point, and to wear for some time an anxious and depressed air.

II.

FOR a number of mornings previous to the one herein commemorated, Miss Hamilton, whose habit it was to sit, with some slight resource in the way of fancy-work, near one of the windows which opened upon the quiet suburban avenue, had observed a tall, sedate stranger advance along the opposite sidewalk, cross the street, and disappear from view. Perhaps her attention was attracted because of the regularity of this episode; perhaps because his appearance approximated her somewhat exacting ideal; perhaps because the first time she saw him he was looking at the window with a certain expectancy. Among the accomplishments she had acquired under Madame Sevier's tutelage was not the grace of humility. The idea was instantly suggested that he had before seen her here, and was on the lookout for her. This flattered her and piqued her curiosity, — all the more because of the regular recurrence of the phenomenon about the same hour. He was a grave man, twenty-five or thirty years of age; handsome in a certain sense, but not in the style that usually attracts the favorable regards of young girls. He had deeply set gray eyes, an aquiline nose, a large, firm chin, a finely chiseled

mouth and flexible lips, about which were lines
that showed a capacity for varying expression.
The strong lower jaw, and broad, high forehead
gave the face a certain squareness. He was clean-
shaven, and his light brown hair was clipped close
to a shapely head. He wore a well-fitting suit of
light cloth, and a straw hat. He was tall, well
proportioned, and — as an experienced observer
could easily have seen — in good training from the
standpoint of athletics. He walked slowly, but at
an even pace, looking neither to the right nor the
left; and there was nothing, apparently, which
broke the monotony of his methodical progress
down the street except the momentary interest
with which he glanced at the front window of the
corner house.

Now, if there had been any recognizable be-
trayal of such interest at this stage of the affair,
or any attempt to inaugurate an acquaintance,
the matter would have abruptly terminated, and
Hugh Kennett would have had only the view
of John Hamilton's closed window-blinds for his
pains; for the young lady, with all her caprice,
her somewhat exaggerated self-esteem, — to put it
mildly, — and her love of excitement, was fastidious, and a devotee to externals. It pleased her
that he should look with covert eagerness toward
the house, that he should distantly and respect-
fully admire her, and that she should subtly divine his admiration. Since, however, the vanity
which receives homage as due is more exacting

than the vanity which asserts a claim, the affair was not likely to go further but for the interposition of accident.

The accident was of an obvious and simple nature — merely an afternoon call.

"I think I should like to take the phaeton and go over to see Amy," remarked Miss Hamilton to her sister-in-law, one day, "provided I can secure the society of the festive Frederick."

It was the habit in the Hamilton family to allude to the eight-year-old son of the house with a sort of caressing mockery, in phrases of doubtful value as witticisms, but of humorous intent.

Mrs. Hamilton replied that it was a pleasant day for the trip, and that the horse and phaeton were entirely at their service.

The "festive Frederick" was four feet high and fractious. To find him was a matter of difficulty. When found, he declared tumultuously that he would rather die than go to call at cousin Amy's, — a reckless assertion, since he was mounted on a bicycle, and destruction seemed to menace him at every yard of his tottering progress. There was a swift exchange of argument and counter-argument. The nephew deftly reclined on his tall steed against a convenient treebox, his distorted shadow stretching along the sidewalk among the dappling similitudes of the maple leaves. A golden haze was in the air; down the vista of the street might be seen a vast spread of clustering roofs; spires caught the light and glittered.

" Very well," said Felicia at last. " I dare say I can go alone. Sometimes there are cows on the streets; probably I shall meet some; and if cousin Robert is not at his house, or if he is too busy to drive me home, I may have to come back by myself."

There was a pause. The boy on the bicycle wore a troubled and thoughtful air.

" They have a good many fires in this city," continued the young lady, discursively, " and when the engines bang a gong and tear along they always frighten me. However, perhaps I can take care of myself."

She turned away resignedly.

The heart that beat so ambitiously on the giddy mount was a chivalric heart enough, after all. There was a short scuffle of descent, and the two set out in amity.

The Reverend Robert Raymond lived in a portion of the city so secluded that it had a village-like aspect. Farther west were miles of staring, new, red brick dwellings and corner groceries, drug stores, livery stables, all important and busy with neighborhood trade; but this retired region the march of improvement, in some inexplicable freak, had spared. Grass and trees surrounded most of the houses, which were old-fashioned, roomy, not altogether convenient according to exacting modern standards, but sufficiently comfortable. Among them was a large, square, two-story brick dwelling, with a wide veranda in front. The

shadows were long on the grass, streaked with the
yellow rays of the afternoon sun, as Miss Hamilton and her youthful escort took their way up the
gravel walk.

A man like the rector of St. Paul's usually has
some hobby. His hobby was the art of gardening. He never accomplished anything very remarkable; the aid of professionals was the sole
reliance before the season was well advanced.
But when he pridefully surveyed the result of
their joint efforts, his calm arrogation to himself
singly of the entire merit of his garden was a
thing to behold; and every spring his faith that
his own work would supply the family with tomatoes and Hubbard squash was as consummate as
his faith in the Creed. Experience taught him
nothing, for cousin Robert was one of those lucky
souls who believe the thing that they wish to believe. Felicia saw him now in the kitchen garden
at the side of the house, plying his rake among
the lettuce; apparently a painful operation, for
he was a long man, and the rake was a particularly short rake, being, in fact, his wife's imple-
ment for use among the verbenas. Felicia's was
not a temperament to sympathize with this sort of
pursuit. "Always pottering," she said to herself,
with half-affectionate, half-contemptuous indignation. "And if he must potter, why *will* he
break his back with Amy's little old rake?"

Her disapproval was not, however, sufficient to
mar the cordiality of her look and gesture —for

she was fond of cousin Robert — as she passed through the garden gate and went swiftly toward him, both hands outstretched and a gay greeting on her lips. Those dewy red lips were smiling; her eyes were softly bright; a rich bloom mantled her delicate cheek; her musical laughter rang out. To the man lounging on the green bench in the grape-arbor near at hand, half concealed by the swaying branches, she seemed the embodiment of the gracious season; as joyous, as brilliant, as expressive of life and light, hope and promise, as the early summer-time itself. For, serious and unimpressionable as he looked, Hugh Kennett had an imagination. His Pegasus had, to be sure, been bitted, and bridled, and trained to run for the cup, but on occasion it might bolt like many a less experienced racer. Thus it was that Mr. Kennett evolved a personation instead of seeing merely a beautiful young woman, moving with ease and grace, speaking with a refined accent, and dressed, with a certain individuality of taste, in a light gray costume, embroidered elaborately and delicately with purple pansies that matched well her dark eyes. Being a man of taste as well as imagination, and particularly alert as to the minutiæ of effect. her attitude, the harmonies of the colors she wore. the dainty details, appealed as strongly, though less poetically, to his cultivated perceptions.

At the sound of her voice, Mr. Raymond turned, with a start. She was a little chilled by a suggestion of constraint in his tones and manner, apparent when he greeted her, and still more when he introduced his companion, whom until now she had not seen. Hugh Kennett had risen; he had a cigar in his hand. He was looking at her with attention; their eyes met.

Madame Sevier's training did not comprehend every emergency. Notwithstanding her habit of society, the young lady was for a moment embarrassed; she flushed deeply, and her perceptible timidity contrasted agreeably with her manner an instant ago.

"You are always busy, cousin Robert," she said, glancing down at the lettuce, and conscious of the extreme flatness of her remark.

"Say, cousin Robert," exclaimed Fred, who had delayed to exchange greetings with a very old, very fat, very dignified pointer on the veranda, and who now came up with the eagerness of the small boy to participate in the conversation, — "say, why n't ye sen' yer peas, an' squashes, an' apples, ter the fair, nex' fall? I jus' know yer 'd git the prize. Say, won't yer sen' some ov 'em this year?"

"Well, I don't know about that," said cousin Robert, leading the way to the house.

"Oh, you bet I would, if I was a man an' had a garden!" cried the boy, attempting to possess himself of the rake of the reverend gentleman, who in turn attempted to playfully elude him, and succeeded in making it apparent that no juvenile amateur gardening was desired.

By the time the party reached the veranda, where two ladies in white dresses were profuse in hospitable greetings and offers of the cane chairs that were grouped about in the shadow of the vines, Felicia's unwonted embarrassment had worn away, and she was mischievously amused by the look of anxious inquiry which Amy cast upon Robert and the shade of discomfort on his face. In her youthful self-sufficiency she suddenly arrived, as she fancied, at an explanation of their disquiet. "Cousin Robert seemed to find the introduction a trial," she reflected, rapidly. "And the other day he wished to prevent me from seeing that they know his friend, whom he apparently desires to keep in jeweler's cotton. Does he consider me so dangerous as all that, — such an ogre that they are *afraid* for their precious Hugh Kennett? I think, I really think, Felicia," she concluded, gleefully apostrophizing herself, "you must give your cousin Robert something to be uneasy about."

By way of accomplishing this purpose she proceeded *per ambages*. Mr. Raymond, accustomed to her vivacity, it may even be admitted her loquacity, was thrown off his guard. Madame Sevier, a very wise person in a certain sense, had numerous theories as to the elements which go to make that finished expression of society, a charming woman, and one of these was apropos of the unloveliness of talk. "Talk," she would declare, "is not conversation. The greatest enemy a woman of mind must contend against is her own tongue. It is not what she *has to say* that matters; it is what she *is.* If a beautiful girl's faculties are absorbed in expressing her ideas, which in the nature of things are not valuable, she loses what is both valuable and artistic, — the charm of her individuality. A certain phase of intellectual adolescence is interesting because of its possibilities and its divinations, but this must disappear as soon as the assumptions of the thinker come to be considered, — especially when they are urged with the fatally didactic manner which seems to be inseparable from every woman who has ' views.' "

Perhaps her favorite pupil had profited by these axioms; perhaps she was silent only because she had become interested in the talk of the others; certainly, to those who knew her best she had never appeared to such advantage. She was a conspicuous figure in her circle, and it was the habit of her friends to discuss her much, comparing her to herself on different occasions, — what she wore, how she looked, what she said. This afternoon there was a sort of still brilliance upon her; though she spoke seldom, her smile held the charm of an indefinite, delightful promise; a certain eloquence of expression shone in her bright, dark eyes.

Sundry theories were not included in cousin Robert's philosophy. It did not occur to him that the young lady talked to him much because she considered him little; he took heart of grace.

" A dashing girl like Felicia would never give a second thought to such a sedate fellow as Kennett," he assured himself.

Deprived of Miss Hamilton's conversational aptitude, the party on Mr. Raymond's veranda presented, however, no aspect of Carthusian or Trappist gathering. His mother-in-law, Mrs. Emily Stanley-Brant, was visiting the young couple, and *she* had no theories as to the unloveliness of talk. She kindly entertained the company.

Now, everybody knows, or ought to know, that it was a great blessing to have been born one of the Stanleys. The reasons why this was a blessing are so apparent as to need no explanation; the Stanleys being so highly reputable and estimable a family, well endowed with this world's goods, and holding additional prominence because possessing certain political and legal magnates. It was particularly appropriate that this representative of the Stanleys should have added lustre to the family by her marriage to a certain notable ex-Governor Brant. Although he was greatly her senior, it seemed as much a love-match as so ambitious a woman might achieve. A man who had gone so often to Congress, and who had sat for many years on the judicial bench, fulfilled the most exacting ideal of which she could conceive, even had his personal character been less valuable than that of the unexceptionable but prosaic old gentleman she survived. He had been long since gathered to his fathers, but still lived

in the reverential, if discursive, reminiscences of
his relict.   How he rose by degrees to eminence;
how he was elected by overwhelming majorities to
the State legislature, to Congress, to the United
States Senate ; his friends, his enemies, the causes
he espoused, the policies he deprecated, — Mrs.
Emily Stanley-Brant's acquaintances sometimes
heard of these things.   The gentleman whose triumphs were thus celebrated had been a respectable enough politician of the old school, and it is
very creditable to human nature that it was possible for wifely pride to transform him into a hero.

Her faith in him served the double purpose of
keeping his memory green, and of warding off
from the endangered company cousin Robert's
account — which he was aching to give — of the
steps he had taken last autumn with the strawberries, and the extremely satisfactory result attained by planting in hills and cutting away all
runners.   The nethermost abysses were not immediately reached.   The conversation was not agri-
cultural, and the worst that the party was called
upon for a time to endure was the mellow contralto of Mrs. Brant reciting her reminiscences.

The ex-governor as a theme was not forced
upon the company.   She was not malapropos; indeed, he was merely introduced *en passant*, in an
allusion to Hugh Kennett's father, — in a tributary
manner, as it were, to the personal conversation.

"Your name is very familiar to me, Mr. Kennett," she said, smiling upon him across the

veranda, as she sat by Felicia's side. " I remember your father well. I saw him a number of times when I was first in Washington. He was quite a young man, but already notable in his profession. My husband had then just been elected to Congress on the Whig ticket, — ah, such a hard-fought contest, Mr. Kennett! Party feeling ran high in those times. People had no lukewarm blood in their veins *then*." Her manner suggested a certain triumph in the political animosities of the old days. " Only Governor Brant's personal popularity carried him through. He had his own views of political measures, and the event justified him, — yes, indeed, always justified him."

She spoke in an even, agreeable voice; the very tone embodied so entire a faith in her own words that it imposed concurrence. She had a handsome face, of a somewhat imperial type; dark, expressive eyes; a small, finely shaped head, held well back; glossy chestnut hair, — showing an occasional gleam of gray in its abundance, — which was brushed in waving masses on each side of her broad, high brow, and arranged in a heavy coil at the back of her head. She was tall and imposing, and moved with a majestic grace; her manner expressed kindness, consideration, even deference, and yet instilled, in some brilliant, subtle way, the idea that she could well afford to be so polite, being Mrs. Emily Stanley-Brant.

Some very thin-skinned people interpreted this

manner of conciliation and subcurrent of satisfaction as condescension, which Felicia Hamilton, in the exercise of a talent that she possessed, the talent of vicariously experiencing, divined that this stranger in especial must find rather marked. Mrs. Brant was almost offensively gracious to Mr. Kennett: she selected him to the exclusion of the others as the recipient of her remarks; she bent upon him her most amiable smile.

"You resemble your father," she said; "yes, very much. And I am told that you inherit his talents. The tones of your voice in speaking remind me of him. Very remarkable man, and very successful, — yes, indeed. My husband at once predicted his success. 'That young man,' he said to me, 'that young Kennett, will rise high, mark my words.' And the prediction was verified, — yes, indeed. Your father held a *high* place in his calling, — no doubt about that."

Her politeness was so extreme that it was flavored with the sentiment of *noblesse oblige.* "How does our gentleman like to be patted on the back in *that* style?" thought Felicia, in secret amusement. She glanced at him, but his face told her nothing. It seemed now a singularly inexpressive face, or he held it in singularly strong control. His gray eyes were fixed on Mrs. Brant's handsome countenance, he made the proper murmur of assent and reply, and this was all; and it baffled Felicia. "Perhaps he is only stupid," she thought, in disgust.

"Your father had a very full, rotund voice," pursued Mrs. Brant. "I should judge that he sang well."

"He only sang a little for his own pleasure," answered the visitor. "He never studied."

"The talent for music should *always* be cultivated," continued Mrs. Brant, never dropping that *soupçon* of condescension. "A beautiful art, Mr. Kennett. And it is such a pity that so much money is spent upon it to so little purpose. Now, there 's my Amy. I said, 'Now, my child, Nature has done her part,' — a lovely natural voice, Mr. Kennett, high and sweet; you would be surprised. I sent her North, I secured the best professors. And the result is " — she held up her soft white hands expressively, palms outward, as if to show the company that nothing was in them — "the result is — all wasted! She has n't opened a piano a dozen times since her marriage ! "

Four pairs of eyes turned upon the abashed Amy, who seemed very youthful as she looked deprecatingly up from under her fair hair. Mr. Kennett's voice took on something of the reassuring tone with which one encourages a timid child.

"Why do you give up your singing, cousin Amy ? " he asked.

"Oh," she hesitated, "Robert does n't care for music."

He glanced at Raymond with a smile. Then his eyes met Felicia's.

"You and Amy are cousins?" she asked, in surprise. "I did n't know that."

"Robert and I are cousins," he explained.

"Oh!" she said.

Was it inadvertence, was it coquetry? While his eyes were still on her face, her lips curved softly into a smile; those dainty dimples appeared on her cheeks; her purple eyes, so dark, yet so bright, were smiling, too. She looked straight at him.

"Do I understand this?" she said, innocently. "If you are Robert's cousin, of course you are Amy's cousin, and Amy is my cousin, — and are you my cousin, too?" She raised her delicate dark eyebrows inquiringly.

Mrs. Stanley-Brant gasped a little. Mr. Raymond frowned. Amy had the air of cowering back into the recesses of her big cane armchair. Hugh Kennett's eyes were steadily fixed on Miss Hamilton's face. He did not quite interpret her. He was not sure if this were *naïveté* or intention. He only knew that a very beautiful woman was looking at him with the most delightful expression he had ever seen. He had had a wide experience of life, sometimes sordid, sometimes imbued with a certain brilliance; he thought he had forgotten, among more tangible aims and emotions, the thrill and vague complexity of feeling which stirred him for an instant. A dark flush mounted slowly to his face. He said gravely that to be even a distant relative of hers would be a great privilege.

The training of Madame Sevier's pupil, if nothing more, made her abundantly aware that her
freak was inexcusable, but it must be confessed
that she experienced no penitence. She was
pleased with the stiffness of his reply ; she was
mischievously delighted with the discomfiture of
the others, although it had begun to greatly puzzle
her.

Cousin Robert was not destined to remain in
disastrous eclipse. In the somewhat awkward
pause that ensued, it chanced that the breeze
stirred suddenly with an audible murmur the foliage about the veranda. It seemed to him very
adroit to call attention to the honeysuckle vines
intertwined in cables about the posts, and tell how
they should be planted, pruned, and trained.
This led, by one of those easy digressions which
come so deftly to men of his profession, to the
subject of horticulture generally, and he elabo-
rated at some length his theory of the proper
system in the case of the tomato plant: that it
should be trained against trellises ; that the principal stalk should be allowed to branch out laterally ; that all other branches should be ruth-
lessly suppressed ; that half the blooms should be
pinched off while yet in the bud, — what did cousin Robert care for Irishisms on a theme like this ?
— that it should be sprinkled generously before
sunrise and after sunset in dry weather. "And
in six weeks," he declared, triumphantly, "I shall
be able to give you tomatoes, cultivated on this

principle, luscious as strawberries, red as blood, and big as my hat."

And while he thus held forth the twilight advanced apace. The afterglow of the sunset sifted through the leaves on Felicia Hamilton's face, all etherealized by the poetic light, and touched with a soft gleam her violet eyes, as they rested on the shadow-flecked turf outside. Far away the rumbling of an occasional horse-car, or the lighter roll of buggies carrying suburban residents homeward, invaded the stillness. There was a lakelet, or perhaps only a miasmatic pool, in the neighborhood, from which frogs croaked in strophe and antistrophe, — the sound mellowed by the distance. The air was imbued with that primal enchantment of summer which belittles all coming later, — the delicious fragrance of honeysuckle; it seemed to have lured two humming-birds from their downy domiciles, and they were evidently gayly bent upon making a night of it, as they quaffed the sweet wine of the flowers in the lingering flush of the red sunset.

"Them hum'n'-birds ain't no good," remarked Fred. "They can't sing, an' they're so little an' teen-ty."

He gazed up at the fluttering things, as airy, as alluring, as vaguely glancing, as a fancy, a fascination, a dream, the impulse of a poem yet unwritten.

"Swans!" he continued, enthusiastically, — "they're the fellers fur *my* money. Them swans at the Pawk, eh, aunt F'lish?"

He rolled over on his side, as he lay at her feet on the floor, and changed the position of his head, which he had pillowed on the old pointer, who moaned and wheezed in meek objection.

"It is my privilege," said Miss Hamilton, rising, "to drive with this young man to the Park every Saturday afternoon, the one meagre holiday that falls to his toilsome scholastic lot. If he does n't go home and get some sleep, he may not be able to make the trip to-morrow. So we must tear ourselves away."

Fred rose nimbly. "An' we have most bully drives ter the Pawk, you bet!" he exclaimed, vivaciously. "An' we ain't missed a Sat'day since she 's been in town."

Mr. Raymond accompanied them to the gate, and assisted Felicia into the phaeton. Soon the clatter of hoofs and the roll of wheels arose, as they disappeared down the street into the purple shadows of the coming twilight.

III.

ABOUT four o'clock on warm afternoons, there was an interval of quiet, almost of somnolence, in the Lawrence Hotel. The rush of lunch was over ; that of dinner had not begun ; no trains were due or departing ; the glare was tempered to a cool half-light; decorous officials lounged behind their desks. When a voice fell upon the air from the direction of the bar-room it seemed peculiarly loud and assertive, being rotund and penetrating in quality, and invading the stillness argumentatively. It was interrupted by another, a deep bass, embroidered, so to speak, by several bursts of rich laughter. Then the marble floor resounded with rapid footfalls. One of the men who entered hurriedly was a slim, wiry, active fellow, perhaps thirty-five years of age ; he was much flushed, his steps were unsteady, and he betrayed a tendency to emphatic gesticulation. His features were irregular and very mobile ; his eyes were gray and deep-set ; heavy wrinkles about his mouth and brow made him seem older than he was. His suit of blue flannel needed brushing, and his straw hat, set far back on his head, also gave evidence of careless wear. His companion was younger, tall, brunette, slim, debonair, point-device as to his perfectly fitting light gray suit, and joyous as to spirits. These two emerged into the office as Hugh Kennett entered from the street. At sight of him the younger pushed in advance of his companion.

"Hello, Kennett!" he cried, in his deep, gay voice. "You 're just in time. Look at Abbott; he 's trying to shirk his just obligations in the shabbiest way," and his full, rich laughter vibrated on the air.

"It 's all right!" exclaimed Abbott, coming to a sudden stop, and confronting Kennett with a grave, flushed face and an argumentative eye. "Fell'r don't want t' be swindled, ye know. Don't propose to pay more 'n ought to pay, — matter princ'ple, ye see."

A clerk from the bar-room, a fresh-faced young man, evidently inexperienced and oppressed by a sense of conflicting duties, the propitiation of patrons and the responsibility to his employers, had followed the two with hesitation. He also quickened his steps at sight of Kennett, and, addressing him by name, explained, with some vague effort to make light of the matter, that this gentleman had "treated" a number of his friends the previous evening, and now complained of the amount of his bill.

"Could n't have drunk all that champagne, Kennett," declared Abbott, looking with tipsy solemnity into the other's eyes, "if we 'd all been damned fishes, w'ales, ye know; give y' m' word we could n't."

The young man in the gray suit again burst into laughter; it was rather loud. He was contradictorily gentlemanly and *prononcé;* he was too dashing for good style, yet he had ease and smoothness. He made a comical grimace, which was at once irresistible and reprehensible.

"The thing's impossible. They're trying to swindle you," he said.

"Don't you think, Preston, you carry a joke to extremes?" demanded Kennett, glancing with annoyance at the group attracted by the loud voices, and wearing faces in which curiosity and contemptuous amusement were blended. Then he turned to Abbott. "You will be late, if you don't look out."

"Nev'r fear, old fell'r. Made a hit last night; goin' t' make a ten strike to-night, — see 'f I don't. Goin' t' fly high, — bet all ye 're worth on that. Goin' t' float with wind an' tide, — see 'f I don't. Goin' t' make my fortune."

He uttered this string of incompatible similes with an airy wave of the hand which, if he had been sober, might have been eminently graceful.

"You have made your fortune already. You had better take a carriage now and go home. He is not fit for anything, Preston. Why don't you get him away?"

But Abbott laid his hand on Kennett's shoulder. "You 're my bes' friend, Kennett," he declared. "You saw what I could do. You understood me. You pushed me. Old Hoax'em never would have

found out what was in me if you had n't put him
up to it.   You 're my bes' — bes' friend."

He began to show alarming lachrymose symp-
toms.   There was a touch of real feeling in his
voice, but also no little of the pathos of alcohol in
various forms.   The spectators grinned.   Kennett shook him off impatiently.   Preston again
burst into laughter, and, catching Abbott's arm,
dragged him to the door, while Kennett walked
back to the bar-room with the custodian of liquid
treasures.

"Sorry to trouble you, sir," said the anxious,
fresh-faced young clerk, as Kennett paid the resi-
due of the bill, which Abbott, in his wisdom, had
seen fit to eliminate.

"It will be all right when he gets sober."

"That fellow seems considerable of a scamp,"
observed an old gentleman standing near, who
took his straight.

Kennett loyally denied it.   "He is a good fellow and very talented," he declared, "but he has
some friends who like to see him make a fool of
himself."

By the time he returned to the office it had resumed the normal quiet of the hour.   He threw
himself into one of the red velvet armchairs,
lighted a cigar, and took up a newspaper.   He
glanced at it a few moments, then let it fall on his
knee.   The noises on the street were languid and
intermittent; nobody came or went.   He took his
cigar from his lips, eyed it meditatively, then,

suddenly, " Why not ? " he said, — " why not ? " and rose to his feet. He replaced his cigar, threw aside his paper, and walked, not briskly, — he never walked briskly, — but with a certain definiteness of intention, to the door. The jangling of an approaching street-car bell grew momently louder, as he waited under the striped awning. He walked out into the blinding sunshine, stepped upon the platform, and was borne with sufficient expedition toward the suburbs.

In the week that had elapsed since he met Miss Hamilton he had seen her once or twice at the windows of her brother's house, and once in the perspective of the side yard, where, among the ornamental shrubbery, there were garden-seats in the shade, and a fountain that played in the sunshine. A lady was with her, and several children. He recognized Fred's voice, half unintelligible because of overweening enthusiasm. It seemed a vivacious family group. For the past day or so, however, she had not been visible. He thought she had probably left town. Last evening this conjecture was disproved. He passed the house about eleven o'clock. It was brilliantly lighted, but the blinds were closed, except in one of the parlor windows. He heard the murmur of voices and laughter. For one instant, through the square of the window, the head and shoulders of the young lady were visible as she crossed the room. In the swift transit something pink which she was wearing poetically took on the similitude of a rosy cloud, from which her face shone like a star. A gentleman was beside her — blonde, handsome, young. They made a pretty picture for the instant that they might be seen. "She is having a fine time," said Hugh Kennett. "I suppose that 's the favored suitor." He laughed at himself, a moment later. "I seem to have a grudge against that youngster," he said, "because she sits at the window — sometimes." And he went on in the light of the summer moon.

To paraphrase a well-known apothegm, if you do not entertain your frivolous young lady, she will entertain herself. Up to this time Miss Hamilton had had every faculty of an alert, receptive, retentive intellect trained to its utmost possibility in an entirely *personal* direction. Affairs of general moment, every phase of outside life, of thought, of culture, had been presented to her intellectual consciousness as instinct with but one vital element, — their effect upon Felicia Hamilton's identity. She had acquired habits of industry and an eager mental activity which, so far, had found scope enough in the scheme of acquisition devised for her, and which, now that the limits of this scheme were reached, gave a certain poignancy to this moment, while her life stood expectant, and demanded of the future, What next? There seemed a vagueness in all possible reply. Her mental discipline had tended to no practical end ; her carefully cultivated social qualifications had no field. If so intense a nature and so alert an intellect had been in the passionate possession of a definite ambition; if, on the other hand, so worldly a woman had commanded a full measure of worldly interests and absorptions, there could have ensued no sense of vacuity. In either case, she would not probably have given as yet half a dozen moments to the thought of Hugh Kennett. The episode of casually meeting him would have slipped into the past with many slight episodes. But in the simply ordered routine of her days there was little to occupy her attention; she was strangely lonely, one would say, seeing her surrounded by the family group. That was the trouble. It was eminently the domestic atmosphere she was called upon to breathe, and her lungs were not trained to this air. She found a certain monotony in a life of which the most lively incidents were preserving fruit or putting away blankets in camphor for the summer, especially as her interest in the matter was that of the entirely disinterested spectator. She was fond of her sister-in-law and the children; their society, however, did not absorb all her faculties. To be sure, this was very objectionable. A woman of fine mind and feeling should be able to discover resources in simple pleasures and an uneventful routine; but *que voulez-vous?* Promise a richly spiced diet of daily excitement, and does not the nutritious oatmeal become insipid?

John Hamilton and his wife were happily and sturdily unaware how limited were their resources

for entertainment as measured from their visitor's
standpoint. They accorded, as they supposed, all
due consideration to the amusement of their young
guest. They took her several times to the theatre;
they drove with her through the parks; they
showed her the notable pictures; they gave her
an "evening." This "evening" bored Felicia to
the verge of coma.

John Hamilton would have laughed to scorn
the idea that society could be anything of a serious
affair; that the best results are attained by experts who pursue it with acumen and diligence,
and with mental exercises that have some analogy
to the careful vaticinations of chances and of elements which a man of business gives to the stock
fluctuations on 'Change. Social life he regarded
with that peculiar sort of half-amused nonchalance
characteristic of a rural magnate, who had found
it an exceedingly simple matter in his village
home and in the large provincial city contiguous,
where he and his family were as well known as
the court-house or the university at which he had
received his collegiate education. To his mind,
people who were not aware that this favored
region was the most delightful on earth, its educational facilities were the most desirable, and its
society was the most agreeable, were people much
to be pitied. He was a man of inherited fortune,
independent of his expectations from his father.
He had of late years greatly increased his business ventures, and, having nerve and money and

luck on his side, he was rapidly making a large
fortune. In extending his operations, the advan-
tageous field offered by Chilounatti had been
pressed upon his attention, and some six months
earlier he had removed thither; taking with him
a certain dash and an enterprise that instantly
began to make itself felt in financial circles, and
taking also his imperative personality, his breezy,
good-humored manner, and his disregard of conventionality in its more exacting sense. It was
owing to various cumulative and ramifying effects
of some of these circumstances and traits of character that the " evening " presented some features
which might distinguish it from many similar entertainments.

A new-comer into any society, with the definite
claims of money and family, is apt to be the recipient of its respectful attentions, and when Hamilton desired to ask a few people to meet his sister
he was at no loss for material. He cast about
and invited somewhat at haphazard among various families who had been especially polite to him
and his wife. It did not occur to him, however,
that while his guests were heavy weights financially
and socially, most of them were equally ponderous
mentally, and that he had not secured a sufficient
quantity of a lighter and more vivacious element
to leaven the entertainment, and render it altogether congenial to a person of the fair benefi-
ciary's age and temperament. The majority of
the company, substantial business potentates, stol-

idly partook of the conversation and the viands, and lent as much of animation to the occasion as did their wives or the armchairs. A few younger people were present; an incipient lawyer, heavy and monosyllabic, with an unresponsive and sus-picious eye; a rising architect, whose reputation for talent he was apparently conscious needed con-stant vindication; he vindicated it by a haughty inclination to silence, and, when he did speak, as much of covert sarcasm as was admissible. There were also two young collegians, Seniors in a locally celebrated university, — one blonde and rather shy, the other a trifle flippant. Both of these seemed very distrustful of Felicia; indeed, all the unmarried men apparently thought it necessary to be on their guard against her, — perhaps as vaguely dangerous, perhaps lest a chance word of theirs might minister, contrary to their intention, to her self-approval, which they divined and ir-rationally resented. The married men regarded her with mild indifference. The ladies appre-ciated her sparkle, her grace, her poise, her gra-cious little coquetry, which they had the insight to perceive she wore like her flowers, as embellish-ment to herself and in compliment to the guests and the festivity; not by way of tribute to her interlocutor, as the young architect, the lawyer, and the collegians fancied one moment, and half angrily doubted the next. These young men had the "touchy" vanity peculiar to immature years and inexperience, when, unfortunately, it is not neutralized by geniality or frivolity. They took themselves, Felicia, and the occasion with the utmost seriousness, not to say tragically.

Mrs. Hamilton's friends had heard much of her sister-in-law, who was, in her way, something of a social celebrity. It was with very genuine curiosity that they looked at the young lady dressed in faint pink, with a wonderful contrast of darkly red roses on her bosom and in her hand. She held a large pink fan with a full-blown rose and bud painted with such realism that she seemed to have robbed her dress for it; she waved it slowly back and forth; occasionally she opened and shut it. She had great ease of manner. However many were about her, she bestowed some words on each, and a gracious smile; she listened with an appearance of deep interest to whatever was said, and replied aptly and spiritedly. More than one of our young gentlemen esteemed this uncandid, — she could n't be so pleased as that with bald-headed old Harcourt, you know, or that blushing fool, young Orton. She looked at them softly and brightly. The mature young ladies thought she " made eyes " at the gentlemen; it must be admitted she made them very impartially.

The burden of the entertainment devolved upon the guest of the evening, and the manner in which she acquitted herself of the responsibility extorted more appreciation than she supposed. She had her reward, however, such as it was, when the guests took leave, to see that there was a trifle of animation and even gayety among them, and in the approval of John Hamilton and his wife.

"What a brilliant, brilliant evening!" cried Mrs. Hamilton, as the door shut on the last guest. "Oh, Felicia, how *exquisite* you look, and how delightfully you made it go off! What *pleasure* it is going to give me to entertain often in this lovely way!"

Felicia hardly knew whether to laugh or to cry. After she had shut herself into her own room she decided upon the latter course, and shed a few tears of vexation and fatigue. How was it, she asked herself, that she could not come across any agreeable people? Were she and cousin Robert the only conversable human beings in this great city? Perhaps it was because she knew so few, so very few. Perhaps — she had not noticed before — it is necessary to meet two or three hundred people in order to winnow the mass, and extract the infrequent half dozen or so pleasant friends who make life endurable. How dull the whole affair had been, this evening, and how insupportable was life! With her temperament and at her age one has no future; the temporary disappointment curtained her horizon with as distinct a cloud as a real sorrow. What better could John have done? she said. He could not help it if he knew nobody who was interesting. She believed there was nobody who was interesting in the place. She could not remember a face with a spark of intelligence, except that of the silent man she met at cousin Robert's. She supposed he had some brains; he looked as if he had. With his face the last image in her mind, she fell asleep.

The next morning she again remembered Hugh Kennett, and at breakfast, after a full discussion of the festivity of the previous evening, she asked her brother if he knew a cousin of cousin Robert's, — a man named Kennett.

"Never heard of him," said John Hamilton, buttering his roll with quick strokes. He was eating in a hurry, for breakfast was late, as is meet after a party. He was in a good humor, however: the "evening" had gone off very well, his wife was pleased, and he supposed his sister was delighted.

"He passes here every day, about eleven o'clock," persisted Felicia. "A tall man who has no mustache or beard, and usually wears a sort of fawn-colored suit, — sometimes blue, sometimes a gray suit."

"Don't recognize the description, — passes here every day at eleven o'clock?" He brushed away with his napkin the crumbs adhering to the long, fair mustache that swept across his full, florid cheek, and fixed his blue eyes on his sister's face. "Felicia," he said, with mock gravity, "don't have anything to say to any fellow — even if he is Raymond's cousin — who does n't go down town till eleven o'clock. He must be president of a bank, a faro-bank."

He burst into a loud laugh at his own witticism, and catching up his hat put it on his head, where it fortunately concealed an expanse of premature baldness, and revealed only a fringe of close-clipped brown hair. He was light on his feet for a heavy man, and in another instant his rapid step resounded down the hall; the door closed with a bang; he dashed into a passing car, and was instantly absorbed in abstruse calculations concerning the possible corner in wheat, as oblivious to the fact of a girl's vague and delicate complications of feeling as though no such subtle and imperative forces were in existence.

When Fred reminded his aunt, that afternoon, of her promise to drive with him to the Park, he was disgusted to perceive that she seemed disposed to shirk her obligation. She was tired, she said; she felt languid, — perhaps it was a touch of malaria. Besides, did n't he see what she was doing? This was the baby's flannel petticoat she was embroidering as a surprise for his mother. Would n't he be pleased to see his little sister wear a petticoat with such deep embroidery? And what a pretty design! — roses and lilies, — so appropriate.

But Fred said he would n't be pleased at all. " I ain't goin' ter let you off fur nothin', — just trine ter cheat me out'n my trip, because you know mamma won't lemme go by myself, when there ain't one bit of danger, nohow," whined Fred.

He raised his stormy freckled face, almost as red with to-day's varied experiences as if it had been parboiled. Expostulation, surly disfavor, impending outbreak, and entreaty were oddly blended in his eloquent blue eyes; his hat was pushed far back on his disheveled flaxen hair, which was beaded with moisture, and stood upright from his brow in damp wisps. His complication of expressions moved Felicia; she began to fold her work.

" An' I think a smart girl like you," continued Fred, with his own inimitable patronage, " might find somethin' nicer ter do than workin' old flow'rs in an old baby's petticoat, when she don't know a rose from a tadpole."

" No doubt you are right about that," said Felicia, with a laugh.

She might have had for her drive more improving and intellectual companionship, but it would have been difficult to surpass Fred on the score of animation. He chatted without cessation, in high feather; now and again his cackling juvenile laughter split the air. Felicia, too, was well pleased. The afternoon was soft, yet fresh; the horse was gentle but spirited, and very fast; the roads were excellent; from the crests of the many slight elevations were fine views of purple hills and green and yellow fields; now and then were visible the silver curves of the river, all softened by the distance and the transmuting afternoon sunshine. She appreciated intensely that quaint combination of ingenuousness, conceit, generosity, and selfishness which characterizes callow male human nature, and she had not been sufficiently long an intimate of Fred's to wear threadbare the interest she took in his peculiarities. It was her habit to conduct herself toward him with a certain *camaraderie*, serious or mirthful according to circumstances; and he accepted her tone in all good faith, nothing doubting that his consequence was as definite as her manner implied.

Thus they bowled cheerily along the broad thoroughfare, overtaking and passing many other pleasure-seekers in vehicles and on horseback; past handsome suburban residences, with lawns and gardens, growing gradually more extensive; past vacant lots, with big placards inscribed " For Sale," conspicuously displayed; past now and then a field, which was some day to be divided into lots and also placarded, and perhaps in the good time coming to be built up, when the " City of Splendid Promises " should redeem some of its pledges to futurity and extend thus far; past here and there sparse strips of woodland. And all at once more houses, although it seemed a moment ago that the country was almost reached, — plenty of them, too; city houses, showy, expensive, and modern. And here was the broad impressive entrance to the Park, crowded with vehicles coming and going, presided over by members of the Park police, and by a great equestrian statue, looking down silent and inscrutable. It

was not disagreeable, after a time, to turn from
the wide, much-frequented gravel drives down one
of the quiet woodland ways. The sunshine and
shadows flecked the road before them ; vistas of
greenery, upon which were imposed the brown
boles of oak and hickory trees, stretched on each
side; now and again the ground fell away in gentle grassy slopes ; here they caught sight of a
great burst of yellow sunshine flooding an open
space in the distance, and here were steep banks
and a stream gliding far below; the shadows were
thick ; the vegetation crowded close about the
water; the horse's hoofs fell with a hollow sound
as they pulled him into a walk, and they crossed
the bridge slowly ; and now on the opposite banks
and away, the ground flying beneath the feet of
the good Kentucky trotter.

In this portion of the Park little in the way of
landscape gardening had been done, the attractions of the place being judiciously intrusted to
well-tended smooth " dirt roads," and forest trees
growing as Nature chose along the hillsides and
about the levels. But upon emerging suddenly
from the shaded ways into the sunshine, the more
conventional aspect of flower-beds, fountains, lake-
lets, grottoes, and fanciful pagoda-like structures
was presented. A stone basin by the roadside,
through which a stream of water was flowing, all
at once reminded Fred that he might introduce
the element of variety into the expedition.

" We ain't give Henry Clay one drop of water

since we started!" he exclaimed, reining up suddenly.

"He can't be thirsty. Don't stop," protested Felicia.

If, however, one makes it a habit to place a boy of eight on a plane of consequence and dignity, it is not improbable that he will indorse the status in a manner and to a degree not always convenient. Fred, willful under all circumstances, was particularly resentful of authority where Felicia was concerned. She had herself to blame for the state of mind in which he composedly descended, paying not the slightest attention to her words, climbed upon a terrace close by, laboriously unfastened the check-rein, and led the horse to the trough. The animal was evidently not thirsty, but he thrust his nozzle into the water and went through the motions of drinking, now and then turning his intelligent eyes contemplatively on the round, rosy face of the boy at his head. The sunshine was bright on his glossy bay coat that shone like satin; the wind whispered through the leaves; a thrush was singing in the clump of lilacs near by ; some few belated blooms sent out on the air their delicate fragrance. Felicia sat in the phaeton waiting, the reins in her hands.

At this moment, unluckily, a boy, a year or two older than Fred, came cantering down the road on a black pony. He stopped upon seeing the party at the trough, and the two boys greeted

each other as Damon and Pythias might have
done after a separation of years, if both were suffering from the infirmity of deafness.   Fred
left the horse's head, and ran to the side of the
pony.   Suddenly, to Felicia's amazement and hor-
ror, she saw him, after a short conference, — loud
enough, but unintelligible to her, — put his foot
into the stirrup and scramble up behind his friend.
In reply to her eager remonstrance, he turned
upon her an excited eye and a grave, sunburned
face.   " You just wait here for me," he said, peremptorily.   " I 've got to go to this boy's an' see
his new rabbit-house.   He lives just outside the
Pawk.   I 'll be back d'rec'ly.   You just wait."

Objection was useless.   Felicia had merely
time to open her lips for the purpose, when the
two equestrians were off like the wind, clattering
toward · the southern gates, leaving the wrathful
young lady sitting in the phaeton, and Henry
Clay looking after them in dignified surprise,
until he bethought himself of the trough and
occupied himself with pretending to drink.

The moments passed wearily.   Now and again,
Felicia, hearing the sound of rapid hoof-beats,
would turn her head expectantly to see only
strangers gallop by.   At length, tired and restless, she descended from the phaeton, slipped the
hitching-rein through a ring on a post that stood
in convenient proximity, and addressed herself to
systematically waiting for the truant rabbit-fan-
cier.   She strolled up and down the walks ; she

gathered a few clover blooms and offered them
to Henry Clay, who accepted them languidly,
looking at her with a touch of contemptuous com-
miseration, she fancied ; she bethought herself of
a book which had been placed in the phaeton,
in order that she and Fred could take it, on their
way home, to a friend of Mrs. Hamilton's. She
returned to the phaeton, secured the volume, and
placed herself on one of the benches that stood
on the grassy margin of the lake. She did not
read, however ; the breeze fluttered the leaves,
and brought to her many perfumes from the fantastically shaped beds of flowers near by ; the
expanse of water dimpled in the sunshine ; a boat,
filled with children and with its pennons flying,
was making its way toward the island ; some
swans, slowly sailing about, arched their necks,
and approached, and receded, until one, bolder
than the rest, waddled up the bank toward the
young lady, with sharp, unmusical cries of insistence. It seemed all at once to realize that it
had mistaken her for some human friend in the
habit of bringing a supply of cake or cracker ; it
paused, gazed at her intently, its head inquiringly
on one side, its long neck stretched laterally toward
her ; it turned as suddenly, waddled off, glided
into the water, and gracefully floated away.

Felicia's smile was still on her lips, when,
observing that a shadow had fallen across her
page, she looked up.

"That seemed a case of mistaken identity,"

said Hugh Kennett, referring to the bird's noticeable manœuvre. He was lifting his hat; the gesture was ceremonious, but he was smiling as he looked at her, — smiling like an old friend.

"It was disappointed," said Felicia.

"I believe you drive out to this park rather frequently with your little brother."

"My little nephew," corrected Felicia. "Yes, every Saturday. He does n't deserve to come again. I can appreciate Ariadne's despair. He left me here, while he has gone to look at another boy's rabbit-house."

She was in the habit of being much attended, and she deprecated that she should be sitting here alone, seeming, she fancied, rather forlorn, but she attempted to carry off the matter as jauntily as possible. "I am very angry with him, but I suppose I shall forgive him before his next holiday. He considers me pledged for Saturdays."

"They have music here on some of the other afternoons."

"But there is such a crowd."

"You dislike a crowd?"

"It is not an interesting sort of crowd," said Miss Hamilton, exactingly; "it is a rabble, with a few nice people sprinkled in."

"After all, human nature is human nature," said Hugh Kennett.

So far he had been standing in the middle of the wide walk. He had replaced his straw hat; he held a little cane motionless with both hands behind him. The attitude showed his sinewy and admirably proportioned figure to much advantage. The fawn-colored suit he wore fitted well, and its soft tone accorded with his peculiar coloring. His complexion, neither noticeably fair nor dark, had a certain warmth, and its delicacy of texture suggested an indoor pursuit. He had the look of a man who conserves an enviable physical trim. Well in health, well fed, well dressed, with nerves, mind, and heart under full control, — this was the impression given by his personal appearance. His eye, now that she saw it close and in a bright light, was full and clear; there were composure and strength in its expression.

Before Felicia replied she hesitated a moment. That moment meant a great deal to her. She was about many things somewhat exacting. Matters of social usage and form were important in her eyes; perhaps she even exaggerated the importance of her own dignity. She knew that he desired her to ask him to take the vacant place beside her, — it was what he was waiting for. She knew that to do so would confer upon him the favor of her acquaintance. She would not confer it merely because he desired it. She deliberately weighed, in that short pause, the reasons for and against this course. That he was Robert's cousin, and that she had met him, a guest, at the Rectory, on friendly terms with the clergyman and his wife, — to say nothing of Mrs. Emily Stanley-Brant, — went a good way, to be sure.   But the meeting was accidental, and not necessarily an official indorsement, so to speak. Mr. Raymond had not introduced him to her brother or his wife, and had not brought him to call.   On the other. hand, the Raymonds were not very ceremonious about such matters, and this omission might have been merely negligence, not intention.   Perhaps he was himself a stranger in Chilounatti ; and again she was reminded how very little she knew of him personally.   Although by no means so thoroughly versed in the ways of the world as she deemed herself, she had experience enough to understand the difficulty in gracefully getting rid of superfluous acquaintances. But was she justified, she argued, in relegating to this circle of the excluded a man whom the most punctilious of men received on intimate terms into his own family, and whose manners and appearance were evidently those of a gentleman?   She said to herself that she was as competent to judge a gentleman as her brother, who was dense in some respects, or cousin Robert, who was flighty.   This reflection turned the scale. She raised her eyes to his.

"Will you sit down ?" she said, gravely.

"Thank you," he returned, as gravely, and placed himself beside her on the painted bench.

It had been a momentous pause ; each realized it, and each knew that the other realized it.

There was silence for a moment; then she replied to what he had said.

"Human nature may be human nature," she admitted, "but all *people* are not human. I know a terrier who has a tailor, — an excellent one, — and eye-glasses, and a mustache. Did you never see a woman like a bird, hopping and perching about, and surprising you every time she handles a fan or a parasol because her fingers are not claws? Why, a moment ago a man passed here whose fat little eyes were exactly like a pig's. Oh, no, some human beings are not exactly human, — I 'm sure of that."

"I had no idea you were such a cynic," he said, looking at her with a half laugh. It was the glance and laugh of an old friend.

She was disposed for a moment to resent this, to consider it a liberty that there should be so distinct an undercurrent of sympathy, already glimpsed, or rather felt, through the crust of formality which characterized their short acquaintance. She arrogated to herself the privilege of any lapse from convention. As she glanced at him in uncertainty, she met his fine, calm eye; it had so evident a reliance on a reciprocity of feelings, whatever they might be, so simple and candid an enjoyment of the moment, that she was disarmed.

"A little cynicism is not a bad thing," he suggested; "it prevents one from wearing one's heart on one's sleeve."

"If one has a heart," she returned, with a little laugh.

"I am afraid we are all provided with that discomfort. Even the rabble, who have such bad manners."

"Bad manners are wicked," said Felicia, with that willful air which cousin Robert could never resist, and which Hugh Kennett also seemed to approve.

"In these cities that have such a rapid growth, other matters take precedence," he remarked. "Many people make money too fast here to care much about manners."

"Manners are more important than money," quoth the pupil of Madame Sevier.

He laughed at this.

"Just as the people about us are more important than the things about us," she persisted.

"I should never have thought you would feel that," he said, suddenly serious. "I supposed environment meant a great deal to you."

He spoke with evident interest; he looked at her expectantly as to what she might reply. He seemed determined to make the conversation very personal. This time she did not relent.

"I was speaking merely abstractly," she declared, indifferently, turning her eyes with a casual glance upon the scintillating surface of the lake, already enriched with gleams of gold and lines of crimson beneath the red and gilded brilliance deepening athwart the soft azure sky.

He was slightly taken aback for a moment. "Ah, well," he said, "an abstract truth merges itself sooner or later into a personal application. In my case, I admit environment means very little. A few close friends, an object in life, good health, and a quiet conscience, — that is a world a man can carry about with him as a snail carries its world."

"A *man* can do that," said Felicia.

"And a woman cannot? Why not?"

"For several reasons. We have no close friends; we can't go into the world and select those that suit us. And we have no object in life, — no definite object, I mean. And health, — you mentioned health, did n't you? — if we have health our occupation is gone; we can't coddle ourselves. As to conscience," — she laughed gleefully, — "we have n't that, either!"

Kennett laughed, too. "I am well aware of that fact," he replied; "I discovered long ago that you have no consciences."

She looked very arch and pretty at this moment: her eyes were bright; her parted scarlet lips showed her milk-white teeth; she had flushed a little. Her toilette, always so felicitously devised as to convey the impression that it was the most becoming she had yet worn, was noticeably simple; to-day she seemed to owe nothing to the embellishments of art. Her white dress was very fine in texture and very plainly fashioned; long black kid gloves, that fitted conscientiously, so to speak, gave her little hands additional daintiness; a straw hat demurely shaded her delicately tinted, brilliant face : she might have stepped from the frame of some old picture, but for the anachronism of a very modern lace-covered parasol with a long amber handle, which she revolved upon her shoulder as she talked. He was a man whom no detail escaped. He noticed, when she raised her eyes, that the iris was a veritable purple ; that the whites were clear and tinged with blue ; that the gold-tipped brown lashes were long and curled upward.

The wind stirred the leaves ; the water of the fountain, falling, falling, in the midst of the rippling lake, was monotonously agreeable. The closely clipped turf was vividly green with the welcome brilliance of the season ; striking athwart the emerald expanse was a wide bar of yellow sunshine, and as a trio of young girls in light dresses passed through the gilded radiance, the red feather which one of them wore in her hat had a suddenly splendid effect, — it was a moment for enchantments. The trill of a lettuce bird vibrated on the air ; the swans floated, and paused, and floated again, their snowy plumage gleaming in the sun.

" Do you read a great deal ? " asked Mr. Kennett, glancing at the volume open on her knee.

" Very little."

" You don't care for reading ? " he pursued, with the accent of surprise.

" Very much. And that is why I rarely indulge myself."

Again he looked at her, with that smile which, beneath its geniality, was charged with a more definite sympathetic quality.

"What unexpected material for martyrdom!" he exclaimed.

"I am not so heroic," she returned, with a laugh. "It seems to me I have no time to read."

"I had an idea — to be sure, I may be mistaken — but I had an idea that people like you have *all* the time."

She explained. "Once I read a great deal, — long ago, when I was young; and it became impressed upon me that I had no time to spend upon any books but text-books. One who intends to *live* has no time to read."

He gave this a moment of cogitation. "I cannot say I am quite ready to accept that doctrine," he declared.

"If you read, you take the views of the writers; you think their thoughts; you live a life made up of their theories mixed with your own circumstances. It is all incoherent."

"You want to conserve originality, I see," he remarked.

"Cousin Robert says Amy and I never look at a newspaper because we are afraid of learning something about politics," she said, with her sudden laughter. "And he is right, — we detest politics."

"Robert does not show his usual acumen in

attributing the same views to you and his wife. You are not at all like your cousin."

"I don't know that you are at all like *your* cousin," remarked Felicia.

"We used to be considered alike," he returned, — "not so much in appearance, perhaps, as in temperament and character. The influences have been so different of late years that we may have drifted apart."

Certainly the talk had become very personal, but she said to herself that, under the circumstances, it was hardly matter for surprise.

"You have known him always, then?" she asked.

"Always. In fact, he was from his early childhood a member of my father's family, until he took that — well, excuse me — that freak to make a clergyman of himself. I must say I regret his choosing the ministry. You see, I am not much of a churchman," he added, deprecatingly, as her face grew grave.

Among the privileges she arrogated to herself was that of any depreciation of religious matters, and she was severe in condemnation of similar dereliction in others. He saw that he was in deep water, but was not sufficiently adroit to know exactly how to emerge.

"I think it does not altogether suit Robert to be a clergyman," he went on, uncertainly.

"He is a very valuable and useful one," she said, stiffly.

" Oh, no doubt," he rejoined, humbly.

" And very eloquent," continued Felicia.

" He has a great advantage in his voice and his fine elocution. He owes much of that to my father."

She was interested, remembering what Mrs. Stanley - Brant had said about Mr. Kennett's father. Was he too a clergyman ? she wondered.

" My father was very fond of Robert," continued Kennett, " and looked after his education with great attention; but he did that for all of us, — my sisters and I received our most valuable training from him. He had untiring patience and gentleness, and the most complete sympathy. Only those who knew him well could realize how fully he could enter into the ineffectual little efforts of others."

He spoke very simply and naturally, always with that candid confidence in her sympathy, as if to an old friend. His quiet gray eyes were fixed absently on the party-colored flower-beds that in the distance suggested huge bouquets; his face held an expression not so much of grief as of remembrance from which the bitterness of sorrow has been refined away, — a sort of calm and tender reflectiveness. Felicia divined that in the years that had passed the dead had come at last to seem only gone from sight and hearing, and not cruelly and incomprehensibly swept out of existence. She did not know exactly what to say ; it was strange to be thus taken into the confidence of a man who was three hours ago so far removed from her by all those strong conventions which she felt were so important; yet his evident unconsciousness of anything unusual in his words made them seem more a matter of course.

"He thinks cousin Robert has talked of him and of his father also," was her conclusion..

The western sky was crimson now; the surface of the lake was richly aglow. The red gold of the sunset was sifting through the air. The shadows were growing long. The breeze freshened. Suddenly the distant peal of the Angelus — that apotheosis of eventide effects — rang out, caught and tossed from side to side, as many a church and chapel repeated the mellow clang.

Adown the leafy vista of the road Fred and several of his friends might be seen advancing on foot, apparently engaged in some commercial transaction. One of them was holding out temptingly a big pocket-knife, which Fred evidently declined to receive; he had two strips of leather in his hand; their voices were loud in argument.

Felicia rose, and joined her nephew. Kennett assisted her into the phaeton. As Fred drove off, she bowed in adieu to her new acquaintance, and she was again impressed by the formality, even the ceremoniousness, of his salutation, and its singular contrast with his extreme frankness.

IV.

In her leisure moments, of which she enjoyed
some superfluity, Felicia meditated much on the
unexpected interview in the Park, and in the
course of the next week she evolved the idea that
it would be desirable to draw out cousin Robert
on the subject of the Kennetts, father and son.
This astute design was frustrated. Hearing nothing from him or his wife, she undertook a pil-
grimage to the Rectory. The fat old dog on the
veranda gave a gentle wheeze of recognition and
a tap or two with his tail. As the bell clamored
through the house, it had an indefinably hollow
sound, and the maid appeared promptly at the
door.

"I 'm thankful to see you, Miss Felicia!" she
exclaimed. "I 'm too lunsome to live, with nobody to speak to but the old dog. You did n't
know Mrs. Raymond was gone, yet alreatty?
Oh, yes 'm, since Chewsday. She 'd a telegram
that her uncle Lucian is sick up in the country at
his house, where her maw is visitin' him. An'
her maw is worn out nursin' him. So Mrs. Raymond left right away alreatty. An' yesterday,
Mr. Raymond got another gentleman to take the
church next Sunday, an' went himselluf. They

never wrote to you, ain't it?   Mebbe they forgot it; they was so confused in their minds."

She looked at Felicia benignly from beneath her fluffy flaxen bangs, that innocently exaggerated the fashion, and almost obscured her blue eyes.

" Ach — how be-eu-ti-ful yez are the day ! " she cried, rapturously. From the Irish cook at her last place she had secured certain choice idioms, which she had engrafted upon her German dialect with a unique effect that appealed delightfully to Felicia's sense of humor.

Our young lady returned home in puzzled cogitation. She realized that it was possible for Hugh Kennett to make rapid strides in forming acquaintance; in a few more such interviews as their last meeting, similar progress would place him on a footing of close friendship.. She desired much to know who he was, what was his place in life, what were his surroundings, his associations, — not so much because of any distinct interest in him as from the wish to relinquish no element of entertainment, and yet to conform to that Mede and Persian law which she had prescribed for her own guidance in such matters.

Shortly after this episode, the young architect, who had been a conspicuous guest on the occasion of the " evening," called at her brother's house. Mrs. Hamilton, actuated by the unwritten but stringent law which, in her own girlhood days, in her village home, conceded the unmarried guest to the entertainment of the young lady of the family, conscientiously conjured up a headache, and Felicia received the visitor alone. There was nothing particularly unacceptable in this young man, whose name was Grafton. He was a little didactic, and not a little conceited ; but he was a gentleman ; he had fair abilities, and had enjoyed good opportunities of cultivating them. His mistake was the not unusual mistake of intolerance. His misfortune was that he did not possess what might be called a sense of divination. He could not vicariously experience emotions, apprehend a train of unexpressed thought, or intuitively attribute the correct intention to a phraseology capable of more than one interpretation. Felicia also was intolerant ; and, although she had plenty of imagination, her stock of patience was scanty. She thought it possible that she could construe Mr. Grafton's deeper nature if she should give herself to the effort, but she did not deem it worth the trouble ; she preferred to translate him through the surface medium of manner and the casual chat of the evening. He seemed to her very unresponsive, self-absorbed, prone to misunderstandings, and almost morbidly appreciative of platitudes. An older woman, of equal mental qualities, or a coquette, might have found entertainment in drawing him out as an exponent of his class, or as a possible victim. Felicia had little interest in types of this sort, and was too proud — or, it may be, too vain — to be definitely and of set purpose a coquette. It must be confessed, however, that, although she would not attempt Alfred Grafton's scalp to wear as a trophy, she did not fail to sharpen the knife, — in other words, she deemed it incumbent upon her to make his call agreeable ; this obligation, according to her code, she owed to herself. He could not, in reason, find fault with her graceful cordiality. At first, he was inclined unreasonably to object to it as insincere. Later, his self-love came to the rescue, and he wondered if this suavity might not be susceptible of a different explanation. Many a man of twenty-four would have thawed under the geniality of this suspicion ; but Grafton's nature was one of those which, accepting the most flattering concessions as tribute, do this with a certain grudging, a certain objection, as if on guard against being surprised into benignity, cajoled, got the better of, in some inscrutable way. It is impossible to say what Felicia would have thought, could she have divined how egregiously he mistook her smile over her big, pretty, gently swaying fan, her gracious eyes, her vivacity, her affability, — that he fancied she was trying to fascinate him. What she did think was something like this : " It is a pity he is such a stick. He is rather good-looking : his eyes are set too far back, but they are hazel and well cut ; his face is somewhat narrow. Still, he looks refined and intelligent, and as if he ought not to be so terrifically tiresome."

They talked a little of the weather, and Felicia inveighed against the dust.

"It gives one a taste of martyrdom," she declared. "St. Simeon Sisanites of Syria need n't have gone on the top of a column in order to be wretched enough to found a sect of Stylites, if he had lived here. And those watering-carts are only an aggravation. One expects so much of them and gets so little."

"I think the street-watering system is perhaps as good here as elsewhere," he replied, looking at her with that expression by which a capable adept can thoroughly chill a conversation without being tangibly rude.

She wondered if she had said anything particularly objectionable; if he had any interest in the matter, — a contract, for instance, to supply the lumbering carts to the city, or the horses. She remembered that he was an architect; for all she knew, the city gave such contracts to architects. Cousin Robert might have mentioned other things she was afraid of learning, besides politics.

It was with a distinct intention of recompensing a possible slight that she smiled upon him now ; under these circumstances her smile was very sweet.

"At any rate, this place has many attractions," she said, "notwithstanding the dust. The parks are lovely, and the public buildings are so interesting. I suppose the architecture is very fine," she added, vaguely.

"The architecture is very bad," he declared, unexpectedly, — "atrociously bad."

She raised her eyebrows. "Indeed? I had fancied the reverse the case. But I confess I know nothing about architecture. A young lady is lucky in not being expected to take, as Lord Bacon did, all knowledge for her province."

"Is not her education expected to teach her something about everything?" he asked; and with him a question could be as didactic as an axiom.

"Oh-h-h — but if it does that, she will be a *bas bleu!*" Felicia cried, making her eyes large, and intimating that this was a dreadful thing.

"I feel assured," he persisted, seriously, "that it is a woman's duty and privilege to be thoroughly well informed."

Her eyes resumed their normal dimensions, and into them came a slight expression of weariness. It seemed to her that it would be difficult to conjure what she called *esprit* into this conversation.

"I am one of those who hold that sex should be no disqualification in education," he continued. "I maintain that women should share higher education equally with men."

"I should think women would find it rather *ennuyant*," said Felicia, with a smile.

"Why do you use foreign words?" he asked. He seemed sensible that she might object to this, for he went on, with some suggestion of the manner of conciliation, "I think we have English words that express that idea."

"Oh, I will talk English, if you prefer, — or

American, even!" exclaimed Felicia, with her light laughter, which was now a trifle forced.

The next hour was, perhaps, the most laborious she had ever known; it was not only the fact of uncongeniality, — it was the necessity to gracefully concede. She found it desirable to maintain a proposition to a certain point, and then relinquish it scientifically, — not too suddenly, — with the judicious amount of argument necessary to keep up the similitude of interest. This is exhausting intellectual exercise, and also a trial to the temper. She wondered why he did not go. The truth was, the reason their talk tired her was the reason it interested him; then, that flattering suspicion afforded a certain agreeable titillation, notwithstanding his stern determination not to be subtly overreached. He did not grow genial, but he was satisfied. He was having what she would have called a good time.

It was abruptly terminated. There came by degrees the roll of rapidly advancing wheels. All at once they stopped in front of the house. There was a sound of quick, light steps, the bell was rung, and, when the front door was opened, a voice, asking for Miss Hamilton, invaded the silence of the hall.

Grafton noticed that, at the first tone of the voice, Felicia turned her head; her color deepened; her expression was expectant. In another moment a gentleman appeared on the threshold. For a second he stood motionless, as he glanced about him ; then his eye fell on the young lady, who had risen, smiling. He darted toward her, tucking, with incredible deftness and quickness, his crush hat under his arm, and holding out both hands.

"My dear f-r-r-iend," he cried, joyously, "how enchanted I am to see you ! "

He was so swift, so vivacious, so unexpected, so foreign, that his entrance was as incongruous as if he were a flash of lightning ; and a veritable flash of lightning could hardly have demolished more abruptly Mr. Grafton's measured enjoyment of the evening and his flattering little theory of the young lady's favor. Was it like this, he wondered, that she looked at the man she loved ? Her eyes, — how lucent they were, how dark with feeling ; how smilingly her beautiful lips had curved; what welcome her face expressed ! He looked — and his neutral glance had at length become tinged with a distinct sentiment — at the visitor. He saw a man of thirty-six or seven ; rather under medium height, in full dress, with auburn hair and mustache, fair complexion, delicately cut features, brilliant blue eyes, a vivacious expression, and an alert and graceful figure. He acknowledged the introduction to Mr. Grafton with a suavity which was at once curiously *empressé* and perfunctory ; then he dropped on a sofa beside Felicia.

"And how did I discover you were here, eh ? The merest accident, ten minutes since, or I should not have dared to call at this unconscionable hour. Met your brother at the opera — went out after the second act to take a — a — smoke — saw Mr. Hamilton in the crowd — caught him — asked news of you — 'My dear fellow, don't you know she is at my house?'" He vivaciously mimicked John Hamilton's voice and manner, and Felicia burst into a peal of silvery laughter. "So I asked the number of his house — called a carriage — 'Drive as if the furies were after you!' — and *me voici*, eh?"

He gave a great wave of his hand to intimate the rapidity of the transition. He used many gestures. He was hardly still a moment; he shrugged his shoulders; he threw up his eyebrows; a turn of his flexible wrist would fill out a sentence; he glanced swiftly about the room, apparently taking in everything instantaneously, but casually. The expression of his eyes, coming back to the young lady's face, and that recurrent "eh?" intimated a friendship that made the impassive Mr. Grafton, looking coldly on from his armchair, set his teeth together with an unwonted intensity of emotion.

He gathered that the stranger was a brother of a school friend of Miss Hamilton's, on a flying business trip through the West. "And a most annoying, disagreeable journey I have had, but for the lucky accident of meeting you. I assure you I am fully recompensed now. And there's no chance of your going back to Madame Sevier,

eh?　Ah-h-h, she is afflicted to give you up!　'Lucille,' she said to my sister, the day before I left,
'the place can never be the same without my
dear Félicité.'　Ah-h, with tears!　I assure you
she wept.　And you like the West, eh?　I thought
not," triumphantly.　Then he turned to make an
amende to the Westerner, who, stiffly erect, sat
regarding him as if he were an escaped wild beast,
— not dangerous, but very objectionable.　"You
have a wonderful country, Mr. — er — Grafton.
Progress, enterprise, all that, — the future of the
nation, all that.　But we don't want to relinquish
everything to you; we must keep the approval of
our own young ladies; we must n't be too generous.　And when," he continued, again addressing
Felicia with his sudden swiftness, "are you coming to see Lucille?　A visit, a little visit, eh, —
you won't deny us that?　She will be enchanted
that I met you."

Grafton thought Mr. Adolphe Devaux the most
odious, insufferable, vain, shallow popinjay he
had ever beheld.　Mr. Devaux commiserated
Felicia's hard fate that she was compelled to play
the agreeable to a conceited prig like that.　Each
attempted to outstay the other, and Grafton succeeded, for train-time is inexorable.　The French-
man, suddenly bethinking himself of the hour,
vehemently apologized for looking at his watch;
despairingly tossed up his eyebrows and his
shoulders at the result; explained comprehen-
sively that he must get back to the hotel, change

his dress, pack his traps, swallow some supper, and reach the train in half an hour from this present speaking; and tore himself away, after adieux which, although rapid, somehow expressed and embodied a vast deal of the genius of leave-taking. There were many messages given him to Lucille; and when Miss Hamilton reached Madame Sevier's turn, her voice suddenly faltered, the color flared up in her cheeks, her violet eyes grew dewy, the hand she had given him trembled in his clasp.

"Ah-h!" he cried, "how glad Madame Sevier will be that you remember her so kindly! She was afraid you would forget her. No fear of that, eh? Adieu, adieu. *Good*-evening, Mr. Grafton. *So* happy to have met you."

When Felicia's remaining caller had also taken leave, she repaired to her own room, where she found her sister-in-law, her round, rosy face beaming with pleasure, awaiting her. This lady, shortly after her graduation from the Young Ladies' Select Institute of her native village, had married John Hamilton, in the chrysalis stage of his career. His semi-rural home, his respectably large provincial business, his juvenile family, and her share in all these phases of life seemed to her to afford full measure of interest, until the wider pageant of cosmopolitan possibilities was presented by their removal to Chilounatti. Now her ideas were rapidly expanding. Her imagination had compassed ambitions, pleasures, pursuits, half realized heretofore. She developed an interest in the matter of entertainments; she carefully read the fashion articles in the papers and the society columns; she collated scraps of information as to the appropriate *menus* for ladies' luncheons and afternoon teas, for dinners and evening parties. On these subjects she obtruded none of her newly acquired wisdom, but listened and observed with great intentness, and held herself always in readiness to amend her code. She was becoming familiar with minutiæ of household management under altered conditions, and had bloomed into a modest splendor of dress on great occasions. Among other phases of this new life upon which she was entering with such zest, Felicia's enjoyments and prospects offered a suggestive theme for congratulatory contemplation. How gay and eventful existence must be to her! She was never a whole day without some agreeable episode, although the "season" was virtually over. Last week, the theatre twice, and the Melville reception; and last Friday the "evening;" and several trips down-town this week; and to-night two delightful callers; and — "Oh, Felicia," she cried, as the girl entered the room, "who was he? —the last one, I mean. I know Alfred Grafton came first. Oh, how delighted he seemed to see you! Is he nice? Is he handsome?"

"Oh, yes, he is a dear little man," replied Felicia, as she removed her earrings and carefully bestowed her big fan in its box, — "a dear, dear little man."

Mrs. Hamilton's face fell. This did not seem exactly on the plane of the status she had conjured up.

"And is he very devoted? Is he in love with you, too?" she asked.

Felicia stared at her. "Adolphe Devaux!" she exclaimed. "Why, he's been married ten years, at least."

"Oh-h-h!" said Mrs. Hamilton, disappointed.

And here was John Hamilton, pretty tired, a little out of humor, and, as he expressed it, frantic to go to sleep.

"I suppose, Felicia, you saw that howling swell Devaux? Rushed at me as if he were crazy. It takes a foreigner to make a fool of himself. Everybody looked at me. I felt like braining him. The opera? Was it good? *I* don't know. Everybody said so. I did n't pay much attention. Gale asked me to meet some fellows — friends of his from Minnesota — at dinner at the club, and nothing would satisfy him but the opera afterward."

As he tramped out of the room, his step sounded as if he were indeed very sleepy.

To-night Felicia took stock, in a manner. So much time, — such elements for filling it. She said to herself that she was, perhaps, abnormally dependent on the personality of those about her: their natures were her bane or her blessing; their manners could afflict or delight her. The expression of kindly feeling or the divination of approval was like the breath of her life, — was like the sunshine to a plant. She said she had no idea how much she valued cordiality until Adolphe Devaux, whom she had esteemed slightly enough heretofore, was contrasted with Mr. Grafton. And, as she considered these matters, she said to herself, with a certain satisfaction, that she had shown good judgment in not rejecting the acquaintance of Hugh Kennett, who had manifested some capacity to understand her; whose ideas were congenial with hers; who had intellectual qualities she could respect, and manners she could approve. She admitted to herself that she was pleased that she had met him, and would be pleased to meet him again. Thus Alfred Grafton's call had the perfectly illogical result of strengthening Hugh Kennett's claim upon Miss Hamilton's acquaintance.

However the routine of the Hamilton household might be interrupted, there was one weekly festival that came with unimpaired regularity, — Fred's holiday on Saturdays; and he was very rigorous in exacting all the rights and privileges which he deemed appropriate to the recurrent occasion. Since Felicia, in an unguarded moment, had promised to drive with him on those afternoons, he had held her to the compact with extreme pertinacity, and apparently took as much pride in the fact of the regularity of these drives as if he withstood some strong temptation to forego them. The slight cloud which had ob-

scured the geniality of the last excursion cleared
away during the week, and on the following Saturday they rolled off in high spirits and complete
amity.

They found this drive the most agreeable they
had yet had. Fred detailed many of his plans,
and described his friends and his enemies —
incoherently. Felicia told him, with point and
vivacity, several stories, in which he came out,
unexpectedly, the hero of escapades which had
considerately slipped from his memory. She mimicked him in the dismay or agitation of these *dé-
nouements* with such genial humor that he laughed
uproariously at the figure he presented to his own
imagination. Her eyes sparkled ; the dimples did
not leave her cheeks.

" You 're a bully girl ! " declared Fred, in high
good humor. " You 're always jolly."

The consciousness of her various mental ex-
ercitations regarding Mr. Kennett had a certain
disagreeable effect on which she had not counted.
As she saw him advancing along one of the picturesque footpaths of the Park which intersected
the principal drives, she became aware that she
was coloring violently. This startled and disconcerted her, and she did not realize that a crisis
of another sort impended until it was imminent.

It chanced that Fred, who insisted on driving,
to her exclusion, also recognized Kennett. He
had not shown any especial enthusiasm in claim-
ing the acquaintance on the previous Saturday,

but now, with the inconsequence of the small boy,
he saluted the pedestrian with a loud, eager ac-
claim, signaled him to stop, pulled the horse
sharply across the road, and drew up at its
margin. This manœuvre was so sudden that the
driver of a great watering-cart, which was just
behind the phaeton, taken entirely by surprise,
went through a wild contortion in his effort to
keep his team from running down the slight
vehicle. His struggles seemed for a moment
about to be crowned with success, as he, too,
turned his horses into the middle of the road;
but his utmost skill did not avail to prevent the
wheels of the big, burly cart from sharply collid-
ing with the wheels of the phaeton. There was a
sudden crash, a grinding, splintering sound, and
an abrupt shock. Henry Clay, disapproving of
the noise and the jar, plunged violently, and
would have bolted but for the restraining hand
of a gardener who was fortunately passing, with
his barrow and tools, at the moment. Kennett
hastened his steps into a run, and helped Felicia
from the phaeton; and she stood looking ruefully at the broken wheel, as Fred and the driver
of the watering-cart also descended from their respective perches and surveyed the damage. Each
of the Jehus indulged in wild criminations, which,
after a time, evolved themselves into a participa-
tion in the pending discussion as to what was to
be done for the broken vehicle, in this emergency.

" I 'll tell ye what it is, miss," said the gardener in an evil moment. " There 's a blacksmith shop about two blocks from the north entrance. Why can't the little bye jist get on the horse, an' ride over there an' tell 'm to send here for the phaeton ter mend it? I can't leave here, or I 'd go me-self!"

Fred accepted this suggestion with enthusiasm. Felicia remonstrated on the score of safety.

"Can't ride Henry Clay!" sneered Fred, in-dignantly, as he hurriedly unhitched the traces. " Why can't I, I 'd like ter know? Harness! what 's harness got ter do with it? I 'll show you I can ride him, if he *has* got his harness on him!" He led the horse out of the shafts.

Kennett, too, remonstrated, infusing as much authority as he might into his manner. Fred looked at him in surly surprise, and for reply scrambled upon the horse's back with great ex-pedition and agility. The gardener, realizing his mistake, glanced, crestfallen, from one to the other. Felicia fired her last shot with all the skill she possessed.

" Oh, Fred, do you think it is right," she cried, " to leave me to go home without you? I shall have to walk to the street-cars alone, — three miles, at least."

Fred hesitated. His sense of his own importance was very great, especially his idea of his impor-tance to Felicia. This appeal for herself touched him on his strong suit. But the counter temptation was also strong. He thought that it *was* something of a feat for him to ride Henry Clay, and he knew it would not be permitted by his parents unless his father were one of the party. Then he prefigured the scene of interest and excitement that would ensue at the shop when he should gallop up on the harnessed horse, with the news of the damaged vehicle. It is to be feared that it was his unexpressed intention to figure as the hero of a sensational story. Under the stress of opposing influences, Fred attempted, as wiser people do in emergencies, to evolve a compromise. He looked over his shoulder at her with serious eyes. "You jus' walk ter where the street-cars start from," he said, imperatively. "There 's plank sidewalks part of the way. You get in the car an' wait, an' I 'll be along jus' as soon as I tell them men ter come after this phaeton."

As if afraid of more remonstrances, he "gave his noble steed the rein," and went off at a gallop and with a wild halloo.

Nothing short of an earthquake could have more thoroughly disconcerted Felicia. The annoyance of being stranded here in the Park was greatly aggravated by the prospect of a walk of three miles, at least, through a region unfamiliar to her. Her swift speculation as to the improbability of procuring a carriage in any reasonable time was interrupted by Kennett's voice. He apparently shared none of her anxiety. He turned to her with a smile. For a moment she almost resented his expression ; it held a sort of friendly reliance, seeming to say in effect, "I am very glad to arrange this for you, and I have no doubt you will be glad to let me arrange it."

"It is fortunate that I came down from town on the river," he declared. "I can save you a dusty walk. The boat-house is just outside the gate, and if you have quite recovered from the shock we will go over and get the boat. I can row you up to the street-car terminus by the time Fred reaches there."

She hesitated. She had found it necessary to amend her theories as to *les convenances* very radically, in view of the difference between Madame Sevier's rule and the more lenient systems prevalent outside those scholastic walls. She had been greatly surprised and a trifle doubtful that people — we are aware that she did not consider all the human race "people" — should permit their young ladies to ride and walk alone with gentlemen, but had realized that the custom of the region makes the law in matters of etiquette. This case, however, held certain other elements of difficulty. She had a reluctance to be placed under a distinct obligation, and an obligation to a stranger. But *was* he a stranger? — Robert's cousin, closely connected by marriage with her cousin Amy and with Mrs. Emily Stanley-Brant. And what else could she do? He glanced at her expectantly, with, she fancied, a trifle of surprise. She had but a moment for cogitation. She rap-

idly decided that in a matter of the sort ultra-
fastidiousness is absurd ; that to refuse to row
with him, and then to plod with him three miles
on a dusty turnpike road, — for he would iusist
on seeing her safely to the cars, at least, — would
make her ridiculous, and would be quite as un-
suitable as rowing on the river, if either were not
convenable, according to the Chilounatti code.
She conceded the point gracefully, putting up her
parasol, giving one last glance at the disabled
phaeton, and turning with Kennett toward the
south entrance.

As they walked on in the soft sunshine and the
alternating spaces of cool shadow, Felicia was
subacutely surprised that her annoyance should
diminish so swiftly. There was something singularly restful about him: in the expression of his
contemplative eyes, now turning upon her as their
desultory talk progressed, now dwelling on the
green slopes or the fanciful flower-beds by the
roadside; in the tones of his even voice ; in the
steadiness of his movements ; in his candid and
natural manner. His manner had, too, a certainty, a definite quality, which had the effect of
placing a sort of appropriateness on what he proposed or did. It began to seem a simple and
suitable thing thus to stroll with him along these
verdure-bordered ways, through the golden afternoon sunshine, toward the Park gates ; already in
sight they were, as well as the broad, low boat-
house beyond.

They mentioned the weather, the beauty of the Park, Fred's singular idea of the duty of an escort.

"Fred thinks I am a useless annoyance in every expedition, like the sermon in a church which has a show choir," declared Felicia.

"By the way, you know that Robert and his wife have left town?"

"I discovered that fact only yesterday. Will they be long absent?"

"Some weeks. He will take his vacation now, while the church is under repair. I believe I have his note with me."

He extracted several missives from his breast pocket, selected one and handed it to her.

"Your cousin is more considerate than mine," remarked Felicia, feeling aggrieved. "Amy has not vouchsafed me a scrape of a pen."

The note was very short, very familiar, very careless, very fraternal. The Reverend Robert stated that he was just about to start for the train. Amy left some days since. Mr. Lucian Stanley quite ill. Could n't say when they would return, — the repairs in the church were more extensive than had been anticipated; not for some weeks, probably. Sorry not to see you again. Good-by, and God bless you.

As she replaced the note in its envelope, Felicia noticed that it was directed to one of the hotels.

"I had an idea you lived up - town," she remarked. Surely some slight personality might be considered in order, since he was not only cousin Robert's relative, but apparently his Damon as well.

"No doubt you had that impression because I pass the house so frequently. I am the most methodical of men. I walk the same distance at the same time every day. I have discovered that serenity is necessary, if a man wishes to put in his best licks, — if you will excuse the expression, — to accomplish his highest possibilities. And serenity is facilitated by long contemplative walks. It is a good habit ; one has time to think. Living in the midst of such a rush as I necessarily do, it is well for a man to take a little time to think."

They had reached the confines of the Park, had crossed the road, and were soon standing upon the river-bank. Belts of blue, of orange, of purple, of a dazzling white, alternated upon the surface of the water. It was ruffled into waves by the breeze, bearing woodland odors from the Park, and sparkled with myriads of prismatic scintillations, as the sun, slowly tending westward, shot athwart the stream. The boat, which had been fastened to the pier, was rocking gently to and fro. Kennett assisted Felicia to a seat, and took the oars. With one long, smooth stroke the little craft shot out far into mid-stream.

"How strong you are!" cried Felicia. "I should never have thought it!"

The ease, the dexterity, the grace, delighted her. She looked at Hugh Kennett with shining eyes.

It may be suggested that no man, however well balanced, who is capable of athletic achievement, is ever insensible to such a tribute. This man had his foibles and pet vanities well in hand, but he certainly felt a momentary thrill, a glow of ingenuous pleasure, a strong, subtle, delicately intoxicating elation. He flushed a little.

" I find it to my advantage to keep in training, to a degree. It is a good point for me. Besides, I am fond of all athletic pursuits."

" There is a class for ladies at the gymnasium," remarked Felicia.

" I hardly think ladies need that sort of thing."

" *I* don't need it. I am very strong," declared Felicia. " I have no doubt I could surprise you, if I should condescend to row, as much as you surprised me."

But when he rose and offered her the oars with a great show of insistence, she laughed and crimsoned, and leaned back in her place, eagerly declining.

" It is not because I can't," she maintained, as he resumed his seat. " I don't want to make you uncomfortable by excelling you."

" Now, that is *too* kind," he retorted.

She had ceased to wonder that they knew each other so well ; it had begun to seem that they had been good friends always. Apparently he had felt this from the first. She had no care what she should say to him ; she knew he would be satisfied with whatever she might say ; he would share her mood, he would understand it. She did not feel it necessary to agree with him; she felt at liberty to argue, even to contradict, if occasion should offer. Occasion did not offer, however. The two natures were vibrant, and when a chord was struck the response was instantaneous and in tune. As the boat glided over the water, sometimes, after a silence which was curiously unconstrained, both would speak at once, and would laugh to discover that they had shared the thought which was uttered.

"The sky is like an Italian sky," she observed, looking up at the delicately yet intensely blue vault.

"I was just about to say that," he declared. "All day the air has been so soft that I have been reminded of days in Italy."

"I was abroad a very short time," remarked Felicia. "I should like to go again."

"You will, some day," he returned.

"Why do you say that?" she demanded, with a sort of pleased credulity.

"You are one of those lucky people who get what they desire. Life is going to be very good to you."

"It is delightful to think that," she said. Her face, above the smoke-colored dress she wore, and shaded by the long gray plumes of her hat, was so radiant that he was again reminded of a star in the rift of a summer cloud.

"It is your birthright," he added. "There is even a prophecy in your name."

"I hope it is a prophecy," she said, more gravely. "I am afraid of unhappiness. But it was my mother's name. She was very happy, but she died young."

"You are the youngest child?" he asked. He was rowing slowly, his steady gray eyes fixed on hers. The exercise had brought a glow to his face; his lips were slightly parted over the white line of his teeth; his attitude revealed the depth of his chest; through his light cloth coat the play of his muscles was suggested; the ease of his movements gave token of covert strength.

"I was her only child. My brother John is my half-brother."

"Oh," he said. Then after a pause, "I imagined — I don't know why — that in your own home you had a mother who was very fond of you, who read all your letters many times, and sent you pretty things to wear." He glanced at her soft gray dress, accented here and there with an indistinct shadowy pattern, which added to its cloudy effect.

"You fancied that because you think I am spoiled. Every one thinks I am spoiled." She would not listen to his protest. "Oh, you can't excuse yourself. You *almost* said it; you implied it. I never forget and I never forgive. I am very vindictive. Beware; Nemesis is on your path!" She broke into a peal of laughter.

It was pleasant to hear; she was pleasant to see, — so young, so happy, so genuine, so freshly and piquantly beautiful. Nature and art had combined their forces very judiciously, he thought. It was charming that she should be spontaneous, even childish, ingenuous, and natural; it was delightfully incongruous that she should have that finish of manner which comes only of elaborate training.

When their mood was graver, they talked discursively of life, of character, of aims. Felicia admitted that once she had been ambitious. That was long ago, when she was very young.

"I pined to do something grand with my life. I did not know exactly what I wanted; to write great books, or to paint great pictures, or even to delve into science, like Mrs. Somerville or Caroline Herschel. I wanted to accomplish something important. I knew it would require hard work, but I believed I was capable of hard work."

"Well?" said Hugh Kennett, expectantly, looking at her with a smile.

"Well, papa thought that was all nonsense. He said that if a woman has capacities she can find ample scope for them in making herself generally cultivated, and that to be a charming woman is as much a career as any other."

"I think he is right," said Kennett, heartily.

"Sometimes I doubt it," returned Felicia, pensively. "How would you like it if there seemed to be no real use for those things which you had spent your life in acquiring?"

"Well, not very much. However, there is this

difference : a woman may be learned or not, as she pleases, if only she is charming ; but a man must be one thing, or he is nothing."

" And that ? "

" Why, a success."

" Ah, you have had ambitions, — that is evident," said Felicia.

He laughed as his eyes rested on the emerald banks. " When I was young, — a long time ago," he said, repeating her phrase. " My ambitions have been like the bag of gold said to be buried at the foot of the rainbow, — when I reach the spot, it is just a little further on."

" That is because you have high ideals," said Felicia, maturely. She sometimes spoke with weight, as of years and experience, and he did not resent her pretty patronage. " That is different from not attaining, from failing. It would break my heart to fail; but pride is my besetting sin."

He would not admit that pride is a sin ; he evolved a theory on the spot.

" Pride has the same relation," he submitted, " to the moral nature that imagination has to the intellectual ; they are the only qualities that soar."

As the boat glided over the glassy surface she more than once pointed out some fleeting effect of the scene that escaped him : the flare of a clump of trumpet flowers growing about the bole of a dead tree ; the fantastic similitude of a whirlpool on the shining water ; the metallic gleam that edged a spray of leaves, definite against the rough gray rocks on the bank, — it might be cast in bronze, she remarked.

"How quick your perceptions are, — how sensitive you must be!" he said.

"It is not fortunate to be sensitive," she declared.

"That depends. Some emotions one need not fear, and others are like vitriol; they spoil everything they touch. Did you ever notice carefully any large collection of people? I have often observed that almost every face — I could point them out, one by one — is burnt by envy, or hatred, or ill temper, or anxiety; most, no doubt, by unnecessary cares, easier, and pleasanter, and more natural to throw aside than to cherish."

"That is rank pessimism," said Felicia. "People don't spoil themselves for pleasure."

"They don't realize it."

"You talk like a very happy man," said Felicia, with her former sedateness. "How would you endure some blow, some bitter disappointment or grief? Don't you suppose the vitriol would burn you, too?"

"You call sorrow vitriol? That does not burn. Sorrow is the pen of the prophet: it writes on the human palimpsest first a mandate, then a history; but it does not necessarily destroy the page. I don't hope to escape sorrow."

He rowed for a time in silence. The clouds were tinged with rose; the waves scintillated with gleams of green and yellow; the willows on shore rustled, as the breeze swept through.

" When a man does see a woman's face," said
Hugh Kennett, with a long sigh, " on which no
unworthy feeling has left a belittling touch, which
is bright with hope like the morning, and strong
with intellect, and gentle, and soft, and all wo-
manly, he should thank God for the favor vouchsafed ; for he has beheld the face of Eve in Para-
dise."

The shadows of the trees, ever lengthening, had
fallen over the water. And now the trees were
fewer, for the suburbs were reached. Scattered
residences surrounded with shrubbery had appeared upon the banks ; and already here was the
boat-house, craning over the water as if curious to
look at its own reflection. And on the slope of
the hill beyond there might be seen an ungainly
flat surface, suggesting the broad back of some
waddling animal, but which was recognizable as
the top of the street car.

Kennett was pulling in to the shore. " Layard,
and Schliemann, and Di Cesnola made valuable
researches," he remarked, as he helped her from
the boat. " They knew where Nineveh, and Troy,
and Salamis were, no doubt; but one other rather notable place they don't exactly locate." He
laughed, musingly. " Who could have imagined
it was so far west ! " he exclaimed.

" What is all that ? " asked Felicia, curiously.

But he only laughed again, and said that it was
not worth repeating and explaining.

As they reached the car they descried Fred,

coming in a violent hurry, flushed and panting. He said that the " boss " at the blacksmith shop had sent a man after the phaeton, who would take the horse home and explain the accident. " He 's got there by this time, with Henry Clay, and told papa all about it," said Fred with a certain satisfaction. Felicia thought Fred manifested considerable acumen in denying himself the pleasure of more equestrian exercise, and the glory of relating his sensational story in the paternal presence. She pictured to herself, with some amusement, his serious, anxious, sunburned face, when he warned the emissary — as no doubt he did — to say nothing of his ride on Henry Clay through the Park, and when he magnified the older charioteer's share in the accident.

The three started in a sufficiently amicable frame of mind. But when Fred learned that Felicia and Kennett had been upon the water, his sky was abruptly overcast ; it was difficult to appease him ; he wanted to begin the afternoon over again ; he wanted a new deal ; he would fain, like Joshua, command the sun to stand still. He bitterly and illogically upbraided them with having gone on the river without him. " Always trine ter beat me out'n my fun," he whined. "An' what do I want with this old knife, ennyhow ? I met that boy again, an' went an' traded my two good whangs o' leather fur it. An' I ain't been on that river fur a month o' Sundays."

All the way home he was malcontent and morose, and meditated bitterly on his grievances, commercial and social.

It was only the lumbering, ungraceful summer car, drawn by two big mules, driven by a red-faced, beery Irishman, presided over by a grizzled and grim conductor. No, no; rather, it was an enchanted chariot, rolling through the warm, sunset-tinted twilight, carrying Happiness and Hope, attended by Love and Constancy and all the Graces. Far away, the city stretched in shadowy uncertainty; already the purple vistas were enriched by lines of yellow gleams, that crossed each other in a tangled maze, like a swarm of fireflies; ruby points, advancing and receding, gemmed the dusky streets; the tinkle of bells was borne faintly on the air; the silver sphere of the full moon, slowly appearing above the eastern roofs, outlined them against the darkly blue sky with shining white gleams.

When the trio of pleasure-seekers approached John Hamilton's house, they saw him smoking a cigar, as he leaned in a sufficiently graceful attitude against one of the big fluted pillars at the head of the flight of steps. The lingering daylight showed the flowers in the grass-plot, and the vines about the walls. The windows were open, and through the lace curtains streamed the subdued radiance of a shaded gas-jet.

"That is like a stage-setting," remarked Hugh Kennett. "In another moment you will see advancing down the right centre the first lady, or the villain, or the heavy father."

"There's the heavy father, now, is n't he, Fred?" said Felicia.

Fred only mumbled that he did n't know, an' did n't care, an' did n't want nuthin' ter say ter her, — always trine ter cheat somebody out'n their fun.

John Hamilton was a cordial soul. When Felicia introduced her companion, though he wondered greatly whether she had met him at Madame Sevier's or at home, he received the stranger like a suddenly found friend, ardently shook hands, and warmly invited him indoors.

Kennett replied that he was sorry he could not come in, but he had not time; he was due downtown now.

"We shall be glad to see you at any time," said the master of the house.

The heartiness of tone seemed to awaken reciprocal warmth. Kennett replied, with the air of very amicably receiving an advance, that next week he should be at leisure, and should be glad to avail himself of the invitation. He expected to spend his vacation in Chilonnatti. It was an agreeable prospect. He had been knocking about from pillar to post for so long, he thought he should enjoy a rest. Delightful weather just now. And then he lifted his hat and said good-evening.

"Glad to have met you, Mr. Kennett," declared John Hamilton, unreservedly; and as the sound of the stranger's footsteps died away, he turned to his sister.

"Who is that fellow, Felicia?" he asked, with vivacious curiosity.

"That is the Mr. Kennett I mentioned to you. He is a cousin of cousin Robert's," she replied, as they entered the hall together.

"Did you meet him at Raymond's house?"

"Oh, yes. He was there one day when Fred and I happened to call."

"What is his business?" asked John Hamilton, somewhat indifferently, now that his curiosity was satisfied.

"I don't know. I never heard him mention business except what he said to you a moment since. I have met him only three times. He was in the Park last Saturday, and, while I was waiting for Fred, he came up and talked to me. He met us again this afternoon, after the phaeton was broken, and I rowed with him from the Park as far as the street railroad."

She said to herself that there should be nothing clandestine about the affair. If any objections were to be made, now was the time to make them. John Hamilton was apparently disposed to advance none.

"Seems an agreeable sort of fellow," he remarked, casually.

V.

THIS year, the summer was very long and hot. From early morning till the reluctant sun sank slowly below the horizon, the heated city rarely felt the thrill of a breeze. Sometimes sudden, short, angry thunderstorms passed tumultuously, and left the air warm as ever, but permeated with a heavy moisture. People plied their palm-leaf fans, declared that it was intolerable, and left town in great numbers.

Hugh Kennett, who had promptly availed himself of John Hamilton's invitation to call, was before long a frequent visitor at the house; indeed, almost the only visitor, so general had been the exodus. The method of entertaining him might have been deemed monotonous, but was in a certain sense flattering. He was allowed to slip into the little circle on the footing of a family friend. He was invited more than once to dinner, quite informally. He fell into the habit of walking by the house late in the afternoon, and there was usually a plausible excuse to stop and chat with the group disposed on the front steps, after the custom in Southern and *quasi*-Southern cities; he had brought a book they had had under discussion, or the illustrated papers, with the last political cartoon; some one would give him a has-sock; the dusk would deepen; the few moments would multiply; the perfume of heliotrope and roses would burden the warm, languorous air; the gentle voices of the women would rise and fall; the moonbeams would slip down on their hair.

It was Mrs. Hamilton's habit, at a regular hour every evening, to repair to the front room upstairs, to put the baby to bed. This conscientious lady would not attempt to overhear the conversation of the young people; she only undressed the baby near the window, and their voices would float up to her. His was resonant and carried well, and was far more distinct than Felicia's. There seemed to be nothing very important said. Some-times his laughter rang out: it was a pleasant laugh, peculiarly rich, full, and musical; it had an appreciative suggestion. Occasionally there were long pauses, and no wind stirred the vines, and the flowers gave out a faint, sweet breath, and the white blocks of moonlight on the streets and sidewalks were unbroken by a passing shadow. The discreet matron made the job of undressing the baby a long and elaborate job, and came down, with an innocent face and the consciousness of duty well performed, to take her share in the talk, — for the most part trivial chat concerning the incidents of the day, or the weather, or that unfailing theme, the dullness of town.

" I should have found it unendurable but for my calls here," he once said, frankly. " I have

not had much of the home atmosphere in my life.
I had no idea that I should appreciate the home
atmosphere so thoroughly as I do."

They grew to know him very well ; but he was
not a difficult person to know. He was transparent, and in fact sometimes lacked tact. He
was not sensitive, — in the interpretation of being
on the alert for slights ; either from pronounced
self-esteem or because of reliance on the intention of others, he was apt to place a kindly con-
struction on anything that was apparently equi-
vocal. He seemed to be tolerant in judgment,
and generous. There was but slight suggestion
of a fiercer stratum underlying the smooth surface of his character. Fred, it is true, had a lurid
theory.

" He's got a orful high temper," the boy remarked one day, when the new friend was under
discussion in the family circle. " Yer oughter
heard him givin' fits ter the man that come so
near runnin' over me on Sixth Street with his
team yestiddy, when I was jus' crossin' the street,
an' warn't thinkin' 'bout nuthin', nor lookin'.
An' Mr. Kennett, he happened to be passin', an'
he jus' jumped off the sidewalk, an' caught the
horses by the reins, an' hollered ter the man ter
mind what he was about. An' he was mighty
mad, Mr. Kennett was, an' — swore."

He said this in a slightly awed voice, and looked
seriously at his mother, doubtful, but impressed.
She rose to the occasion.

"You shock me," she said. "How could Mr. Kennett do so ungentlemanly a thing as to swear!"

Felicia glanced up quickly, as Fred left the room.

"Why should n't Mr. Kennett swear, if he likes?" she demanded, aggressively.

"According to Fred's account there *was* no reason," replied Mrs. Hamilton, with a mild giggle.

Notwithstanding her partisanship, something in this episode grated on our fastidious young lady's ideas of the fitness of things, and it might have been with a lurking intention as to the effect of a subtle, unrecognized influence that she contrived, at the first opportunity, to steer the conversation into the subject of self-command, and to lay down some impersonal, and it might even be said elementary, propositions touching the triviality of character suggested by an incapacity to control the temper. "It is as ludicrous and weak for a man to stamp about, and break things, and swear because he is in a rage as it is for a woman to mope and cry because she feels nervous," said the young Mentor, didactically.

And Mrs. Hamilton, who happened to overhear this, noticed that Mr. Kennett wore a bland and innocent unconsciousness, which induced in the matron of a decade the reflection that, if Felicia were ambitious of a missionary career, the heathen offered a more promising field than the one she seemed to have in contemplation.

He was mild mannered and peaceable enough, however, so far as they knew of their own knowledge, and Fred's story might require a grain or two of salt.

In their long interviews he was somewhat given to silence; he talked little about himself, and was little inclined to reminiscence. Once he spoke of his mother, who had died when he was growing into manhood. She was very strict, he said, very stern and uncompromising; she was the most devoted of mothers; she had no happiness save in the welfare of her children. His father he mentioned occasionally, with that tenderness which Felicia had earlier divined had survived a bitter and long-felt grief. Of his sisters, the elder, three years his junior, had died at twenty-two. That loss had broken his father's heart; he did not live long afterward. The younger sister had married about a year ago, and had been abroad ever since. He said he had been disappointed; he thought she deserved well of fate; she was very beautiful and talented. Her husband was a good fellow, but commonplace.

This, in effect, was all that was revealed, in those summer evenings, of Hugh Kennett's past. To Mrs. Hamilton, afterward, it seemed very meagre, though at the time she felt no lack. And as for him, — when a man is happy he thinks little of his past. He was doing what few can do in a lifetime, — he was living his present; he was interpreting that problem which eludes us when it is attainable, and mocks us when it has slipped by, at once the simplest and the most complex element of existence, that tantalizing mystery, *Now.* His past was narrowed to what was said and glanced yesterday evening; his future was bounded by the possibilities of to-morrow.

Felicia, too, was alive in every sensitive susceptibility to the influences which permeated the intense momentous present of these radiant summer days. Life had come to be enchantment to her; the prosaic episodes of the daily routine were transfigured and dignified; monotony,— it was an unrealized and a forgotten force; thought was reverie. She, too, had no longer need for memory or anticipation. Her beauty had acquired a new softness; there was a sort of tender appeal about her, and yet the delicate and ethereal exaltation which possessed her had a less poetic element, for she was prosaically good-humored; annoyances that would once have tried her sorely had become merely unexpected opportunity for mirth; she had developed sympathy and tact; she was gentle and amenable, and easily pleased. "A girl in love is a very agreeable visitor in the house," was Mrs. Hamilton's comment,— a mental comment, for she was a prudent woman, and in silence smilingly watched the little drama, in which the actors were too deeply absorbed to remember the spectator.

All this time John Hamilton was absent from

home. The day after he met Hugh Kennett, he had been called away to certain famous Dakota wheat-fields. He was going into very heavy enterprises ; he proposed to himself that his operations in the near future should be still heavier ; he aspired to be the Napoleon of the next great " deal." Fortune, so far, had favored him, and he was liberal as well as ambitious. He was ready to give appropriate exponents of his increasing prosperity, and had bought a particularly eligible corner lot, on which he was building a fine house. One of Mrs. Hamilton's reasons for liking Hugh Kennett was the fact that he had so much taste and acumen in the matter of the new house, and she frequently consulted him.

" Don't you think the walls of that east room should be Pompeian red, Mr. Kennett ? " she said one day, fixing her eyes on his face as if she would read his very soul. She was constantly growing more assured as to manner, and her increasing prosperity expressed itself more distinctly, still with circumspection, in the appointments of her house, her carriage, and her dress. She was not the less eager, however, to avail herself of the advice and experience of others, and kept her own views in a condition to be instantly modified by circumstances. " Pompeian red, with panels, — those large panels, with arabesques in shaded reds. I showed you the design."

" Well, to be perfectly candid," he replied, " it seems to me those panels are too pronounced, too theatrical."

" *Do* you think so?" she said, and meditated deeply on this view.

They were going, this afternoon, to look over the new house. Mrs. Hamilton — her plump little figure encased in a gray and white India silk, which seemed refreshingly light and cool — walked in front with Kennett. Her face, flushed with heat and exercise, under the soft brown hair that waved on each side of her candid brow, was a study of anxiety and complacence. Her round, gentle, inquiring eyes took in all the details about the ambitious mansions they passed. Her little remarks were not sufficiently absorbing to prevent his hearing every word uttered by Felicia, who, with Fred as escort, made up the party.

It chanced that, in the course of the expedition, Mrs. Hamilton was in the hall in consultation with the architect, on the endless subject of the staircase, Fred had strolled off, and the other two found themselves in the great unfurnished drawing-rooms. Felicia had been much exercised about various points under discussion, and had given her opinion with frankness and vivacity. " When those changes about the sliding-doors upstairs have been made and the frescoing finished, it will be almost perfect; don't you think so?" she said, appealing to Kennett.

He did not reply. He was leaning against the window-frame, his eyes fixed on her, as she stood in the middle of the floor. She had come at a moment's notice, in the lawn morning-dress —

white flecked with pink — she was wearing.
Nothing could be simpler. She was without
gloves. Her garden hat shaded her face. She
seemed to him fair and fresh as a flower.

"Do you know," she exclaimed, suddenly, "this
is the first time I ever saw you out of spirits.
You look dismal. What is the matter?"

"I was thinking," he returned, a trifle embarrassed.

"So I perceived ; but of what ? "

"Well, to be candid, I was thinking that you
ought to have a house like this, — a house of your
own."

"Oh," cried Felicia, "I should n't like it ! "

"You seem very fond of all this sort of thing,"
he persisted. "You were describing with actual
enthusiasm the upholstery they have selected for
this room."

"I *am* interested — for other people."

"Frankly, now, would n't you like it for yourself ? "

She glanced about her critically, — at the big
rooms opposite, the big hall, the sweep of the
stair-case, the carved newel-post, which had cost
Mrs. Hamilton several nights' rest lest it should
not be exactly what was desired. She tried to
imagine it all when finished, — the rich and ac-
cordant coloring, the pictures, the deep, soft carpets, the sheen of mirrors. Then she turned her
eyes on him with a smile.

"I hope it is not discreditable to me," she replied, — " an irresponsible, Bohemian way of looking at things, — but, frankly, I should n't care to have a house like this. Sophie is going to find it a white elephant ; a good thing in its way, but a great responsibility."

His face was less grave, but he shook his head. " I am afraid you don't understand relative values," he said.

" Why, you are doing me injustice ! " cried Felicia, crimsoning suddenly. " This is the first time I ever knew you to do any one injustice. You must think me very frivolous to care so *much* for things, — mere *things*."

" No, no ; you misunderstand me," he protested. " I was only a little curious as to how you feel about such matters. What *do* you care for most, if not for ' things ' ? "

" Well," began Felicia, appeased, — she was easily appeased, " I believe I care most for people, agreeable, bright, cheerful people ; not glum individuals, who stand in a window and quarrel about nothing. Then I like change and variety. I am fond of things, too, — pretty things ; but principally I like people. I have seen so much deadly dullness in the best houses. That is what I hate, — dullness."

All the light had come back to his face.

" What you like," he said, recapitulating, " is brightness, and what you hate is dullness."

" Yes," said Felicia, with her sunny smile. She had perched on one of the carpenter's saw-horses, and leaned her elbow among the shavings scattered about the big, rough work-bench; she supported her head on her hand. She had been running up and down stairs; the expression of her eyes showed that she was tired.

"And it would not be a bitterness, a trial, to you to give up — I have often thought it a great sacrifice a man situated as I am would ask you to make, if he should tell you — that he — that — that I" —

He was agitated; he hesitated, yet he glanced around in intense impatience because of an interruption, as Mrs. Hamilton came suddenly into the room.

"Felicia," she began, with excitement, "don't you see that carriage stopping in front of the door? Who can it be?" She had rustled to the window. "Why, it is Mr. Raymond!" she exclaimed.

A gentleman had alighted from the vehicle, and was advancing up the pavement. He saw the group at the window, and as they emerged into the hall to meet him he entered at the front door. His face was grave.

"They told me at the other house you were here," he said hurriedly, as he greeted Mrs. Hamilton. "I have bad news. Mr. Stanley died last night, very unexpectedly. The physicians had pronounced him convalescent. I must ask you and Felicia to give some orders for Amy and Mrs. Brant, and" —

He paused abruptly as he caught sight of his cousin; there was much surprise in his face as they shook hands. "Have you been in town all summer, Hugh?" he asked.

"All summer," replied Kennett.

Raymond looked hard at him, the troubled perplexity deepening on his face. Nothing further was said, however. He turned to Mrs. Hamilton to reply to her interrogations and remarks touching the news he had brought, and gave Felicia a note from his wife, — hasty and blotted with tears. There were tears in her sympathetic eyes as she read it.

"You can go now?" asked Mr. Raymond. "The stores will be closed in an hour or two."

Felicia assented, and started toward the door.

"Won't you have time, Felicia, to put on a street dress?" cried Mrs. Hamilton, in dismay. She had adopted not a little of the young lady's exacting code of externals.

"Oh, what does it matter at such a time!" exclaimed Felicia; and Hugh Kennett thought loyally how petty, how trivial-minded, were the best of women — Mrs. Hamilton was one of the best of women — in comparison with a supremely lovely nature like this. He did not accompany the trio.

"I will take Fred home before I go down town," he said, as he stood on the sidewalk, by the carriage door.

As they drove away, Mr. Raymond remarked, "You seem to know Kennett pretty well."

" Oh, yes, indeed ; he has been such a pleasant friend," said Mrs. Hamilton, enthusiastically. " He is *so* agreeable, and high minded, and well informed, and *such* a gentleman."

Felicia's shining eyes — dewy and dark with feeling — were fixed on the speaker ; her lips wore that curve which expresses more happiness than a smile. Robert Raymond thought he had never seen her so childlike, so beautiful, so unconstrained, as she sat opposite him, in her simple dress, with her soft, ungloved hands lying lightly in her lap. " How her face reveals her heart ! " he thought.

" Yes," he said, " Kennett is an agreeable fellow. Does Hamilton know him ? "

" They were introduced to each other the evening before John received the telegram calling him to Dakota. By the way, I am looking for John every day, now."

" He is just back," announced Raymond, suddenly. " We met on the train to-day."

" Oh, dear, perhaps I ought to go home ! " cried Mrs. Hamilton, in a flutter.

" No ; he knew I should see you, and he asked me to tell you that he could not leave the office until late, — there is so much to arrange."

" Oh, well, then," said Mrs. Hamilton, settling back contentedly. To be sure, the opportunity was a melancholy one, but even the duty of ordering a friend's mourning is its own recompense, and spending money on so sad an occasion affords the Mrs. Hamiltons of this world a gloomy joy.

It was evident that the time for the purchases was very short, yet as the two ladies were about to enter the store at which the carriage stopped Raymond detained them. He was greatly disquieted; his eye was anxious and wandering; he began more than one sentence, and broke off in its midst.

"There is still something I must see about," he said, uncertainly. "I will come back here and say good-by — or — no — I shall not have time. Perhaps, Mrs. Hamilton, you will drive down to the depot. I will meet you there." ·

He left them abruptly, and Mrs. Hamilton stared at him as he went. "How funny he is!" she said, wonderingly.

The truth was, the Reverend Robert's conscience was after him, and it pursued him in a lively fashion till he reached the office of Hamilton and Gale — Commission Merchants.

He was very nearly left by the train, this afternoon. Mrs. Hamilton and Felicia, sitting in the carriage at the depot, had waited half an hour; the locomotive had pulled into the building; crowds of passengers were boarding the cars before they saw his face framed by the window of a hack that was driven furiously down the street. He had barely time for hasty adieux. "Good-by, good-by!" he exclaimed. "It is very kind of you to take so much trouble."

He looked hard at Felicia; she did not understand his expression. It was tender; it curiously

blended a sort of compassion and a sort of entreaty.   After he had started hurriedly from them,
he turned back suddenly, took her hand, and held
it in a strong clasp.   "God bless you, my dear
child," he said.

"He is very, very odd to-day," said Mrs. Hamilton, again gazing vaguely after his receding
figure.   "How strange, his coming back to bid
you good-by again, Felicia, and how strangely he
looked at you ! "

"I suppose it is because Amy is so fond of me,"
said Felicia.   "Now that she is grieved he feels
very kindly to any one she loves."

But she did not quite accept her own explanation, and pondered on that pitiful expression of
his in pained bewilderment.

VI.

THAT night seemed afterward to Felicia like the beginning of a terrible dream. It opened with a bitter experience, — for the first time in her life she received a cruel look, directed point-blank into her eyes. To be admired, quoted, commended lavishly and injudiciously, — this had been her lot so far; and to her half-brother, — who was almost double her age — she was indebted for more than a fair share of praise and petting. To receive from him a prolonged stare, keen, critical, — no, was it not more? even angry, bitterly angry, — it was like receiving a blow in the face.

As there was no visitor this evening, she had shared with Sophie the diversion of getting the baby to bed. She was sitting on the floor, with the child in her arms, when Hamilton's step and voice sounded in the hall below, and his wife ran downstairs to meet him.

As they entered the room, Felicia called out gayly, without rising, " See how strong the baby is, John! See how she has learned to stand alone while you were away! Stand alone-y, precious, for your auntie."

She looked up, startled, as her brother spoke; his voice was cold and hard.

"Pack your trunks at once, Felicia," he said, abruptly. "We shall start for the East to-morrow, and you will go with us."

She rose to her feet in surprise, the child still in her arms.

"Going East to-morrow?" she repeated faintly. Then it was he bent upon her that cruel look.

"You don't seem pleased," he said, with a short laugh. "I thought you would be delighted to get back to your beloved Madame Sevier again."

"I — I don't want to go now — it's so — so hot," said Felicia, hesitating.

"We'll hunt a cool resort; Mount Desert, perhaps. Or maybe we'll try Long Branch, Cape May, Saratoga. I don't know where we'll go. We'll have an outing. You and Sophie have been penned in this dull hole all summer." Again he laughed, his eyes still fixed on hers.

For a moment she did not reply; then she faltered, "This is very strange. It is not proper for me to go off on a pleasure trip so soon after the death of a near connection of my mother's. Papa will be very angry."

"This trip is *my* affair. *I* propose to account to father for your movements," returned Hamilton, significantly.

She did not, as might have been expected of one so indulged and so spirited, resent his tone. She was amazed and startled, and she quailed a little. She lifted her eyes with a propitiatory look. "You are not angry with me, brother?" she said, almost meekly. She usually addressed him by his name; he softened a moment, then hardened again.

"Why should I be angry with you?" he demanded. "Give the baby to Julia, and go to your packing. We leave in the morning at five o'clock."

Felicia went to her room. She stood meditative and motionless, near the window, her eyes upon the scene without. The moonlight alternated with parallelograms of black shadow; very quiet was the street; the stars burned faintly; the wind had died; fireflies gleamed fitfully among the foliage of the shade trees along the sidewalk, whence she was wont to catch the advancing red glow of Hugh Kennett's cigar. She walked slowly to her desk, seated herself, and began to write. Her brother, lounging on the balcony of his own room, watched her curiously through the vista of doors, left open that any welcome vagrant breeze might enter. He saw that she hesitated as she wrote; that she made more than one beginning; that she read over the few lines hurriedly, placed the sheet in an envelope, and directed it with a precipitancy that contrasted with her previous deliberation. He saw her hand it to the maid, who had been packing the trunks, with the injunction to run across the street and place it in the letter-box.

"To-night, Miss Felicia?" asked the girl, in surprise.

"Yes, now," she replied.

John Hamilton rose, entered from the balcony, and walked downstairs composedly. When the servant had laid aside the articles in her hands and descended with the note, she came upon him pacing up and down the hall, his hands in his pockets, and a cigar, which he had just lighted, in his mouth.

"What's that?" he demanded, glancing at the envelope she held.

"It is a note Miss Felicia wanted me to post," the servant answered.

He held out his hand silently for the note, and as he read, "Mr. Hugh Kennett, Lawrence Hotel," he turned the envelope so that his wife, who chanced to be coming downstairs, could see the address; then he handed it back to the maid, who passed out of the open door into the moonlit street.

"When I asked you, Sophie," he said bitterly, to his wife, "how far this affair had gone, you said it would not amount to anything. I thought then you were mistaken, and I think so now more than ever."

Mrs. Hamilton made no reply. She had a scared, anxious look; all her little complacence, so satisfactorily growing and putting forth new shoots, had wilted in an hour. She had never seen so stern an expression on her husband's face. Much bronzed his face was by his trip; his hair and mustache had grown luxuriant; he was

stouter than when he left home. Big, strong, and
prosperous, his was the very face and figure for
placid satisfaction ; but his eyebrows had met in
a heavy frown, he gnawed his lip under his flowing mustache. " We are going to have the devil
and all of a time with that girl," he prophesied,
grimly.

The sunrise was hardly more than a rosy glow
over the landscape when the Hamiltons started on
their " outing," and the neighborhood was greatly
amazed because of the suddenness of the flitting.

Heretofore Felicia had been an excellent trav-
eler, always ready, well, entertained, good-humored. The new faces, the variety of incident,
even the rapidity of motion, gave her that keen
sense of delight impossible to one less healthy,
young, and joyous. Now the zest was lacking to
the journey. She did not look with interest at
the people about her, and busy her imagination
with their histories, the comedies and tragedies of
their lives ; the landscape slipped by unheeded.
Once she would have found Fred and his idiosyn-
crasies under these new circumstances great fun ;
now his eager talk tired her ; the warmth of the
weather oppressed her ; she was irritated by the
sound of the train, the bustle, the confusion, the
swarms of people.

When the party reached New York, and later
Boston, she had the shock of a painful surprise.
Among the letters which had been sent on from
Chilounatti, there was no reply to the note she

had written Hugh Kennett the evening before
she left town. It had been a simple little note,
merely telling him of the unexpected departure
and wishing him good-by. But she had confi-
dently expected a reply, and his silence bewil-
dered, pained, and cruelly mortified her. The
complication of feelings developed gradually into
the first deep depression of spirit she had ever
known. There was little opportunity for distraction in outside interests. John Hamilton's idea
of summer pleasuring seemed to be expressed by
a swift, transit from place to place ; to see all that
was to be seen and to buy all that was desired in
as short a time as possible. His plan was to take
the cities first, then the watering places. There
was much of isolation in this style of enjoyment.
Felicia's New York friends had all left town.
The party met few acquaintances, and found but
scant entertainment in the spectacle of metropolitan life out of season,— a dismal spectacle enough ;
like a moulting bird, an absurd caricature of itself.

To Felicia it was very tiresome to wander
through the picture-galleries, and gaze vacantly
at the works of art designated by the catalogues
for intelligent admiration ; still more tiresome to
force herself to take interest in the endless discussions concerning carpets, glass, and china at
the various fashionable stores, where the party
came to be well known, and where John Hamilton's liberality and his wife's taste extorted high

commendation. Perhaps something was extorted
on the other side, but as the Hamiltons were satisfied with their purchases we need make no moan.

Felicia's unhappiness was very evident, and
now it was that John Hamilton should have taken
the field in force with a bountiful supply of am-
munition in the way of tact. If Felicia had been
the recipient of the customary kind consideration
from her sister-in-law and of his half-jocular, half-
tender petting, she would naturally have turned
to their affection, and the impressions of the last
few weeks might have loosed their hold. But
Hamilton proved himself grievously lacking in discernment, in adroitness, even in common policy.
He was a man of strong will and high temper;
when he was displeased he was very likely to
make the fact more patent than the occasion required.

There was something hard in John Hamilton.
Many of those who knew him best never suspected
it. The expression of his florid face, his jolly
laughter, his free, frank, hearty manner, afforded
no suggestion of the underlying iron in his nature. His habit of success had given him an im-
periousness of intention and expectation. He
would not contemplate adverse circumstance; he
would not tolerate opposing will. He was at no
time disposed to subject his thoughts and feelings
to scrutiny. He did not reason on the matter in
hand. It was not his intention to break his sister's spirit; he was simply displeased, and it was

his instinct to sweep out of existence whatever displeased him.

This silent, bitter antagonism was an unfortunate course to pursue with Felicia. In many respects she and her brother were alike : in her nature, too, there was hard metal ; she, too, was intolerant and imperious. When she first became aware of that inexplicable antagonism, pervading the moral atmosphere like an impending thunderstorm, she made some effort to place affairs on a less sombre footing. Her attempts at conversation and vivacity were met with anxious uncertainty on Sophie's part, and a cold unresponsiveness from her brother. Disconcerted and abashed, she fell again into her absorbed musings, with the changed manner of her companions for a new theme. Under these circumstances traveling was not unalloyed pleasure. She would have given up the trip and returned home, but that she had received a letter from her father to the effect that the house was shut up ; that he was off on the circuit, and expected to have no vacation until the early part of September, when he would meet the party in New York, and take her home with him. Obviously no radical change was possible, but a new element of feeling was unexpectedly infused into the situation.

During the early portion of the journey she saw but little of her brother. In the cities they visited he had his own engagements. While in transit he occupied himself in playing with the baby or reading the newspapers, or he was absorbed with a note-book and pencil and abstruse calculations. One day, however, when he chanced to be seated beside her, she broke a long silence by saying, with a sigh, that she supposed they would receive no more letters until they should again become stationary for a time.

He looked at her quickly, keenly, suspiciously. She did not understand it, — she did not understand him, — and she spoke on the impulse of the moment.

"Are you displeased with me?" she asked, suddenly.

"Why should I be displeased with you, Felicia?" he demanded, curtly. He was rising as he spoke; he had taken out a cigar; in his other hand he had a match. He looked down at her, and his face held so tyrannical an expression — an expression at once angry, cold, and overbearing — that the smouldering fire of her pride kindled in an instant.

"I am sure I don't know," she retorted, with spirit. Their eyes met. Perhaps there came to him at this moment some belated inspiration of policy, for, after a second of hesitation, he turned on his heel and made his way into the smoking-car.

Felicia's pride, once ablaze, did not again smoulder. The infusion of animation into her manner was genuine enough, after this, but it was not the light-hearted joyousness of old. She

was on the alert at last, on the defensive; she
was even ready to engage the skulking antagonisms.　Nothing was expressed; nothing was so
tangible that explanations were in order; her resentment only shone in her eyes, vibrated in the
ring of her voice, curved with her upper lip,
which had drooped lately and given her a certain
pathos to enhance the pallor of her face.　She
was not always pale now; she flushed easily and
brilliantly; she carried herself proudly; she became somewhat addicted to sarcasm.　Hamilton
interpreted all this, perhaps correctly enough, as
defiance.　"Did n't I tell you, Sophie," he said
to his wife, discussing with her one of these mani-
festations, "that we were going to have a devil of
a time with Felicia?　I suppose you see how rebellious she is?"

"Perhaps, dear, if you were a little more gentle with her"—suggested Mrs. Hamilton, meekly.

"Gentle!　Blankity blank!" exclaimed John
Hamilton, hotly.　The good lady cowered whenever he fell into expletive.

It would, perhaps, have been lucky for the ter-
mination of this affair, looked at from his own
standpoint, if Hamilton had married a terma-
gant instead of his acquiescent Sophie.　It is
well enough for a man to be afraid of no man;
it is not a bad thing for him to be afraid—in
reason—of some woman.　John Hamilton was
afraid of nobody, least of all, of Felicia.　He
met her tacit defiance with tacit counter-defiance.

He did not dream how unhappy she was; perhaps he would not have altered his course if he had realized it, so incapable of concession was his nature. She was too intense, too untamed, too young, to accept wretchedness save with passionate protest. Sometimes, after a day made up of the weary daze of shopping and sight-seeing, or the laborious idleness of watering-place life, when shut at last into her own room, she would sob for hours in the light of the summer moon or the white stars.

Underlying the pained bewilderment and indignation induced by the latent domestic discord was the complication of emotions caused by Hugh Kennett's inexplicable silence. Often she said to herself she would be reasonable about this matter. Did she not know him well enough, she asked herself, to decide if it were consonant with his character to inflict a slight upon any human being? He was very tender-hearted, — she had often noticed that; he was almost weak in that respect; it was a little absurd to be so ultra-careful of the feelings of other people; and would he, who would not wound Fred, who spoke with consideration to the servants, to the very beggars on the street, put an affront upon any one, — upon *her?* For a time this train of thought would comfort her; but when again alone, the reverse side of the question would present itself. He would not put a slight upon her, — of course he would not; but her note was a matter of such little moment to him that he could not imagine it was important to her. He had forgotten her note, — that was all. Her ingenuity in self-torture was as uncharacteristic as her self-depreciation. As to what she had fancied he was about to say that last day, — she had been misled by her vanity. This reflection made her humble enough. In an evil moment an elaboration of this theory occurred to her. Perhaps he, too, had reviewed those words of his, which seemed to hold a momentous meaning, a meaning he did not intend ; and if that were the case, what of encouragement did her note imply? Did it seem to lure him further when he had said nothing, — when he had nothing to say? And his silence : was he silent in scorn, divining her misinterpretation ; in mercy, that she might have no opportunity to commit herself further? So warped was her judgment, so morbid had she grown, that this wild theory came to be an actual fact to her mind, and all the pangs that had gone before were as nothing to the poignant anguish of her writhing pride.

Toward the end of August, John Hamilton's party found themselves for a few days in Philadelphia. ·One warm afternoon, the choice was presented to Felicia to go with Sophie to select lace curtains, or with Fred to the Academy of Sciences. She yielded to her nephew's ardent insistence, thinking that it would be cool in the Academy building, and she need not talk ; it was not even necessary to go through the form of replying to Fred.

The building was lonely. In all the half million — plus — of inhabitants in the city there seemed to be nobody but themselves disposed toward science. The big halls responded with hollow echoes to the sound of their steps. Fred's raptures, when they reached the skeleton of the Megatherium, were difficult to control; he met the gigantic bones as if he had found a long-lost brother. Felicia, tired of his noisy comments and his monotonous accent, as he laboriously read the valuable paragraphs devoted by the catalogue to the admired object, strolled away. As she stood at some distance, looking absently about her, she was surprised to hear her own name. She turned her head quickly. A gentleman was standing near her, his hat in his hand, a smile of greeting on his lips.

VII.

ABSORBED in her own reflections, she had not noticed an approach, and Alfred Grafton was now so foreign to her thoughts that for an instant she had a trifle of difficulty in recognizing him. That supremacy in small crises conferred by her training came to her aid, and the hesitation with which she extended her hand was not perceptible. He stood in a bar of sunshine that lighted him up with unwonted effectiveness; his dark hazel eyes had yellow gleams in them; he was smiling; for once his face had an entirely simple expression, — the expression of unaffected pleasure; the summer suit he wore was becoming; he looked very well.

After a few conventional inquiries as to the health of the family, "I suppose," he said, with an indefinite wave of his hand at the materialized learning in the cabinets about them, "you find all this very interesting?"

"The bones? No, to be quite candid, I don't enjoy them; I don't care anything about them."

His momentary geniality had already disappeared. He replied with an intonation of objection, — not strong enough to be resented as a rebuke, but which irritated by its suggestion that

he esteemed his own views the exactly appropriate sentiments.

"I should think a lady of your intellect might
find much to instruct and entertain her here."

"I am not a lady of intellect," returned Felicia, perversely. "I am a very frivolous person.
I can entertain myself, and I don't want to be
instructed."

They were walking together down the long hall.
She swung her parasol lightly, and glanced about
her indifferently. Grafton may have been
vaguely conscious of her strong subcurrent of
painful emotion, and, aware that his words were
in some way repugnant to her, have yielded to an
infrequent impulse of magnanimity; he may have
been only desirous to propitiate her. At any rate,
he made the one approach to an apology of which
his record can boast.

"I hope I did n't offend you," he said, almost
with deprecation.

"Oh, dear, no," declared Felicia, heartlessly.
"I did n't care."

He could not complain now that her suavity
was too pronounced for sincerity. The tone in
which she said this was hardly civil, but for a
certain tense vibration which, notwithstanding his
stilted code and contracted horizon, he had sufficient discernment to interpret as the manifesta-
tion of acute mental disquiet. He turned his
bright, deep-set eyes upon her, as they walked on,
side by side. Her face had lost somewhat in

color, in roundness of line, in animation; it had acquired something he did not understand, — something not joyous, but replete with meaning; it seemed to him to have become susceptible of taking on subtle and complex expressions. As the momentary irritation faded, there came in its stead a certain dignity, and that ethereal look which much thought or much feeling can confer. Added to the fascination of her smile which he had known — she glanced at him and smiled presently, as if in reparation, and her voice had gentle intonations — was a new fascination which he could not analyze.

He was cordially welcomed by both Mr. and Mrs. Hamilton, when he appeared at the hotel that evening. They, as well as Felicia, had found their method of pleasuring rather dismal. "To go about among strangers all the time is poor enjoyment, no matter how many new things one buys," declared Mrs. Hamilton. He was a somewhat cool subject for Hamilton's *camaraderie*, but was, as that gentleman remarked, "a confounded sight better than nobody." The young man hung about them while they remained in Philadelphia, and a few days after they reached the seaside he joined them. He explained, with some embarrassment, that he was awaiting the arrival of his mother, who expected to place his sister at boarding-school in New York, and would return home to Chilounatti with him.

What attracted him was soon apparent enough.

He made no attempt at subterfuge after that simulacrum of an explanation of his presence. He was constantly at Felicia's side. He brought her books and flowers. He arranged sailing expeditions. They often rode down the avenues, kaleidoscopic with the pageantry of vehicles and equestrians that defiled between the palpitating sea and the long line of big hotels, with their fluttering flags, and clanging bands, and flower-like groups of women and children bedecking the piazzas. She wondered at his persistence. She had not intentionally given him reason to persist. When, however, a man interprets himself as the expression of his highest ideal, the translation acquires so much dignity that it is not very difficult for him to believe his version is accepted by others. Felicia found it less annoying to maintain a state of seeming acquiescence than to give herself the luxury of indulging her irritability. To make sarcastic speeches to him involved the necessity of reparation, retraction; and this sort of tact required rapid and fatiguing thought. After some experimenting, she discovered that it was not impossible to induce him to talk much on subjects that interested him. He was a man of taste, to a certain degree, and would not intentionally have indulged in monologue; but she was adroit, and so managed that he was not consciously egotistic. She found, too, that she could give him a modicum of attention, enough to apprehend his talk, — the surface of her mind, so to speak, while along the

deeper current swept her own absorbing reflections.   How was he to suspect this dual process?
Her violet eyes would rest softly on his face; her
lips would part now and then with her enchant-
ing smile; she would occasionally utter some per-
tinent comment, or a judicious word of acquiescence or dissent; and he was satisfied.   He told
stories of his college days, — generally stories of
intellectual triumph; for he had been a shining
light, and was proud of his record.   There were
even a few animated *contes* of "rushes" and haz-
ing; but he evidently looked on this as youthful
frivolity, and unworthy, from his present plane of
development.   Sometimes he chose deeper themes,
and instructed her on subjects of national and
scientific importance; and then Felicia found it
necessary to rouse herself from her mental trance,
and lure him from what she might have termed
" Pliny" to his own immediate personal interests.
This pleased him, as it might have pleased a wiser
man.

Strangers looked on as at the presentation of a
romance.   The two were the noticeable couple of
the place, that summer: she with her delicate yet
brilliant beauty; he with his cold, narrow, intelligent face, his clear eyes, his formal manner, his
evident devotion.   After all, this world is very
sentimental.   It was a presidential election year;
there was a war in Europe; the races were in
progress: but during the stay of the Hamilton
party, all other themes yielded in interest to the
love-affair.

John Hamilton was puzzled. " Is she in earnest, or just giving Grafton a chance to make an idiot of himself?" he asked his wife. There was complacence in his face and in his heart, though he tried to moderate it. " That girl looks well in a boat, and well when she dances, and well when she drives, and well on a horse. I taught her myself to ride, and I'm proud of the job. She was always a plucky little thing from the first time I tossed her in a saddle, the day she was four years old. When they started, just now, her horse shied, and Grafton's heart was in his mouth, but she, — she was as calm as a May morning. Grafton is not a bad match, and he's a right good fellow, too. Maybe we were mistaken about the other affair, Sophie."

" I dare say we were," said Sophie, hopefully. Her conscience was all right. She believed exactly what her husband wished to believe.

" She is rather sharp to Grafton, now and then," continued Hamilton, meditatively, — " sarcastic and that sort of thing."

" Sometimes a girl treats a man that way when she likes him," said wise Mrs. Sophie.

He turned this over in his mind a moment, as he sat tilted back in his chair and pulled his long yellow mustache ; his straw hat, pushed far back, revealed his bald head, and his blue eyes were fixed on that section of the big blue sea where a shadowy white sail defined itself daintily against the soft horizon.

"I think you mean when she is sure *he* likes *her*," quoth John Hamilton, astutely. He was disposed to be particularly complaisant to Felicia now; but his incipient benignity received a sudden check.

On the evening before the day set for the departure of the Hamilton party, the two young people strolled out on the broad deserted piazza. The salt breeze blew crisp and fresh from the ocean; the band was playing, — the rhythmic beat of a waltz fell on the air; a lane of molten gold lay on the surface of the water, and was lost in vague shadows far away; a big, red, distorted moon was tilted above the illimitable palpitating waste.

"A waning moon is so melancholy," said Felicia, looking at it with wide, soft eyes that had grown melancholy, too. "I wonder why?"

"I don't see that it is melancholy," Grafton declared.

"No, I suppose not," she rejoined. "I dare say you see a planet which suggests to you apogee, or perigee, or nodes, or something wise. I see only the rising moon, and it seems to me particularly ominous to-night. I am afraid. Something unexpected — perhaps something terrible — is going to happen."

She affected to shiver with fear; then, as the breeze freshened, she shivered a little in reality, and drew about her head the fleecy wrap she had brought out with her. He rose from his chair and deftly arranged it. "That will do," she said, shrinking from him. He thought this a little shyness. He had been flattered, as he often was, by her allusion to his superior intellectual gifts and culture; he could not discern the mockery. It was his nature, however, even in satisfaction and complacence, to lay down the law, to dictate, to assert his supremacy.

"You seem a little superstitious," he suggested.

"Oh, yes, very," replied Felicia, as if admitting something creditable.

"Pardon me," he said with the precision of intonation, indicative of displeasure, which she especially disliked, — "pardon me if I do not accept that assurance. No well-regulated mind is capable of such weakness as superstition."

"I have told you before that I have n't a well-regulated mind," replied Felicia composedly. "On the contrary, I am rather goosey in my mind."

He deemed this tone inexcusably frivolous. But then she was so pretty, — so pretty, as she sat in a peculiarly graceful attitude, thrown back at her ease, one arm hanging over the side of the cane chair, the other hand holding the white wrap about her throat, the outlines of her rounded yet slight figure, in its dress of some soft white woolen fabric, definite against the shadows. He had never seen her so unconstrained; their interview seemed all at once peculiarly informal. He had supposed that he particularly approved of a certain ceremoniousness in her manner, a matter of attitude, of gesture, of intonation, indefinable yet definite, like the perfume of a flower; now he had a swift realization how potent must be her charm in the untrammeled ease of home-life. This sudden sense of closeness quickened his pulse, but he did not lose his head. Alfred Grafton in love was still — Alfred Grafton.

"You do yourself injustice," he said. "I am sure you have a very well-regulated mind. Otherwise I could not feel toward you as I do."

She roused herself from her easy attitude, and turned her eyes upon him. He was perfectly self-possessed and confident, even expectant. She was sitting upright now; she opened her fan; she looked back at the moon. The delightful vague sense of familiarity with which the previous moment had been filled had suddenly vanished.

"I suppose I ought to pretend that I don't understand what you mean," she said with coldness.

"It is better to be perfectly frank," he rejoined, with his air of laying down valuable moral axioms.

"Well, then, frankly," returned Felicia, "I do know what you mean, and I think you had better say no more about it."

There was dead silence. When she glanced at him, she was startled by the change in his face. All this time, absorbed in her own suffering, she had taken no thought of his capacity for suffering.

" Do you understand " — he uttered the words slowly — " that I ask you to marry me? You have long known that I love you."

There was another silence.

" It can never be," said Felicia.

As she again met his eyes, she saw that he was not only bitterly wounded, but very angry. She was surprised to find how deprecatory she felt. At his first word of blame, however, her self-reproach vanished.

" If your own conscience does not accuse you," he said, — his face was white, and set, and stern; he articulated with difficulty, — " I need urge nothing."

" Accuse me ? Of what ? " she demanded in a voice that trembled a little.

" Of trifling with me. In courtesy, I will not say willfully deceiving me, but I did not expect this answer."

" You do me great injustice ! " cried Felicia. " I have accepted your attention as I would that of any other friend, especially if thrown together in this way, — so far from home. I did not think of anything like — like this, till to-night. I had other things to — to think of. Whatever I have done, I have not encouraged *you !* "

" You have encouraged some one, then ? " he said quickly.

She looked at him angrily, but checked the reply on her lips, and turned her eyes again to the quivering, shining sea.

" Pardon me ; I have no right to ask," he resumed, with sarcastic humility. " I have no right to do anything but endure, when a woman lets me dangle around her for weeks, and then calmly tells me that she did not imagine anything like this. I supposed my meaning was distinct enough. I think it probable that most people have apprehended it."

Felicia made a mistake.

" And if I had understood," she cried, " how could I have altered matters? I cannot be expected to refuse a man before he has offered himself."

" A sophism is ample justification for a social triumph, such as it is," he said sarcastically. " To my mind it is a poor enough triumph, but no doubt a young lady estimates such matters differently."

" I did not think of it in that way," she declared.

There was another long silence. All at once she looked at him with an almost piteous appeal in her face ; tears stood in her eyes ; a tremulous smile was on her lips.

" Don't let us quarrel," she said coaxingly. " Let us be friends again."

Even Alfred Grafton was not proof against that look. He faltered ; he was mollified ; he took her soft little hand and held it closely. But he was not the man to be cajoled into accepting half a loaf for a whole one.

"You and I cannot be 'friends,' " he replied. "It is everything or nothing. Now let us look at this matter calmly. I love you dearly. I can safely promise to make you happy. Our tastes are similar; my people would be very fond of you; I think your brother would not object."

"And I should not care if he did object!" cried Felicia fierily, suddenly drawing away her hand. "He is welcome to object as much as he chooses. He shall not interfere with my affairs."

Grafton looked hard at her. Her tears had risen again, but they were angry tears. She brushed them away with an impatient gesture; he saw them glisten, in the moonlight, on her filmy handkerchief. His white heat of rage had returned. "I see," he said slowly, "there is some one else."

Felicia rose. "It is growing cold," she declared. "I must go in." They walked down the piazza toward the parlor. He stopped her before they reached the open door, and looked down into her uplifted eyes.

"I shall never forgive you," he said deliberately. "I shall always believe you did it intentionally."

"You will think better of that some day," replied Felicia, appalled by the strength of a feeling that had seemed to her a slight thing, that had hardly sufficiently attracted her notice to secure intelligent contemplation.

"I shall never forgive you," he repeated.

Late that night, John Hamilton, coming from the billiard-room where he had been enjoying the unwonted luxury of a game with an old friend, — a man like himself adrift in this sea of strangers, who almost wept for joy at sight of that familiar roseate face and rotund figure, — late that night, Hamilton, coming thus from the billiard-room, flushed with success, perfumed with sherry cobbler and cigar smoke, suddenly met Alfred Grafton. The younger gentleman was evidently ready for a journey. He was wearing his traveling gear; his name was conspicuous on a trunk among other luggage awaiting the baggage-wagon. A bell-boy preceded him with a satchel. He looked annoyed at sight of his friend, but faced the situation with composure.

"Hello! Where are you going, Grafton?" inquired Hamilton, with round eyes.

"To Philadelphia," replied Grafton.

John Hamilton reflected rapidly.

"Anything the matter?" he asked tersely.

Grafton, strange as it may seem, shared our common human weakness. He craved sympathy with the eager craving of less gifted mortals. He realized, too, that there was no use in attempting subterfuges with Hamilton, who would no doubt soon be perfectly well aware, without explanation, of the state of the case.

"The matter!" he repeated bitterly. "She has thrown me over, — that's all."

"The devil she did!" exclaimed the brother, with lively sympathy.

" Did n't suspect my feelings — hopes we shall be friends — all very proper and pretty," returned Grafton sardonically. " I ventured to suggest, by way of inducement, which my case seemed to need, that my people would be delighted, and that I thought you would not object. She said, very angrily, that she did not care if you did object. I fancy there is some man to whom you *do* object. Stop ! " he cried, as Hamilton was about to speak excitedly. " I have no right to know. I have no right to revert to that, — it is none of my affair. My affair is overboard, and I have no more to say or hear on the subject."

When John Hamilton repaired to his own apartment, it was all his wife could do to prevent his arousing Felicia from her bed, in the small hours, to give her what he termed a " solid talk." It was owing, too, to Sophie that this was warded off the following day, on their railway trip to New York. She made pretext after pretext to detain him by her side; whenever she saw him look with a scowling intention across the car to where Felicia and Fred sat together, she evolved some immediate and absorbing subject of interest. Here was a letter about which she had spoken to him, — or indeed had she remembered to mention it ? — from the carpet-manufactory people; he must read it, and help her decide. And again, oh, had he seen the baby kiss her hand ? She did it this morning. " Kiss your hand, darling, to papa."

These tactics were kept up after taking the
boat.   He escaped, however, just before reaching
New York, and joined Felicia, as she stood with
her eyes fixed on the vast spectacle of the great
city, its innumerable spires glittering in the sunshine, its hovering smoke a shadow in the distance against the intense blue of the sky, its forest
of shipping also only a dainty shadow.   The
breeze swept over the intervenient spaces of the
sea, and brought briny odors ; it flushed Felicia's
cheeks, and blew backward the draperies of her
trim traveling dress, and waved the brown feather
in the jaunty hat that surmounted her brown hair.
She glanced up as her brother placed himself beside her.   He had pushed his hat back, and an
expanse of bald forehead was aggressively visible ;
his hands were in his trousers pockets ; he wore a
natty suit in shaded gray checks, which was very
becoming to his richly tinted face.

"What did you do to Grafton, Felicia ?" he
demanded curtly.

"Has he a black eye?   I suppose I must have
given it to him."

"I am astonished at you," her brother continued severely.   "Leading a fellow on and flirt-
ing!   I had no idea that you were such a flirt."

As a matter of course she resented this.   "How
dare you say that to me!" she exclaimed, her
eyes flashing, her cheeks aflame.

"I understand how all this comes about," persisted the misguided brother ; "it is all on account of that fellow Kennett."

" You shall not speak of him to me ! " she cried, turning away.

" See here, young lady," persisted Hamilton, laying his hand on her shoulder, " father is going to meet us in New York, and we shall see what he will say to these vagaries. He will take your case in hand."

She drew herself away, and walked proudly to the other end of the boat. These unlucky strictures completed an estrangement already sufficiently bitter. She felt that she could never forgive him. She was placed before the beginning of a contest with her father in the mental attitude of resistance. She promised herself she would not be cowed. And yet, a contest about what ? About her acquaintance with a man whose friendship she could hardly claim, who had forgotten her, who had ignored her letter. Her heart was bruised, sore, unendurably heavy; she had much ado to refrain from tears, — from crying out in her pain, humiliation, and despair, — as they disembarked, entered a carriage, and rolled along the interminable streets to their hotel.

It was in this frame of mind that Felicia came upon the turning-point of her life.

The rooms had been engaged by telegraph some days before. As she entered the one assigned her, she noticed a quantity of mail matter on the bureau. One of the letters was directed in a handwriting she did not recognize. The envelope was covered with addresses : it had been sent first to her own home, thence to her brother's house in Chilounatti, and had afterward evidently followed her from place to place. Still in her hat and wraps, she sat down with it in her hand.

Before she opened it she divined who was the writer. She attempted to collect her startled faculties. For some moments she remained motionless. Then she opened and read the letter. It was dated six weeks before.

Hugh Kennett began by explaining that he had been greatly troubled by her sudden departure; all the more because he was very anxious to say to her what he had attempted to say the afternoon before she left, — that he loved her, and desired to ask her to be his wife. He feared his effort was somewhat premature, in view of their short acquaintance, but he would be only too happy to submit to any term of probation she might require. He would ask nothing except the opportunity to make himself acceptable to her. He hoped for a reply and gave an address in Chilounatti, as well as in New York, to which latter city he was going in a few weeks. He added that he should send this letter to her home, as he had not been able to obtain her present address. There was little of protestation. The phrasing was extremely simple; it was almost business-like. Felicia thought it a very strong and manly way to write a love-letter; she fancied she detected a ring of tense feeling in the few terse sentences; she said to herself that it was perfectly in character, — like everything he did.

With the sudden revulsion of feeling an extreme tranquillity had come upon her. It amazed her now that she had not divined the exact state of the case; that she had not had more patience, more confidence, more strength. She took herself to task for not comprehending him better. The memory of the anguish of soul induced by those weeks of domestic discord she dismissed from consideration with a contemptuous indifference, which argued ill enough for the influence, in a possible contest, of the natural strong ties of kindred and association.

"Was I insane," she demanded of herself, "that I should have cared an instant for anything John and Sophie could do, or think, or say?"

Only one influence prevailed with her now. She gave herself up to it; she sank into a vague, delicious reverie. She recalled, as heretofore she had not dared to do, all the incidents of those happy weeks in the early summer, — the introduction at Robert's, the rowing on the sunset-tinted river, the long talks in the quiet moonlit evenings, the tones of his voice, the look in his eyes, the words he had spoken. How strange that she remembered them so well! They were not such wonderfully wise and witty words, she said to herself, with a happy laugh; she knew in her heart that she believed them to be both. And she could write to him. She would see him soon. Possibly he was in New York, somewhere near to her, now. In a few days — it might be a few hours — and then — and then —

Sophie, coming to her door after a time, was greatly surprised to see her still sitting motionless in her traveling attire; but she sank into a chair, and waited while Felicia hurriedly rearranged her hair and changed her dress. Mrs. Hamilton's face was flushed and her manner discomposed.

"Oh, Felicia, I am so annoyed!" she exclaimed. "All my plans are in confusion; and it is John's fault. You know the Graftons are here, at this hotel."

The brush, gliding along Felicia's bronze tresses, was arrested; she met her sister-in-law's eyes in the mirror with an inquiring stare.

"You know," continued the speaker, "Alfred was to meet them here, but — but" — she stumbled — "but for some reason he has gone to Philadelphia, and telegraphed to his mother to join him there next week. Well, Mrs. Grafton is a good deal put out, naturally, you see."

"Really, Sophie," said Felicia with a hard laugh, "you have a large contract on your hands, if you undertake to become responsible for all of Alfred Grafton's movements, perfect as he is."

"Of course that's not it. But while she was sitting in our parlor fretting about it, Nellie, her daughter, happened to say she should not have cared except that Alfred had promised to take her to some operatic matinée this afternoon. She is to be left with Madame Sevier on Monday, and she seems to think this is her last chance to go to any place of amusement."

"She will see more opera in one term with Madame Sevier than with Alfred Grafton in ten million years," declared Felicia, hyperbolically. "I wonder that he encouraged the frivolity of one matinée. She ought to be reading about Cosmic Force."

"She seems to think Madame Sevier's is a sort of nunnery. And John, instead of leaving well enough alone, sent a bell-boy off and bought tickets, and said she should n't be disappointed."

"Lucky for Miss Nellie," remarked Felicia, coolly. "I don't perceive the hitch."

"Why, Felicia, can't you understand? *I* can't go with them. I must see West and Ware about the drawing-room lambrequins that we ordered when we were here before. A most frightful mistake has been made. They are half an inch too short. I have just received a note about it. Oh, if I had it all to do over, I would buy every solitary thing at home. Such a forlorn, toilsome summer I have had. And just think how perverse John is! As soon as he found that I could n't go he managed to call me into the other room, and swore — most frightfully, too — that he would n't go to a matinée this afternoon to save his life. Oh, Felicia, dear, don't you think you and Fred will do? Won't it be appropriate enough if you and Fred represent the family? I must see about my lambrequins. If my lambrequins are spoiled, my heart will break." She rose from her chair and walked precipitately about the room. Domestic tragedy has its opportunity.

Felicia was disconcerted. She had not intended to answer the letter to-day, but she wanted to think it over, to get used to it; it was so sudden, so momentous. With the cessation of her own anxieties, however, gentleness and tolerance had come to her. " Sweet are the uses of adversity." That sounds well, but it is a mistake. We are beneficent when we are lucky. Felicia sacrificed her preference with a generosity possible only to the happy.

" Well, well, Sophie," she said with a sigh, " I will take charge of Mrs. Grafton and her daughter, and I 'll excuse you gracefully."

Mrs. Grafton was a mouse. To be sure, a mouse accustomed only to the best houses, to velvet carpets, to fine china and linen and glass, to sweetbreads and cake crumbs, — a mouse of the first quality, but still and always a mouse. She was swift, daring, timorous, cringing, bullying, indefinite, by turns and as occasion justified. You never knew exactly where to find her, — like a mouse, — yet you were very sure she would have a distinct personality when you did encounter her. Sometimes you would be positive she was in your immediate vicinity, and she was as far from you in effect as at one of the poles. When you lost sight of her and well-nigh forgot her existence, here she was, — again just like a mouse, — startling you out of your senses. You

were always absorbed in amazement that anything so insignificant could be so aggravating.
She even looked like a mouse, as she sat on a
sofa, in a dove-colored dress and a lace cap ornamented with dove-colored ribbons; and her ac-
knowledgment of the introduction of Felicia was
the perfection of furtive meekness.   There was in
her glance something as well of analytic scrutiny,
and this in her daughter — an awkward girl, at
once shy and forward — had developed into down-
right curiosity, as she stared at Felicia with hard
black eyes.   Our young lady had a sudden rush
of indignation, divining that the son of the house
had written of his pretensions much as if they
were *un fait accompli*.   She controlled her irritation, however, and entered with what zest she
might into the afternoon's festivities, making
Sophie's excuses with such tact that the two
ladies willingly overlooked the informality of Mrs.
Hamilton's absence; and after lunch the party
set out, with Fred as escort.

"Fred will be entirely *au fait* by the time he
gets home," remarked Felicia.   "He learned all
about natural science at Philadelphia, and navi-
gation at the seashore, and hunting in the Adirondacks, and now he is to become a connoisseur in
music and acting."

"I 'd a big sight ruther go ter the dime mu-
seum," grumbled Fred, "an' see the tattooed man
an' the three-headed lady."

Felicia's silvery laughter had an infectious joy-

ousness it had not known for many a day. Mrs.
Grafton wondered, however, if she were not a little
flippant for Alfred, who was so difficult to please.

"It is always well to learn, Fred," observed the
old lady, meekly, smoothing one gloved hand with
the other; "we can learn something almost any-
where."

"So I tell him," said Felicia, commanding her
countenance with an effort, at the sound of Fred's
unintelligible muttered reply.

That afternoon, contrary to her anticipation,
afforded her keen delight. She had expected to
be bored; she was, instead, in a sort of exaltation. The sudden removal of trouble, in itself
cause for happiness, supplemented more tangible
cause, so deep, so strong, that she dared not dwell
definitely upon it; she only felt herself vaguely,
blissfully, drifting like a leaf upon the current.
The large assemblage of unknown, unnumbered
faces strangely exhilarated her, but she did not,
according to her mental habit, disintegrate the
crowd. Ordinarily, she knew in five minutes —
or thought she did — those whom she was wont to
call "interesting," those who were mere human
animals, those who had been lifted from that plane
by some drama of their circumstances. The
young man at the end of the next row, she would
have said, would be a commonplace banker or
lawyer but for some daily heart tragedy, — a
broken ambition, a wretched home. And there is
a woman with a face like sunshine, — one feels

sure she has a nature to match. That old gentleman has little capacity save for the exercise of
piling cent per cent on brain and heart. And
there is another old gentleman, sixty in years and
twenty-five of soul, with a benignant smile and a
buttonhole. bouquet. She made no deductions
now; she saw them as if she saw them not; she
had appropriate words and smiles for her companions; in her deeper consciousness she ignored
their existence. She looked about her with
dreamy, brilliant, happy eyes; she sat very still;
her voice was soft; her lips wore gentle curves
that expressed a still and blissful content.

Mrs. Grafton, scanning her furtively, admitted
to herself that Alfred's choice was very satisfactory, so far as appearances went. Felicia was
pretty and distinguished in manner, and perfectly
dressed; and if Madame Sevier had taught her
those attitudes and that poise of head, — as easily
erect as a flower on a stem, — it was well to have
selected Sevier Institute for Nellie, who would
lounge and would n't hold up her shoulders. As
for Nellie, she gazed at Felicia with the definite
intention of discovering the charm of a young
lady who had secured the ultimate object, in her
opinion, of a woman's creation, — a lover. Nellie's vanity was sufficiently stalwart. She did not
comprehend how Felicia managed to be fascinating, but she was fully persuaded that in time she
herself would discover the secret and use it as
successfully.

The curtain rose after a little, and the audience went for a time into that strange, delightful world where destinies round themselves in an hour or two; where trials accent triumphs; where virtue is lovely and prevails, and vice is odious and is defeated; where retribution and reward come up smiling in the nick of time, and life is dignified, picturesque, consistent, and grand, and very much more worth living, ideally speaking, than our poor little affair, which it modestly proposes to portray.

The troupe was good, but not preëminently excellent; the music was well within the powers of the singers; the stage-setting, costumes, and the chorus were admirable. Felicia, in her absorption, was vaguely responsive to the music, which pervaded her consciousness as the perfume of violets pervades a May afternoon. Like most clever amateurs, she had not been scientifically trained; she experienced no want which these melodious numbers could not satisfy; she did not partake of the musician's intellectual and somewhat strenuous enjoyment; she merely absorbed the representation with more or less vividness through her senses.

As the building was greatly crowded, it was some little time before they made their way out. Nellie, who between the acts had become somewhat well acquainted with her new friend, commented on the performance with her own inimitable admixture of forwardness and shyness.

"Oh, my, was n't it lovely!" she exclaimed, with a fidgety giggle of delight and embarrassment, as they passed out upon the sidewalk, already dusky with deepening twilight and enveloped with the gloom of low hanging clouds. "Oh, was n't that last duet *too* beautiful! And the tenor, — oh, Miss Hamilton, I 'm dead in love with that tenor, ain't you ? "

"The tenor is most admirable," returned Felicia, sedately, not entering into the spirit of her prattle.

As she said this Felicia chanced to raise her eyes. They encountered those of a gentleman who was standing in the brilliant radiance of the electric light. He lifted his hat, and she recognized Hugh Kennett. She returned his salutation. She observed that his face was very grave. The agitation which she had unconsciously held in abeyance all day was upon her with such intensity that she could not distinguish if it were pleasure or pain. When they reached the hotel, and her companions had repaired to their own rooms, she opened the door of the private parlor her brother had taken. It was empty. She entered, sank into a chair, and attempted to rally her self-control, so strangely and suddenly vanished. Her breath was coming quick through her half-parted lips; her face was suffused with a deep blush; she removed her hat, — its weight was all at once unendurably oppressive; she fixed her feverishly bright eyes on the dark, moonless, starless sky. As she thus sat motionless in the centre of the lighted room, there was a knock upon the door, and a servant entered with a card. She looked at it in silence for a moment, then said, "You can show the gentleman in."

When Kennett was ushered into the room, she rose, and advanced hesitatingly a few steps. She was turning the card nervously in her fingers; the gesture was in marked contrast with her usual self-possessed manner; her face betrayed some of the agitation which she sought to control.

"I am glad to see you," she murmured.

Kennett took her hand. "That gives me courage," he said. "Did you receive my letter?"

"I received it only this morning," she replied.

"Only this morning!" he cried, in dismay.

"It had been to a great many places," said Felicia. "It had been following us for weeks."

He was at once infinitely disappointed and relieved. "I could not believe you would intentionally keep me in suspense," he declared.

"And you were in suspense, too!" cried Felicia, impulsively, with a sudden delighted realization of the fact.

"Were you?" he exclaimed, quickly. "Did you want to hear from me, to see me again? It is asking a great deal, I know, Felicia, but won't you give me an answer to my letter now? I love you with all my soul. I have undergone the torments of — of — well — a great deal of unhappiness since I saw you. Can't you — don't you care for me?"

He was still holding her hand; she fixed her fast-filling eyes on his eyes; her sensitive lips were quivering.

"And I have been unhappy," she said. For all her tears, which presently ceased to flow, she felt that there could, in the nature of things, never again be unhappiness for her. She recovered her tranquillity; words came to her; her silvery laughter rang out. Soon she was questioning him as to his proceedings when he had no reply to his letter; she rejoiced to hear him say that he too had been unhappy. In this she differed from him; her assertion had given him a keen pang. She brought him back more than once to this point.

"So you were worried when you had no letter?" she said, with a flattered laugh that was all he could reasonably desire as protestation or admission.

"Worried!" he exclaimed. "I was nearly out of my mind. I wrote again and again to Robert, and — I cannot possibly account for it — I have never received a reply from him. Finally I went to your brother's office, in Third Street."

"For what?" she demanded.

"To discover if they had your address."

"Away down there, — among the bulls, and bears, and other wild animals!" she cried, with her happy laughter. "That was romantic and thrilling."

"It was not very congruous, I admit, but it

was my only chance.　Your brother's partner declined to give me your address."

She stared at him ; his eye glittered ; his lips were compressed ; his face, with the expression it wore at this moment, had a certain ferocity.　He was evidently very angry, and controlled himself only by a strenuous effort.

"Mr. Gale did that?" said Felicia, in amazement.

"He was very polite in manner, but very firm. He said he had your brother's express instructions that in case I should ask I should be refused."

Her cheeks were aflame.　"How insulting!" she cried, angrily.　After a moment's reflection she asked, "Why should John do such a thing as that?"　She was remembering her brother's bitter antagonism, and divined that she was coming upon an explanation.

"I can only account for it upon the hypothesis that he has very strong objections to my profession.　Some people have, you know."

She looked at him with a sudden smile.　"I don't know," she declared, "because I don't know what your profession is."

His face showed that he was startled.　"How can that be?" he said.

"I never heard you speak of it," she replied, growing more grave.

"Is that possible?" he rejoined, reflectively. "But surely Robert must have mentioned it?"

"Never," she returned. "And if you don't object to terminating my suspense, I should be glad to know it now."

There was a pause, in which the sounds in the street invaded the silence of the room.

VIII.

So long the silence continued, so strangely did it all at once seem imbued with a momentous meaning, that there was evident trepidation underlying the impatience in Felicia's voice when she again spoke.

"What *is* your profession?" she asked.

"Felicia," said Kennett, looking into her eyes, "I am a singer.   That is my profession."

"A singer?" she repeated, vaguely.   "Do you mean a professional singer?   In opera?"

"Yes."

She gazed at him blankly.

"Now that I think of it," he continued, "I cannot remember ever mentioning it.   But how could I dream that you did not understand!   The name is so well known.   It is placarded on every blank wall; it is in every newspaper."

He glanced about him, observed the programme she had thrown, with her hat, on the table, rose suddenly, and walked swiftly across the room. As her eyes followed him, she realized now that a quality which she had thought a natural gift — his grace, a certain deftness and suppleness of movement and attitude, and even his appropriateness of manner — was only the prosaic result of professional training in gait and pose; a sordid acquisition, worked for, paid for, part of a stock in trade, an available asset.

It was with a certain inconsequence that because of this utilitarian value she felt, in the midst of the whirl of emotion in which she was abruptly involved, a definite sharp pang,—she, whose talent in what might be called the art of deportment had also been assiduously cultivated for merely ornamental purposes. Her sudden chagrin that he was thus deprived of an endowment of æsthetic worth, with which her respectful estimate had invested him, was only a sentimental grief, but at the moment it was almost a sense of bereavement.

He returned to his place with the programme in his hand, and showed her that printed opposite to Prince Roderic was the name of Hugh Kennett.

"You never heard of me?" he asked.

There are many degrees in notability. He could hardly realize it, but she never had.

"It is strange that you never heard of me," he said, meditatively. "Did they never take you to the opera, when you were at school here in New York?"

"They took us to the Italian opera on Patti nights, and when there were other great stars, and they often took us to the German opera," said Felicia, "but they did n't seem to — well — to think a great deal of English light opera."

He was a polite man, and, what is more to the

purpose, he was in love. He did not openly sneer, "Fine judges!" but there was much of resentful protest in the sarcastic gleam in his eye.

"You did not know me, then, this afternoon, in costume?" he resumed.

"No," said Felicia, faintly.

"And you did not recognize my voice?"

"No; I never heard you sing."

"But sometimes there is speaking."

"I remember that once or twice when he spoke — when *you* spoke — I was affected strangely, but I only thought it was a resemblance. I did not dream of anything more. How could I! Then the singing recommenced, and I began to think about — about something else. I did not even look at that programme. My mind was absorbed. I did not notice anything very much."

"I thought I spoke of my profession to your brother, the evening I was introduced to him, though I had no definite purpose in doing so. I supposed he knew all about it, as a matter of course."

"You merely mentioned business."

After a pause he said: —

"I knew *you* this afternoon, in a moment, among all those people. As soon as the performance was over I changed my dress as quickly as possible, and hurried to the street in the hope of seeing you. And when you said to your young friend that you considered the tenor most admirable I overheard it. I thought you felt that you had treated me badly in not answering my letter, and wanted me to hear it. I thought you said it under a sudden impulse to make amends."

"Oh, no, no. I did n't imagine that *you* were the tenor. It was the merest accident."

There was another pause. Then he took her hand. "You are not going to let this come between us?" he said. "There are singers — and singers. I have a very respectable place. I may say without vanity that I stand high. I expect to stand much higher."

He lifted his head with a quick movement; his eyes were alight.

"I shall do some good work!" he exclaimed, the tense vibration of elation in his expressive voice. "Some day I shall sing the great Wagnerian tenor rôles as they have never yet been sung. I don't talk and boast beforehand, but I will do much to be proud of. So far I have only lacked fair opportunities, but they will come; and I am ready for them."

That latent capacity for expression, ordinarily not more than suggested in his severely regular features, was distinctly manifest now. His face was transfigured with the light, the hope, the exultation, upon it. He wore the look of a man on the verge of achievement, — perchance on the threshold of some discovery in physics which was to revolutionize mechanical science; or thus, perhaps, might look a general suddenly evolving a feat of strategy whereby the enemy would be surrounded, a statesman holding the destiny of a nation in his hand.

So intent of purpose, so prescient of success, so reverent of faith in the worthiness of those aims he held dear, was his face with that expression upon it, she might only gaze at him in wonder.

She had as much of fashionable musical feeling as might remain to her of her fashionable musical education. She might speak knowingly, in the estimation of unmusical people, of notable productions. If in those moonlit evening talks they had ever chanced on the subject, it might have amused him to have heard her prattle enriched by such expressions as "tone color," "close harmony," "technique," "phrasing," "contrapuntal effect." In her naive assumption of dilettanteism she was perfectly sincere. With the happy confidence of ignorance she fancied she knew something of the art; she even had some faint idea that as a science it held certain values, perhaps important values; she was aware that there are schools and movements in varied directions; she apprehended, too, that there is an ascending scale in lyric achievement, — gradations, for example, between the rôles of Nanki Poo, Don Cæsar, Manrico, Vasco di Gama, and Lohengrin. But in essentials, regarded from the sensible and mundane vantage-ground of a fine social position, with the conservatism and common sense of its atmosphere and traditions, what did this amount to? They were all tenor rôles, the possibility of an aspiration infinitely removed from any sympathies, except of a purely æsthetic and impersonal sort, which she might be expected to entertain. That such achievement might be the serious ambition, invested with force, dignity, absorption, of an earnest nature, endowed with a highly intelligent, even a highly intellectual organization; that such a goal could be lifted to so elevated a plane of endeavor, she first realized from the look in his face.

That exultant look passed. He drew a long sigh.

"Ah, well," he said, his eyes seeking hers with a smile, "a wise man will not forecast futurity. We had best confine our attention just now to the present; that is simple and practical. The present, as it happens, is sufficiently satisfactory. I am in demand with managers. I get a good salary. As to the profession" — He hesitated; his color rose. "I don't apologize for the profession. I am not ashamed of it. Although I am a singer, I hope I am a gentleman."

Felicia withdrew her hand from his. "Don't argue it with me," she said. "Let me think it out and decide for myself."

She crossed the room to the window, and stood leaning against the frame, while he sat silent, watching her. It was well for his peace that he did not realize the struggle in the mind of Madame Sevier's pupil and John Hamilton's sister. To admire the tenor was one thing; to be in love

with the man was a different and a much more
complicated matter. Her natural bent and the acquired influences that had made her what she was
placed her in revolt against this culmination. The
atmosphere she had breathed was as aristocratic
as the free air of a republic can be. She understood remarkably well — especially considering
the fact that she had never known their deprivation — the worth of an established position in
society, the value of fortune, its subtler as well as
its practical value. Heretofore she had been unaware that she had gauged these things, — one
does not consciously appraise the air one breathes.
Now that it was brought before her she could
accede to the proposition without fully realizing
it, that outside of her world there was a world
with other standards of excellence, other estimates of values, other objects of ambition. It
might be a very talented, highly artistic world,
but it was not hers. The John Hamiltons, the
Mrs. Stanley-Brants, the Madame Seviers, the
Mrs. Graftons, — the code they exemplified, the
life they typified, the status they expressed, —
these made her world. And even in that alien
sphere of his he was not eminent ; he was merely
a notable member of a moderately meritorious
organization. In a crisis like this dormant intui-
tions abruptly develop into knowledge. She was
suddenly aware that there are many gradations in
that world whose existence she had ignored. He
evidently stood high in a certain line, but his line

was not high; possibly he would never reach any-thing higher; and he would devote all his powers to the attempt. What an ambition! What a future! To consecrate his varied and excellent capacities to success in a pursuit at its best gro-tesquely unworthy of them and of him! Could she share a life pledged like this? Her pride was on fire.

"Would you be willing to give it up?" she asked, without turning her head.

"My profession?" he said, wonderingly.

She assented. There was a pause.

"Do you realize what you ask?" he replied at last. "I cannot give it up. It is my living. I am fitted for nothing else. I have been in train-ing for fifteen years."

Again she was silent, and he marveled that she should take it so hard. He was becoming a great man in his world, — so like, yet so unlike, her world. He was applauded and praised by the public, held in respect by the magnates of his craft, admired by his associates, revered by those below him, whose ambition it was to have in some auspicious future the opportunity to imitate him. He was as far from comprehending the issues which led to contemptuous aversion for his voca-tion as she was from comprehending those which led to pride in it. When he spoke, she detected something in his voice she had never before heard.

"I cannot understand why you object so seri-ously," he said.

She kept her face turned persistently from him. She promised herself that she would not be influenced. She would not be touched by his sense of injury, his wounded pride. It had come to a choice, — that was evident; she could not hope he would relinquish his profession. And the choice should be a deliberate one.

The stealthy wind was rising, hardly distinguishable above the muffled noises on the streets; the air was saturated with a heavy moisture; the mist was accented at intervals by the yellow blur of the invisible lamps; faint lightnings, fitful, vague, like indefinite, piteous phantoms, skulked across the black sky. And ever the treacherous wind was rising.

She must choose. To give him up? That meant a great deal. She realized her inordinate sensitiveness to the disposition and temperament of those near to her. To be comprehended thoroughly; to be her truest self without effort, explanation, or qualification; to discover in another mind and heart the complement of her own thought and feeling; to experience, in thus sharing the thought or feeling of that other mind and heart, its deeper, fuller development; to delight in the delight which her presence, her words, her glances, could give; to find her exacting taste satisfied, her intellectual nature met on its own level; to feel the hours imbued with a happiness that never palled, the fulfillment of a joyous expectation, — this was what those weeks of early summer had given her. Having once known so perfect an accord, vouchsafed to few even of the most fortunate of mortals, could she, did she dare to voluntarily relinquish it? The recollection of all she had endured during their separation surged over her in a wave of bitterness. She remembered, too, how needlessly and cruelly it had been enhanced. But she said to herself she would be dispassionate; she would admit that her brother had great cause for annoyance, disappointment, even dismay,— he could hardly have felt these more acutely than she had done this evening; his wife might well be distressed. But what of the conciliation due from a brother who loves his sister; what of the sympathy one woman gives another woman's heartache! She resolutely withdrew her thoughts from this branch of the subject; she would not risk her happiness, she declared to herself, to be revenged on John and Sophie by making a marriage they would bitterly deprecate. They should not influence her. The decision involved only her future and Hugh Kennett's. No other consideration should have weight.

How should she decide? To give him up? Could she do it? To marry him? To place in controversy the human heart and the implacable forces of conventionality?— it was a dangerous experiment.

The rain was falling heavily and the wind was loud at last. And as to the menace that the future held, as to the pallid potentialities of regret, disappointment, despair, could these vague gleams slipping about the horizon, contend against the effulgence of love and hope? Only a room bounded by four walls, or a realm vast as the universe? And darkness had come, and the prophecy of winter was on the turbulent air; or were light and summer here, and all sweet promises and dreams?

When she suddenly turned, there was a strange commingling of expressions on her expressive face; that tumult of thought and perplexity which had torn her with a sort of mental anguish, and had stamped her features with its intensity and its trouble, was still upon them. But a radiance was dawning in her eyes, and an amazed delight that this feeling which she could not conquer was stronger than her will. She held out her hands to him. "I cannot give you up," she said, simply. "I thought I could — and I cannot."

That night Kennett sang and acted like a man inspired. His elaborate stage training, which had been a conspicuous element in the excellence of his work heretofore, was now merely a subservient adjunct — valuable, but imperceptible — to the fiery and tender exaltation which possessed him.

"Oh, Lord! if you 're going to keep this up, Kennett, you 'll walk over the course away from all of us," said young Preston, during one of the waits, as, arrayed in ruby-tinted velvet, he threw himself into a chair in Kennett's dressing-room, and elevated his feet to the back of another chair. He lifted a glass to his lips and drained it with a grace of gesture that would have done justice to '28 port, but it was only beer.

"Kennett must be a little tight," said Abbott, dryly. "A man is always at his best when he is a little tight."

Kennett only laughed. He was a notable figure as he stood among them, gay and triumphant, and with brilliant eyes. Small wonder that Felicia had not recognized him in costume. That which had met the requirements of her stringent taste, a certain neutrality, a conservatism, gave him the look of an unobtrusive and serious man, and had even rendered inconspicuous certain qualities of his personality, — the regularity of his features, his symmetry and grace of figure and gait; for the stage hero these had a market value, and were brought out and accented by his auburn wig, his rouge, his slashed black-and-gold costume, his long, supple, easy stage stride.

IX.

Judge Hamilton reached New York the next morning.

In comparison with his father, John Hamilton might be deemed meek. There was a strong likeness between the two in appearance; the elder man being a trifle more florid, stout, bald, and hale than the younger. What little hair he possessed, however, was gray; his mustache was short, bristling, and white; he was more vehement and rapid of speech; he had an emphatic gesture of the right hand brought down upon the open palm of the left which the son had not yet acquired. He also had a habit, in excitement, of throwing back his head, widening his eyes, and dilating his nostrils, which were flexible and open, with a sound resembling a snort of indignation or of intense affirmation. At such moments he suggested a horse subjected to unusual cerebral activity.

When, his shaggy white eyebrows contracted over his big, indignant dark eyes, he listened to the reasons which led to the summer " pleasuring," his first impulse was to settle accounts with his unlucky son.

" I thought it was better to take her away from

there," said John, concluding his report. " I thought that perhaps in changing about from place to place she would lose interest in the fellow and maybe forget him."

The old gentleman, when his son ceased, bounded from his chair with an elasticity wonderful in a man of his years and weight. He was almost inarticulate in his wrath, as he dashed about the room, accenting his words by a sounding thump on the floor with his stick, and now and then facing round on his anxious son.

" By the Lord Harry," he roared, " you ought to be in the lunatic asylum, sir! You ought to have a guardian appointed, sir! You are not fit to manage your own affairs! Any man who can't take better care than that of a girl like Felicia ought n't to be trusted with business."

He stood still suddenly, beating out the words impressively on the marble-topped table ; and the decanters and glasses — ordered by his son in the hope of a mollifying preparatory influence — rang with the vibrations.

" Good Lord, sir, I would n't have believed it ! I send my daughter — the best child in the world, and the most docile — to your house to make you a visit, because you and Sophie insist on having her, and because it is dull for her at home, and you let her fall in love with an *oper-y* singer ! "

It is beyond the possibility of the printer's art to intimate the scorn which the old gentleman infused into these words. He spoke them, too, with a certain remarkable nasal, rustic drawl, suggestive of extremely rural regions. Perhaps he had picked it up in the more remote counties of his circuit. Whenever he chose, in scorn and anger, to affect this tone, it always made his daughter wince with a disapprobation that was nearly akin to pain. He was an able lawyer, a logical reasoner, an intellectual man, accustomed to good society, but occasionally, in some crisis of temper, his personation of an ignorant country boor would have been useful in the profession he contemned.

"An oper-y singer," he drawled; "light oper-y! Comic oper-y, I suppose. They tell me that's lower than the other kind. Comic oper-y! Mighty comical, I'll swear! And you have the grit to tell me that you and Sophie hope it will not amount to anything serious! It's damned serious! And you tell me you hope he'll disappear from here, do you? A man, too, with a sort of claim, — kin to that blamed fool Bob Raymond! Kin to the pa'son, sir, — kin, in a sort of way, to her cousin Amy. And you *invited* the man to call! You found out nothing about him, — his business, his character, his habits, his friends! You only *invited* him — *a perfect stranger* — to your house — just because he was kin to dear cousin Bob, the pa'son! Then you took yourself off to Dakota next morning, and he came to the house every day or so! Met a girl like Felicia mighty near every day! And you hope a fellow with that much chance and that much claim will never be heard of any more! God bless you, John, what a fool you are!"

It might be supposed from these strictures that the old gentleman's wrath would soon exhaust itself. Such an expectation would be based on a very slight knowledge of the resources of his temper. He shared none of John's ideas as to the policy of non-explanations. Almost his first words to his daughter were on this subject. She came in with delight to meet him, having for a moment dashed aside her anxieties. She threw herself into his arms, with tears in her eyes. There was great fondness between them. He petted and spoiled her, rebuked and praised her, lavishly, inconsistently, and inconsiderately; and his demonstrative and tyrannical affection had never seemed to her so precious as now.

"See here, Felicia," he exclaimed, after a hurried kiss and a tremendous hug, "what's all this they tell me about their having introduced strangers to you? When did you see that fellow Kennett?"

Perhaps it was the courage of desperation which nerved her to reply with calmness: "I saw him yesterday afternoon, papa."

Though Judge Hamilton became purple with wrath, he cast a glance of triumph at his son, — a glance which said bitterly, "What did I tell you?"

"I find that the man is an opera singer. Did you know that?" he demanded.

"I have known it only since yesterday," said Felicia.

"Ah — um — is that the case? Well, I don't blame you," with a gulp; the old gentleman was trying to be just. "But he is not an appropriate acquaintance for you. It is a low business, — comic opera is."

"I dislike it as much as you do," said Felicia, in a low tone.

"That's a reasonable girl. I thought you would look at it that way," said Judge Hamilton, with great approbation. "Yes, yes, it's a low business; don't wonder you disapprove of anybody connected with it. You shall not meet that man again."

"I don't think I can promise you that, papa," said Felicia, still more faintly. "I am going to marry him."

The color suddenly left Judge Hamilton's face, then surged back in a deeply crimson tide. "Hey! hey!" he demanded, as if he doubted his sense of hearing.

At this moment, after his customary annunciatory tap, the brisk bell-boy entered with a card, which he handed to Judge Hamilton. Then he stood still awaiting instructions.

Judge Hamilton hurriedly examined his pocket for his spectacle-case. He did not find it, and with a growl of impatience he gave the card to his son, for the benefit of his younger eyes. One glance at John's perturbed countenance as he read the name was sufficient.

"That's the man, is it?" said the old gentleman sharply. "Yes, I thought so. Show him in, you, sir!" He glared at the startled bell-boy with a fierceness intended for Kennett. "Show him in immediately!"

As the servant vanished he walked up and down the room in a sort of angry elation. "I'll settle this matter at once!" he cried. "Stay where you are, Felicia," for she had risen to make her escape. "Sit down," he ordered peremptorily. "I intend to put an end to this affair; I'll settle it." He thumped the floor with his thick cane, in his excitement.

At the sound of the opening door, Judge Hamilton faced about suddenly. The sedate, almost saturnine gentleman on the threshold did not accord with his idea of an opera singer in private life. His mental ideal was of a more pronounced type. However, he stepped quickly to the middle of the room. The hand holding his stick was trembling violently; his eyes were very fierce.

"If I am not mistaken, sir, your name is Kennett," he began. "Yes, I thought so. Now, sir, I am a man of few words, — a plain man. I am told you have been visiting my daughter. I don't approve of it. I won't have it. I know nothing against you personally, but I won't have an opera singer among her acquaintance. You will be so good as to discontinue your calls."

John Hamilton, now that he was relieved of the responsibility of the crisis, was able to look at

Kennett, at this trying moment, with a certain dispassionate criticism impossible earlier; and in this calmer mood he marveled at Felicia's infatuation. No man could fully gauge another man's power in a matter of this sort, he reflected, but, making all allowance, what could she see in this fellow? He looked like an honest man, with the proclivities of a gentleman, of somewhat more than average intelligence. It was perhaps the best which might be said for him that his was a lucid nature, with a certain dignity, a certain strength. Surely this was not remarkable; there were doubtless hundreds and thousands of men equal to him in these respects, in the conventional walks of life. How had she happened to fancy the man? She was not a fool to be attracted merely by the tawdry glitter appertaining to his vocation. What a commentary on the perversity of women that she, with her ultra-fastidious notions, should be seized upon by an infatuation like this, without even the absurd excuse of dash, romance, fascination, in its object to explain it!

Judge Hamilton's look and tone, in their arrogance, their intolerance, were hard to endure without protest more or less insistent, but the habit of self-management had been the business of Kennett's life; the exercise of tact, of policy, was a daily necessity. It was with a judicious admixture of firmness, of self-respect, and of respect for Judge Hamilton's seniority that he replied.

"Your daughter has promised to marry me," he said, "and I shall use every effort to induce her to keep her promise."

Judge Hamilton shifted his hand from the head of his cane, and, grasping it in the middle, brandished it with a wildly threatening motion.

"But I tell you, sir, I won't have it!" he exclaimed, in a stentorian roar.

"She has promised to marry me," repeated the young man.

Is every able jury lawyer an actor as well; has he something of that wonderful faculty which can instantaneously master a situation, experience an emotion, gauge and apportion its reflex action upon the natures of others; or was there hidden away in Judge Hamilton's intellectual being an exceptional gift of which he was half unconscious? His face suddenly cleared; he let his cane slip through his fingers, which lightly tightened upon the gold head; he gently tapped the floor; he nodded two or three times, with an expression denoting perfect faith in his own words.

"She will never do it," he said. "She will marry no man without my consent." He turned upon his daughter a beautiful look of tenderness and confidence. "She is fond of her old father," he added, simply.

It was a fine touch and very well done; all the actor's sensitive perceptions made Kennett keenly alive to its artistic merits. The others, less discriminating, were more emotionally, and consequently more vividly impressed. Evidently this had told heavily against him. He was beginning to lose his calmness; he attempted to argue.

"If her happiness is at stake," he said eagerly, "does it not occur to you that my personal character is a matter worthy of some consideration? I think a little inquiry would satisfy you on this score. I can "—

"I need inquire no further, sir, than your business," returned Judge Hamilton, lapsing into anger. "To me it is intolerable, unendurable. Allow my daughter to marry a singer, an operatic singer! Sir, I would not for one moment entertain the idea."

If he could have stopped here, the affair might even yet have adjusted itself on his basis. Since that fine little stroke of delicate sentiment his daughter had grown white; there were tears on her cheek. He loved her so, — her father, — and she *was* fond of him; what must she do, — what must she do?

When, however, Judge Hamilton's astuteness and his temper were weighed in the balance, the chances were in favor of the temper as the more definite element. It shortly effaced the impression his tact had produced.

"There are other considerations "— persisted Kennett.

"Can't you take No for an answer?" interrupted the old gentleman, aggressively. "There is no use in discussing the matter."

Kennett turned suddenly to Felicia. His self-possession was gone at last. She had never thought to see him so shaken. His voice was strained; the hand that held his hat was trembling; the look of appeal he bent upon her, charged with a sort of helplessness in significant contrast with his strength as she had known him heretofore, was very potent with the woman who loved him. Her heart beat fast; she looked at him piteously.

"I will take my answer only from you, Felicia," he said.

The tone in which he pronounced her name, the fact that he dared utter her name at all, set the old gentleman's blood boiling. He again grasped his cane in the centre and made a hurried stride forward; then he turned sharply and fixed his angry eyes on his daughter.

"Give him his answer," he commanded; "his answer is *No!*"

She made no reply.

"I will be obeyed, Felicia!" he thundered. "Send the man about his affairs! Give him his answer; his answer is *No!* You *shall* obey me! Send him away — or I'll disinherit you — I'll write my will this night, and cut you off without a cent!"

"Lord, Lord!" groaned John, in his corner. "To threaten a girl like Felicia! And he calls *me* a lunatic!" But John groaned this reflection very *sotto voce* indeed.

Felicia had risen; her color had come back in a brilliant spot on either cheek; her eyes were bright.

"You bring money into this discussion, papa," she said. "I will not obey you for such a reason. I will not send him away so that I may inherit your money. I feel very well satisfied that he will take care of me. Besides," she added, proudly, "I am not a beggar. I have my own property that mamma's father left me."

The old gentleman glared at her in a baffled way during this defiance, and as she concluded he gave a loud snort of scorn and anger.

"Lord, yes," he exclaimed, contemptuously, "you have got that! I'd lost sight of that vast estate. Oh, yes, you've got your mother's share."

"And you can leave your money to whom you please. *I* don't want it!" cried Felicia, unappeasable now.

In this spirit of mutual defiance the contest was waged afterward. There was no more of softening on either side. Felicia could not forgive her father's threat of disinheritance; it had kindled even more resentment than John's mistaken and disingenuous policy of silent antagonism. Judge Hamilton, on his side, could not forgive her infatuation, and it held for him the element of dismayed astonishment. He was one of those men whose critical faculty is not disarmed by partiality. His very fondness for his daughter made him keenly alert to her faults, and he had decided, upon what he deemed abundant evidence, that a pronounced worldly-mindedness was one of those faults, — that she had an undue appreciation of a fine establishment, of the newest and most desirable attainment in equipage, diamonds, laces, the triumphs of the dressmaker's and milliner's arts. He desired that she should enjoy these good and valuable things, that she should appreciate them fully, and yet that she should in some sort spiritually ignore them. The reverse danger, the unreasoning relinquishment of all this gilded and refined mammon, he had not felt called upon to fear.

In this emergency he took Madame Sevier into his confidence. His feeling toward this lady was somewhat contradictory. When, ten years before, he had opened his eyes to the fact that his daughter was growing into a tall, dreamy, awkward girl, extremely fond of books and abnormally ignorant of everything else, he selected a notable French boarding-school as offering the influences likely to ward off the danger that she would develop into a desultorily intellectual and socially untrained woman. With the result of the experiment he was not altogether satisfied; yet he could hardly say what was lacking. She was, as he desired, educated, yet not over-educated; her taste was schooled, her social gifts were cultivated; she had a good French and Italian accent, and spoke both languages fluently; she sang and played on the piano and harp very creditably, according to the authorities, — he admitted his incapacity to judge in this regard ; she understood life and society, — there was no doubt about that. Sometimes he called the vague fault he found in this product of Madame Sevier's civilization frivolity ; sometimes, vanity, petty - mindedness, artificiality. It not occur to him that he had desired an impossibility : worldly training with simplicity, intellect without its self-assertion, social culture without its imperative demands and its intolerance. He was as greatly surprised that the moderately near approximation to his ideal which his daughter embodied should not be content with the society of Blankburg divinity students, thus negativing her intellectual tendencies, as that she should ignore her worldly training by giving a serious thought to a man in Hugh Kennett's position in life. He forgot now all that he had said in disapprobation of Madame Sevier, her methods and achievement, and turned to her for aid, as he had done ten years before.

She gave him her most ardent sympathy, — who feels another's woe so keenly as one whose own interest is also involved ? She threw up her hands ; she elevated her fine gray eyes, her delicate black eyebrows, and her thin, expressive shoulders. And she said with the intensest and most sincere feeling, " A-h-h, mais mon Dieu, c'est trop terrible ! " An eloquent dismay was depicted on every feature : on the curves of her short upper lip; on the thin dilating nostrils of her classic nose; in the flush that overspread the clear pallor of her cheek; on the delicate network of wrinkles that corrugated her frowning brow, and extended to the dense black hair streaked with gray which she dared to dress, in this day of curls and bangs, in the fashion of forty years ago, — in soft loose waves on each side of her broad low forehead. Her favorite pupil, the show young lady of the Institute, who had been with her for ten years, whom she was accustomed to point out as an exemplification of what she and the Institute could do, — her Félicité, of whom she was so fond and so proud, — to marry an opera singer, and thus reinforce the fascinations of the stage hero for silly school-girls! She, the model, the intellectual, — it would have surprised Alfred Grafton, the extent to which Felicia's intellectuality was esteemed at the Institute, — she, the clear-headed, the solid-minded! Ah-h-h! such an example to the other young ladies! What could Madame Sevier do but call upon her *bon Dieu*, maintain that this was *affreux*, and promise to see Felicia at once?

She was eminently calculated to influence Felicia. The magnetism of her presence, her superior mental qualities, the adroitness of her tact, the graceful tenderness of her demonstrations of affection, the force of long association, all conspired to bring their strength to any cause she might espouse. This time, however, she was too thoroughly interested to avail herself fully of these aids. Her tact at a moment of peril was not equal to her earnestness, — which affords gratifying evidence of the sincerity inherent in the human soul. Beyond this Madame Sevier was at a disadvantage. An argument which can be supported only by commonplace truisms — so obvious that nobody denies them — is necessarily weak. She could only declare in varied phrase that marriage is a serious matter; that a passing fancy should not be allowed to jeopardize solid happiness; that only in romances is emotion the all in all of existence. It might have been better if she had stopped here, but —

" Ah, ma chère, c'est trop affreux! Only reflect. How public! how notorious! And your father and brother are so violent, so imprudent. Ah-h-h, my dear, these family storms will be heard of. You are notable. The Institute is *so* notable! There will be paragraphs. Ah, yes, indeed; the reporters are hungry for items. Paragraphs in the newspapers about the beautiful heiress, a former pupil of the well-known Sevier Institute, who is bent on marrying a singer! Ah, just Heaven! I would not have that happen for a great deal. Give it up, my dear Felicia. Think of the Institute! Think of ME!"

It may be doubted if Judge Hamilton's partisan did his cause much service.

So strained and unnatural a situation could not long remain unchanged. It was radically and very suddenly altered one afternoon, when Felicia walked down to the public parlor of the hotel, met Hugh Kennett, and accompanied him to St. —— Church, where they were quietly married.

In an hour thereafter, Judge Hamilton, his son, Sophie, and the children had left New York; the two gentlemen metaphorically shaking the dust from their indignant feet, and literally bestowing hearty maledictions on the devoted city and all it contained.

X.

THE jets in the great chandelier were slowly lowered; the large semicircle of the auditorium, over which the flutter of fans and ripple of smiles suggested the fugitive effect of breezes and butterflies about a bed of flowers, sank gradually into deep shadow; the footlights became suddenly brilliant; the prompter's bell tinkled; the curtain glided upward; the second act had begun, and Prince Roderic advanced down the right centre to a soft pizzicato movement of violins, through which floated the melody, sustained by cornets and flutes.

A round of applause greeted him. The curtain had fallen upon him as the central figure of an effective scene, and the situation was one which appealed to the sense of pity and the sense of justice, thus moving the popular heart. And now was introduced in hiding in certain woods this potentate, vaguely described as prince, deposed from his indefinite high station through his own confiding nature and the machinations of a false and trusted friend, whose office seemed to embrace all the functions of a Grand Vizier. Abundant opportunity was afforded for soft and deft stepping about and for graceful attitudinizing, as the prince assured himself that no hidden foe lurked in ambush among the trees and rocks. Satisfied that he was alone, save for a thousand or so people in the audience, who do not count, except in the sordid computations of the ticket office, he gave himself up to despairing reflections on his situation, supplemented by vows, in sufficiently heroic strain, of vengeance. His voice, rich and robust, embodied a certain nobility, and the covertly martial orchestration heightened the effect. The contrast to sudden tenderness — expressing the idea of an amazed incredulity and grief because of the perfidy of his friend — in the succeeding movement was so well done, assisted as it was by a very soft and taking melody, that it brought down the house and extorted an encore.

It is seldom that any prince, on or off the stage, is watched with such a complication of feelings as those which animated a pair of violet eyes in one of the proscenium boxes. Felicia had been married six months, and this was her first acquaintance with the prince — as a prince. To the mere man she had given much intelligent appreciation and her tender heart. Now, what of the prince? She was proud of him; she could not help that, — he did it so well. Her musical training had been sufficient to enable her to admire enthusiastically his voice and gauge the extent of its culture. She was ashamed of him, — that he, bedizened in stage finery and with a painted face, should display himself and his capacities so that all these people, who had paid their money, might be entertained, might approve or disapprove at their good pleasure! She pitied him. To her it all seemed so small, so false, so utterly unworthy of him; and yet he was so thoroughly satisfied with it, and — he did it so well. And she had discovered that it was no light task, — to do this well. She had had glimpses of the incessant labor; the unceasing exercise of judgment, of patience, of memory; the tense strain on the nerves; the exhausting attention to detail, which go to make that airy structure, a success on the lyric stage, which presents the very perfection of spontaneous inspiration.

She had arrived late, and had missed the first act. When he came walking down the stage in this new guise, so strange to her, she felt her heart beating fast and heavily, and the color slowly left her face. It returned with a rush when the sound of clapping hands broke the silence, and she leaned slightly forward, watching him with a grave face and intent eyes.

Thus she was looking at him when he caught sight of her.

There was little change in her since the enchanted days of last summer; none but a keen observer might detect a subtler expression on her expressive features. Something was suggested of the emotions of a woman who loves entirely and is entirely loved. There was beside something more complex than this, — not pain, not restlessness, yet partaking to a degree of each, and contending with that deeper, stiller look which happiness had given to her face.

This was a good deal to see in one half minute, but Hugh Kennett saw with his intellect and his heart as well as with his eyes, while, with long golden curls hanging beneath his plumed hat, and arrayed in a costume of violet velvet, combining two tones, very faint and very dark, which gave back the lustre of the footlights, yet held rich shadows, he stepped deftly about in his search for Prince Roderic's implacable foes among the tangled intricacies of the canvas rocks and bushes.

As the tenor finished his encore, the baritone came on in a green hunting-suit, apparently winding a silver horn, which office was judiciously delegated to a member of the orchestra. Felicia gathered that the baritone and the prince were rivals in love, and that the baritone had left the court in dudgeon because of the prince's presumptive success with the lady previous to his exile, brought about by the perfidious Grand Chamberlain. There was a melodic defiance, pitched on a high key, and later, when matters were explained, much graceful and musical magnanimity on both sides. With the offer on the part of the baritone to join the usurper's forces, and to introduce the prince in disguise into his own dominions, in an effort to regain his status, the scene closed; the silver horn was again wound; the prince, by agreement, passed up the left centre; and a party of huntsmen came into view at the back of the stage, to the prelude of a dashing chorus chronicling the joys of the chase.

The face with which Hugh Kennett dropped into a chair in his dressing-room, after changing his costume, was not Prince Roderic's face, nor was it the serene face he usually wore. The paint did not obscure its expression: it was anxious; it held some impatience, some depression, some uncertainty. "How did she happen to come?" he said to himself. And then, "I suppose she considers me a sort of Harlequin," he reflected, bitterly.

Abbott entered a moment later. He too had changed his dress, substituting for the green hunting-suit a blue and white costume very resplendent with silver lace, supposed to be the acceptable court attire. He flung himself into a rocking-chair, lighted a cigar, and for a moment the two men were silent.

The room was small and in disarray. Much-bedizened costumes were tossed about the chairs; several pairs of stage slippers were on the floor; the gas-jets on each side of a mirror were alight, and from the elbow of one of the brackets depended a blond wig. The hair was very long and curled, and the effect was that of a decapitated head as the locks waved in the breeze, for the window was open. It was a warm night for the season, — the first week in April; there had been rain, and the air was heavy. Abbott picked up a palm-leaf fan, and as he swayed back and forth he fanned himself. His mobile, irregular face was in this brilliant light ghastly and unnatural, with its staring contrasts of red and white; those heavy lines about his mouth and brow were plastered over, but there were black semicircles under his eyes. His nervous temperament was manifested by the restlessness of his movements: he changed his attitude abruptly; he glanced about him with eagerness; he plied the fan with energy; the very act of rocking was done with a rapid, uncertain motion.

"Your wife is here," he said, suddenly.

Kennett glanced at him.

"I don't mean in here," said Abbott, with a laugh. "Outside, — in the audience — in one of the boxes."

"I know it," returned Kennett.

There was a short pause.

"She does n't honor you often," remarked Abbott.

Kennett made no reply. These men had known each other long and well; each was perfectly aware of the other's thought, — nay, Abbott even divined his friend's impulse to declare that her absence was through his own desire, and the instantaneous rejection of the half-formed intention as useless for the purpose of deception. And Kennett knew that Abbott was triumphant because she had not come before this, and was contradictorily and characteristically resentful of her neglect.

"Sometimes I think," Abbott went on, reflectively, "that it is best for a man not to marry out of meeting, as the Quakers say." He himself had married, while yet a chorus singer, a young girl with a rustic style of beauty, also a chorus singer, who had left the stage before progressing beyond that point.

Kennett again said nothing.

"The identity of interest,—that's the thing; the sympathy, you know. I suppose it is impossible for an outsider to feel it exactly."

"If you lay down a general rule, no doubt you are right," returned Kennett, coolly.

Abbott looked at him hard, with a feeling which is somewhat difficult of analysis. His was a nature in which the sweet and bitter were mixed in exact proportions. There was something feminine in his disposition, illustrated just now in an impulse to say that which would cut and rankle; yet his affection for his friend was strong and sincere. His unreasoning and unreasonable perversity went hand in hand with magnanimity. He could throw himself with ardor into another man's effort, sincerely sympathize with his defeat and rejoice in his achievement; and he could no more refrain, when in the mood, from gibe and fleer than a freakish woman, in irritation or disappointment, can leave unuttered the word that stabs the heart she loves best. He had, at the time, deplored Kennett's marriage as a calamity. Judge Hamilton and his son might possibly have enlarged their estimate as to the scope of human impudence, if they could have divined Mr. Abbott's point of view. Since that event he had not altered his opinion.

After a pause he spoke again.

"Marriage is a mistake, and don't you forget it," he said, thoughtfully; "that is, for a man with ambitions. It does well enough for mediocrity."

Kennett looked at him fixedly, with set teeth and compressed lips, which brought into play the latent fierceness his square lower jaw could express; there was a steely gleam in his gray eyes.

The crisis required only a look. Abbott retreated in good order. He glanced innocently at his friend and vaguely about the room, fanning himself and smoking.

"Good house," he remarked, with a nod in the direction of the audience.

"The duet went well," said Kennett.

"You bet," rejoined Abbott.

His quick sense caught the step of the advancing call-boy before the door was opened. He sprang from his chair to the mirror, took a swift, comprehensive look at himself, readjusted with a dextrous hand the collar of stage jewels about his throat, and vanished without another word.

Kennett, left alone, rose and walked to the window. His step was heavier than its wont.

A warm, dank breeze was blowing; the clouds were low. The sounds from the street, the rattle of wheels as a carriage drew up near the mouth of the alley, the pawing of a horse, the accents of a voice raised in objurgation, the distant tinkle of car-bells, came muffled on the thick air; an almost imperceptible drizzle of rain made itself felt on his face. It was an imprudent thing for him — the most prudent of men — to stand in his airy attire at the open window, and it was almost equally imprudent to give himself up to his purely personal interests, in this interval which belonged, as distinctly as active duties, to his professional work. Instead of devoting the wait to mere mental and physical rest, or to the anticipation of what remained to be done in the next hour, his mind was busy with a brief review of the last six months and the effect of a foreign influence on his life. Abbott's ill-natured dictum came back to him with malignant iteration. Was his marriage a mistake? For his own heart, his happiness, he indignantly denied this. But for his ambitions, his future, his artistic development?

So far the foreign influence had been merely negative. Felicia had held apart from his professional life; she had ignored as much as was practicable the fact that he had any life except the one she shared. In the early weeks of their marriage, the perception had come to him that her persistent pretexts for declining to accompany him to the performances and rehearsals were part of a premeditated plan. When he realized this he ceased to urge her, and without explanation there came to be a tacit agreement that his stage life was a thing apart from his domestic life. It was very quietly but very firmly accomplished. He winced under it, but his pride was roused, and he accepted the situation without protest. Now he was asking himself how it was that a merely negative influence could chill. He did not believe that a difference was as yet perceptible in his work, for thorough training and the habit of a lifetime go far as substitutes for ardor, but he sometimes knew — and it was growing upon him — a deep-felt want; he recognized it, — it was a lost impulse, a lost inspiration. While still in his possession it had dignified his calling, it had made toil light, it had invested the tedious details with recurrent interest. Now that he missed it he appreciated its worth both as a sentimental possession and as a tangible factor in achievement. He wondered how this would end; he wondered if a. change impended; he wondered how she happened to come here to-night. He wondered again if she rated him as a bedizened Harlequin, — it must all be buffoonery to her.

The call-boy stuck his head in at the door.

" Stage waits."

The reflections that had absorbed the last ten minutes narrowly missed being a singularly unfortunate preparation. For the first time in many years Kennett experienced, as he left the wings, the poignant anguish of stage fright. He pulled himself together by a great effort; he called up all his faculties. At this moment he met her eyes again; she smiled, and her face wore an expression he often saw in that closer life which had come to be so much dearer to him than his public life. Under the impetus of the thought that perhaps after all she might reconcile those diverse existences he regained his self-command, but he was vaguely aware of a sub-current of surprised dismay that her approval or her objection should exercise so strong a control. His capacities had responded to that smile of hers like a horse to a touch on the curb.

The representation continued to a felicitous conclusion. The usurper, unconscious of his impending doom, robed in power and red velvet, made welcome the stranger — all unsuspecting the prince in disguise — in a fine bass solo, embodying some elements of self-gratulation and braggadocio which afforded the opportunity for an arrogant and mocking ha! ha! peculiarly rich and full. Laughing and dying were conceded to be this gentleman's province; and he presently demonstrated his claim to superiority in the latter accomplishment when the counterplot culminated, and, overwhelmed and despairing, he stabbed himself, circumventing the representatives of justice, who would fain have dragged him to a dungeon, by dying melodiously in E minor. The rightful prince was restored to his possessions, including the heart of the soprano; the baritone made the timely discovery that he had mistaken his feelings, had been unawares interested in another young lady, and was satisfied with her hand; the faithful adherents vociferously proclaimed their joy; the orchestra sympathetically and vivaciously accented their sentiments; the tableau formed itself swiftly and incomprehensibly into a glittering semicircle of brilliant colors and flower-like faces; the lights in the auditorium brightened; the curtain slowly descended; there was a final crash and bang of instruments, and the performance was over.

As she stood watching the audience making its way out of the building, a note was brought to Felicia. It was signed with Kennett's initials, and merely asked her to wait for him a few moments. In a short time he entered the box.

An old lady, whom he had not before observed, was with his wife, — a sedate old lady, dressed with punctilious regard to the fashion in some respects, and in other respects disdainfully ignoring it. She regarded him intently when he was presented, and the three made their way across the street to the hotel. At supper, of which she was induced to partake, she gazed at him with a covert curiosity, which had in it something at once ludicrous and embarrassing. She accorded the gravest attention to whatever he said, and seemed to weigh carefully her somewhat commonplace and obvious replies. Before the conclusion of the meal she demurely bade them good-night, adding that she was unaccustomed to such late hours, and betook herself to her own room.

"Who is she?" asked Kennett, as the rustle of her black silk dress died on the air.

"She is the wife of one of my father's old friends. Her husband and she happened to be passing through the city. I met her in the hotel parlor, and asked her to go to the opera."

"She seemed to think me a queer fish."

Felicia laughed. "You must forgive her," she said. "This is a remarkable experience; she never before took supper with a singer and a singer's wife."

He did not quite comprehend her tone, and he was vividly conscious that for the first time she had mentioned him as a singer and herself as a singer's wife. Nothing more was said on the subject until they returned to their own room. She threw herself into a low chair, and he lighted a cigar and stood near her, with his elbow on the mantelpiece.

"This is a new departure, is n't it?" he asked, after a pause.

She raised her eyes slowly. "It is an experiment," she replied.

"Why did you come?"

"I thought the other experiment had been tried sufficiently."

"Has it failed?"

"I think it has."

He walked up and down the room for some moments, with his hands behind him; then resumed his former place and attitude.

"What was your experiment, Felicia?"

"I wished to prove to myself that in marrying a singer I had not necessarily married his profession."

"And you did not prove it?"

She did not reply directly.

"A woman who marries a lawyer takes no thought of his clients; a woman who marries a doctor,—what does she care for his patients or their diseases? I suppose Sophie hardly knows whether her husband deals in cotton, or wheat, or dry goods. Your vocation is business, like any other pursuit: women have nothing to do with business."

"You dislike it so much," he said, not interrogatively.

"Oh, so much!" cried Felicia, impulsively. Then she checked herself. "I take that back. I should not say that. You chose your line in life long before you ever met me; it has the prior right. I don't complain."

"If you dislike it so much," he said, disregarding her retraction, "you need see very little of it. Why not continue as we have begun?"

All at once he was made aware that while he was enacting mimic woes a drama of real feeling had been going on very near to him. Again she lifted her eyes, and now their expression cut him deeply; her lips were quivering.

"I am so lonely," she said, simply.

It is a bitter thing for a sensitive man to see that look on the face of the woman he loves, and to realize that he is to blame that she should be called upon to endure the feeling which elicits it. For the first time he took into consideration the fact of his own absorptions; of his eager and un-failing response to the demands of his profession. He saw in a swift mental review what her life must be as a whole. He realized the gaps of time that she must sit alone in the hotel bed-room, with its dismal simulacrum of comfort, and occasionally of luxury, in the huge caravansaries which marked their progress eastward or west-ward. What could she do with the hours while she thus waited for him to come from rehearsals and the evening performances? Write letters? To whom? All her valued friends she had alien-ated by her marriage. To be sure, there were books, painting, fancy - work. These, he realized with sudden insight, are the resources of people who are not living their own dramas. Of what did she think in those long hours? Did memory take possession of her? So young a woman should have nothing to do with memory. Ah, had regret too made acquaintance with her heart, while he was away? He appreciated that she must have experienced much of the sensation of isolation. Her connection with the little world of theatrical people amounted to a formal bow to certain members of the troupe, in the hotel dining-rooms or on the trains, and for many reasons he hardly cared to have this otherwise. He recalled now — it had made scant impression at the time — the gleeful interest with which she recounted, one day, in Buffalo, an interview she had had with a little girl, who had stopped her in a corridor to tearfully relate her woes, exhibit a broken doll, and be consoled. Once when she had attended a morning service in Washington, — alone, for he was no church-goer, — the white-haired old lady to whose pew she was shown had spoken to her, and hoped she would come again. She had recurred to the circumstance more than once; saying wistfully that she wished they could stay longer in Washington, and that they knew some one who could introduce them to that old lady, — it would be "so pleasant." And once in New York Madame Sevier had called; he had fancied, that evening, there were evidences of tears on his wife's face, but she said nothing, and the incident slipped into the past.

This had been her social life for the last six months, — she whose instinct for human companionship was so strong and had been so assiduously cultivated. Even of his leisure he had been unconsciously chary, giving much of it to the details of his work; only to-day she had waited long by the piano until he satisfied himself that certain passages were susceptible of no further improvement.

In this sudden enlightenment other facts acquired new meaning. There seemed now something pathetic in the touches of ornamentation about them. He had been amused by her efforts to give a homelike look to the stereotyped rooms of the hotels at which they had temporarily lived, in their ceaseless progress " on the road." She had provided herself with vases, portières, books handsomely bound and illustrated; the tables were draped with embroidered covers ; the two armchairs were decorated with scarfs. He had called these things her " properties," and had laughingly threatened to send them on ahead with the stage effects of the troupe. Now he was touched by the feminine longing for a home and its associations which this tendency implied. For himself, his personal tastes were of the simplest ; perhaps the attention to matters of effect and fabric incident to his professional life had satisfied whatever predilection in that line he possessed.

When a man has been successful, flattered, admired, and always in the right, and when he suddenly discovers that he is in the wrong and his feeling is deeply involved, expressions do not readily present themselves. Kennett's thought was — and at the time it was perfectly sincere — that his insensibility had been brutal. To her he said nothing for some moments.

" Try to like us ! " he exclaimed at last, with emotion. " There are some good men and women among us. There are even some agreeable people among us. Idealize us a little. Half the

world lives and is happy by means of illusions;
why not you?"

But even while he spoke there came upon him
a stunning realization that many conditions were
utterly metamorphosed by the changed point of
view. His toleration in judgment, which she had
once noticed, was exercised instinctively, good-
humoredly, but always impersonally. These men
and women, for example, whom he mentioned,
many of them sterling, hard-working, talented, —
he could approve of them as members of society,
as his own casual associates, his comrades, his
friends. But it had not before occurred to him
that he had judged them leniently because he had
held himself a little — just a very little — above
them; that for many complicated and subtle reasons he condescended; he felt himself a little
above the profession. It was a fine thing in its
way, and eminently calculated, taking into view
his peculiar order of talent, to advance *him*. He
felt that this was an absurd position for him to
have assumed. He was with the stage, he was
of it; his family was identified with it, his father
and grandfather having been actors of considerable note; his interests were identical with the
interests of those he had unconsciously patro-
nized; they were his circle; they must necessarily
be his wife's circle, unless she preferred isolation.

The next day she went with him to rehearsal.

There was much to interest her in her new experience, and she did not observe that she herself

was the object of curiosity and covert attention on the part of members of the troupe, as she sat in the dim twilight of one of the proscenium boxes. The huge empty semicircle of the auditorium was unlighted save by a long slanting bar of sunshine that shot adown the descent of the dress circle. The stage also was dim, although several gas-jets were burning. A number of men and women in street attire were grouped about, presenting a very different appearance from the glittering throng of last night. Many of the faces were at once curiously young and old. Some were care-worn; some were anxious; some were bold; some were hard; many told no story and held no mean-ing. A man evidently in authority was talking loudly and vivaciously; now and then he walked about fitfully, and occasionally he gesticulated in illustration of his words. Most of his hearers had so bored and inattentive a look that it might have seemed worn of set purpose. The members of the orchestra lounged in their places, their instru-ments ready.

The weather had changed in the course of the night; a cold wind was blowing. The building was not well heated, and from some opening at the back of the stage came a strong draught, bringing a damp, vault-like taste and odor. Feli-cia, who had removed her wrap, an expensive fur garment, more in keeping with her previous cir-cumstances than her present, shivered slightly. Kennett rose and readjusted it about her.

"Don't signalize the occasion by taking cold," he said.

A voice behind him broke upon the air, — a mocking, musical, penetrating voice, subtly suggestive of possibilities and of meanings not to be lightly understood.

" ' Benedict, the married man ' ! " exclaimed the voice.

Kennett turned his head. "Is that you, Abbott?" he said. "Come in."

Abbott entered, and seated himself near them.

"Don't let your husband lavish his care," he continued. "It will not do for him to be thoughtful and attentive, like any commonplace, good husband."

"I think it is very proper for him to get my cloak," returned Felicia, a trifle aggressively.

"That is only a little thing, but it shows which way the wind blows."

"The wind seems to blow every way to-day," interpolated Kennett, lightly.

"He has, or has had up to this time, a sort of divine right to immunity from small cares; it has been his prerogative to make himself comfortable."

"Abbott thinks I am selfish," said Kennett.

"You are if you know what's good for you, and don't you forget it," retorted Abbott, quickly.

Felicia, irritated by the imputation and offended by the slang, was silent for a moment, but her interest in the subject prevailed.

" Why should he be selfish? " she asked, stiffly.

" Because, when a man has a great future, he can't give himself a thought too many."

" Has he a great future ? "

Abbott looked at her steadfastly, then at his friend. Kennett's fine gray eyes rested tranquilly on Abbott's unquiet, expressive face, cut by deep lines of hope, of disappointment, anxiety, excesses ; his eyes, too, were gray, but eager, fiery, restless, penetrating. The two men exchanged a long look.

" Well? " said Kennett, smiling.

" I don't know," answered Abbott, shortly. He turned his face toward the stage.

Changes were in progress there. The talking man was loquaciously retiring, looking over his shoulder. A lady in a gray dress and cloak, and with a black feather in her hat, had detached herself from the others, and advanced toward the footlights. She glanced about her hardily, and shrugged her shoulders with a show of contemptuous impatience as the stage-manager's prelection seemed suddenly to take a new lease, and he continued speaking. All at once he came to a standstill. " Now there 's your cue, Miss Johnson," he said, — " ' Me hopes, me honor, and me broken heart ! ' Go 'n ! " very peremptorily.

She began to declaim in the loud, hard stage voice which has so unnatural a sound in an empty theatre.

A man with a worn face and a *blasé* air had

placed himself near her, and at his cue took part in one of those dialogues so useful as connecting links of the story. Little of action was required, but even that little was not satisfactory; the talking man found it desirable several times to dart forward and eagerly correct, explain, and suggest. At last there came a rap of the conductor's baton, — the members of the orchestra were tense and alert in their places; another rap, — the dialogue developed into a duet, and the duet was succeeded by a chorus.

It had seemed to Felicia that disproportionate care and work were requisite for individual excellence; she now saw that even more were necessary to produce a good *ensemble* effect. Again and again the sharp raps of the baton resounded with a peremptory negative intention, which brought a sudden silence, invaded in a moment by the melancholy voice of the Gallic leader, with unexpected pauses and despairing inflections.

"That was 'orrible, 'orrible, 'orrible!" he said, definitely; or, "A mos' slovenly *attac'*!" or, "Tenors, you sing a minor third instead of a major third;" or, "*Mon Dieu!* Sopranos! Sopranos, you are *fl-l-l-at!*"

When at last the chorus was progressing smoothly Kennett rose.

"*Au revoir*," he said to Felicia; and she fancied that there was something propitiatory, even appealing, in his expression. Did he recommend Abbott to her leniency, and vicariously deprecate her criticism?

"Now Kennett will warble O. K., you bet your life," Abbott said.

He misunderstood the haughty displeasure on her face. All the nicer issues of social training were as a sealed book to him. He did not dream that the rudeness of his phrase was in her estimation intolerable; that she deemed slang — unless, indeed, it were the trick of expression of "the best people," and not fairly to be called slang at all — an affront to her and a degradation to him. He placed his own interpretation on her evident intolerance.

"Confound the little idiot, she is ashamed of him!" he thought, angrily. "She must have married him in a freak. She considers herself too good for him. And he with the best voice of its class in America!"

He looked at her resentfully.

Her attention had become riveted on what was in progress before her. She had noticed, the previous evening, the marked effect of Kennett's presence on the stage. Life was infused into the inert business; among the other singers there was sudden alertness of glance and intention; the action began to revolve about him as if animated by his controlling thought; smoothness and ease replaced mere mechanical effort, under the strong influence of an intelligent enthusiasm and a magnetic personality.

The manager, at the back of the stage, leaned against the frame of the canvas, took off his hat, mopped his face with his handkerchief, and uttered an audible "Whew-w!" in which were infused both fatigue and relief. Abbott called Felicia's attention to him.

"The governor feels easier now that Kennett is on. He's worked pretty hard to-day. Looks all tore up, don't he?"

Felicia disdained to say that the governor did or did not look "tore up."

"You see that woman with dark hair, in a black dress? She is under-studying Miss Brady. She can sing if she only has a chance. You bet your sweet life she goes into some church after every rehearsal, and prays God Almighty and the saints that the other woman may get run over by the street-car or the fire-engine, or something." He looked with a laugh into Felicia's horror-stricken eyes. "For a fact she does. Told me so herself. You see she's waiting for her promotion. She used to be with the Vilette Company, until they went to pieces last fall; then she" —

Felicia lifted her hand imperiously, imposing silence. "He is going to sing."

There had floated upon the air a prelude familiar to her. She leaned slightly forward, her eyes on him while he sang, all unconscious that Abbott's eyes were on her. No man, especially with the soul of an artist in him, could misinterpret that expression; her face was for the moment transfigured by the emotion upon it, so proud, so tender, so absolutely enthralling, was it, — as intense and as delicate as white fire.

Abbott looked at her meditatively. " The man," he said to himself, " has got a big possibility in the future; and the woman thinks small beer of his future, and don't care a continental for his best possibility; and, God help 'em, they love each other. Now, what are they going to do about it ? "

He cogitated on this subject for some time. Finally he rose, left the box unobserved, and went to wait for his cue at one of the wings.

Under the ethereal fire of those violet eyes, the man with a possibility in his future sang well that day. The members of the orchestra laid down their instruments and applauded. The stage manager bawled that it would be an easier world if there were more like him. The other singers looked at him with eyes animated by every degree of intelligent admiration and appreciative envy. It seemed to Felicia that it was distinctly an ovation he was receiving; she wondered that adulation had not spoiled him. She did not realize that with a fully equipped capacity ambition dwarfs possession.

As he went off, he encountered Abbott in the narrow passway between two " sets." Each placed his hands on his friend's shoulders and looked long into his eyes.

" Well ? " said Kennett, in the tone with which he had uttered the word an hour before.

" If this world does not offer you everything heart can desire in the next five years, it will be your own fault — or your wife's fault!" cried Abbott, with the thrill of sincere feeling in his voice.

"I shall have everything that heart can desire!" exclaimed Kennett, airily. "There's your cue, old fellow." And he went back, with a satisfied smile, to Felicia.

He noticed, as the rehearsal proceeded, that Preston often looked with some wistfulness at their box, as he lounged at the back of the stage and about the wings. During one of the waits he stood near them, and Kennett called him in an undertone.

"I must go on again in a few moments," he said to Felicia, "but Preston will come and talk to you."

Preston was evidently pleased and flattered, but to Felicia's surprise he was inclined to taciturnity. He was bold enough among men, — in fact, he was sometimes accused of impudence, — and not too gentle and meek with the women with whom he was usually thrown. In the little world of the troupe he was considered by the feminine members a singing Adonis, and was greatly approved; with them he was gay, boisterous, flippant. But with Felicia he was shy. He was quick of perception: when she bent her violet eyes upon him and allowed her gracious smile to rest on her lips, he apprehended that the gentle demonstration was merely a surface effect; it was not the flattering and flattered smile he was accustomed to receive. He appreciated the dignity underlying the soft exterior of her manner, and realized that she probably had a distinct ideal of the proper thing to be and to feel, to which he might not altogether conform. This sort of influence makes many a man restive and defiant, and it is to Oliver Preston's credit that he was a trifle timid and propitiatory.

Their conversation, constrained at first, grew gradually more easy. She drew him on to talk of himself. She saw presently that he was not by any means so young as his boyish manner and regular, delicate features made him seem. With her alert interest in the vivid drama of life and character, she speculated on this existence of his, and the strange fact that excitement and variety do not make the inroads on mind and body which are compassed by inaction and tranquillity. He had happened to mention that he was thirty-two years old. " At that age men in little country towns are advancing into middle life," she said to herself, " while he has the buoyancy, and to all intents the youthfulness, of twenty."

After a time she was struck by something unfeeling in his tone, — the more objectionable in that he was unconscious of it. When the contralto was sharply reprimanded for a mistake in a short interjectionary phrase, which threw the other singers out and necessitated repetition, he laughed with genuine gusto that she should become confused, blunder again, then dash at her phrase with ludicrous precipitancy. "What a fool!" he said, contemptuously. "And flat besides."

He listened with great attention while Abbott sang a solo, and said at its close: —

"Abbott will never get much further than he has already gone. He is limited," he added, with a certain complacence.

"I think he has a very beautiful voice," remarked Felicia.

He reflected a moment.

"Yes, it is sympathetic and true, and it has a vibrating quality, but it is uneven; both the upper and lower registers are better than the middle. Then he works spasmodically; he is kept down by his habits. Sometimes he does pretty well for a while; then he 'll take to drinking. He drinks like a fish. And he gambles; and that keeps him poor as Job's turkey, as he often says himself. He always has hard luck and he always expects a streak of good luck. So he is continually in a state of anxiety and agitation. And that is very bad for the voice. He used to be ambitious. He used to think he would make a great success, but I believe he has given up all hope for that now."

"Oh-h!" exclaimed Felicia, regretfully.

"Abbott says," continued Preston, "when he sees how Kennett is running for the cup, he feels like a man who has been buried alive. He says, though, he wants Kennett to win the race. That is what he would do if he could get out from under the ground."

This figure of a despairing and buried ambition, and this wistful and generous acceptance of an humble share in another man's triumph, denied to him, touched Felicia. She looked with meditative pity at Abbott's ugly, expressive face, with its spent fires and spoiled purposes. His melodious voice was at its best in the soft melancholy of love-songs; he was singing a serenade now, and the building was filled with the insistent iteration of tender strains.

"'Buried alive,'" she repeated. "I think it is very sad that he should feel that."

"I think it is very funny," said Preston, with a rich ha! ha! He really thought so. Tragedy of feeling was, in his opinion, good stuff to act; as to sympathizing with a man's heart-break, how could he understand a language as foreign to him as if spoken by the inhabitants of Jupiter or Mars? He lived in another world.

"Why does he drink, then?" he asked, after a pause, as if realizing that something deeper was expected of him, and vaguely defending himself. "No fellow pays him anything for drinking."

He was regaining his usual mental attitude, which was a trifle dictatorial and tyrannical, as that of a spoiled young fellow is apt to be. When he presently went on, he said in a grumbled aside to Abbott that Kennett had all the luck, got *all* the plums, — a big salary, and managers always patting him on the back, and now marrying "a tip-top woman like that."

As the rehearsal drew toward its close, a marked change was perceptible in the spirit of the performers. An air of great fatigue had come upon them, and the lassitude which accompanies continuous and exhausting effort of brain and body. With the physical break-down the moral supports gave way; they were evidently as cross as they dared to be. The stage-manager was more eager, excited, and far more impatient than when the morning's work began. The conductor sometimes laid down the baton, rubbed with both sinewy hands the wisps of scanty hair on each side of his brow, took off his spectacles, replaced them, and resumed the baton with a loud, long sigh. Of the singers, Kennett only was unharassed. "I suppose that is part of his system of 'running for the cup,'" thought Felicia.

It seemed to her that the performers took pleasure in annoying each other, and presently this theory received confirmation. One of the chorus — a small girl, with a dainty figure, a pert face, black hair, and a somewhat conspicuous dress of red and black plaid — had been more than once called sharply to order for inattention. After the last of these episodes, as the music, which was in valse time, recommenced, she defiantly placed her arms akimbo, tossed her head saucily, and began to balance herself with the perfunctory dance-steps which, with appropriate costumes, serve for the ball-room illusion in the modern light opera. She looked mischievously at the tenors near her, and a few of the younger men laughed, but the others discreetly kept their eyes before them, and forbore to smile.   The manager, in a rage, stopped the orchestra, and advanced upon her with an oath that was like a roar.

"Quit that damned monkeying!"   He caught her arm and thrust her back to her place; then, as he turned, a sudden thought struck him.   He wheeled abruptly, and, with a grotesque imitation of her attitude, ludicrously caricatured her dancing.   She shrank back, blushing and discomfited, as a peal of appreciative laughter rewarded the managerial pleasantry.

When he had advanced upon the girl with that loud oath, Felicia had cowered as if herself threatened by a blow.   She glanced at the other men, in expectation of their interference.   Abbott's mouth was distorted by an abnormal grin.   Kennett was looking with a contemptuous smile from the absurdly dancing manager to the equally absurd victim.   Preston's handsome head was thrown back; his white teeth gleamed under his black mustache, while the building echoed with his delighted laughter.

The chorus was the last work of the day, and as Kennett rejoined his wife he found her standing at the entrance of the box with brilliant cheeks and flashing eyes.

"Why did n't you strike him, Hugh? Why did n't you knock him down?" she cried, impulsively.

" Who ? " he demanded, in amaze.

" That man, — that stage-manager."

" For what ? " he asked, completely at sea.

" For swearing at that girl, and pushing her, and mocking her."

He looked at her in silence.

" Felicia," said Hugh Kennett at last, with a long-drawn breath, " I would not imperil my prospects by striking a stage-manager for the sake of any chorus-girl on the face of the earth."

She thought at the moment that this was cruel and selfish to the last degree.

XI.

WITH something of the spirit, the serious absorption, the singleness of aim, the intensity, the concentration, which animate the student in pursuit of learning, or the man of affairs in the conduct of enterprise, Felicia entered upon the untried phase of her dual life; her rôle was now that of the singer's wife. She familiarized herself with the details of her husband's work. She accompanied him to every rehearsal and every performance. She promised herself that she would not permit extraneous matters to assume an importance which did not of right attach to them. Money, luxury, society, congenial association, — these were merely accessories, unimportant compared with the great fundamental fact of duty. She told herself that she had no right to come into his life, aware of its incongruities, and injure his future. As to the worthiness of his career as a career, who was to judge? She acknowledged the artificialities of her standards; she admitted to herself that if the world — her world — held his vocation in as high esteem as the law, medicine, literature, politics, the army, the navy, she would not object to the thing itself. As to the influences, he had become what he was perhaps in spite of them, but certainly subjected to them. She would not be petty-minded, she declared. The man had a gift and an ideal; she would help him conserve the one and attain the other. She would control her exacting taste; after all, taste should be a useful servant, not a tyrannical master. She would see deeper than the surface of Bohemianism, into the lives of these people with whom she was surrounded, — their pathos, their struggle, their strength, their fervor. She had known life in one phase only, so far; she would know it in another, widely different. In the contemplation of these new conditions she would grow wiser and stronger, clearer of vision, more calm of purpose, more tender of heart; development was her duty as well as his.

It was dreary work. All her natural instincts and the strong effects of her education were marshaled against her will. She could not always recognize and adequately gauge excellence of achievement, she had not reached the very vestibule of the great temple of art; yet she was constantly incited to revolt when she was brought face to face with the spectacle of warped sensibilities, solecisms of manner, the grinding and belittling influences of a desperate struggle for precedence and a constant contention for place. She saw much selfish scheming, much infirmity of temper, much envy and jealousy. These people were banded together by a common interest, — the success of the troupe; they were opposed to each other by the intense antagonisms of professional rivalry. That any should not succeed injured the others, yet each grudged every round of applause as the deprivation of a vested right. Thus capacities which would appear to admit of no comparison were bitterly contrasted : the contralto hated the tenor because of his encore for the love-song, and the basso could not forgive the soprano for the trippingness of her execution. The chivalrous instinct seemed dead among the men, who were as envious and small-minded as the women ; the instinct of conciliation seemed lacking among the women, who were as assertive and antagonistic as the men. It was an army vigorously at war with the enemy while torn by internal conflict. For them to indulge in the tender and ennobling luxuries of generosity and self-abnegation was to bare the throat to a willing sabre close at hand, without waiting for the possible minie-ball of the public a little later. To rise above such a mental and moral plane was, through exceptional gifts and the tyranny of a life dedication, to grow by slow and painful degrees to the state of *facile princeps* among them.

Kennett, somewhat indefinitely apprehending the maze of conflicting emotions which possessed her, had, with some eagerness, asked her impressions of that first rehearsal.

"You found it very entertaining, did you not?" he said, in the tone of one who would fain constrain a favorable opinion.

Yes, she had found it very entertaining.

"You are interested in human nature," he continued, in the same spirit. "You like to study people, and think you understand your fellow-creatures. Can you analyze those two men to whom you were talking to-day?"

"I think," said Felicia, meditatively, "that Mr. Abbott is a kindly disposed man, but he can do and say very unkind things. He pines to make other people suffer with him. 'I will burn, thou *shalt* sizzle,'—that's Mr. Abbott's motto."

Kennett thought this over in silence for a moment. "Rather a good guess," he admitted. "And Preston?"

She laughed. "Preston is — *Preston*," she said; "and so are all philosophies, and creeds, and arts, and sciences,—all Preston. If this city and the troupe were swallowed in an earthquake, what would he care, if he were left! There are other cities with opera - houses, and other troupes in need of a basso, and other friends to be had for the asking. That is Preston."

Kennett had become grave. "Felicia," he said, "your insight is almost terrible."

"There was at any rate one interesting person on that stage to-day," declared Felicia, suddenly. "That mezzo-soprano; don't you remember? She is intelligent and gentle. She has a nice face."

He looked at her with slightly raised eyebrows. "She is Mrs. Branner," he remarked. He was silent a moment; then, with a slight laugh, "I take back what I said. You have no insight at all."

In this life of his before the public, Kennett was much like a man on a trapeze : every moment was a crisis. However strong a matter of feeling might be, other importunate considerations pressed rival claims which could not be put off or lightly estimated. Thus it was that he did not entirely apprehend the complication of motives which induced Felicia to offer to play the accompaniment, one day when he was about to practice. He agreed, after a scarcely perceptible hesitation, and relinquished the piano-stool.

From an amateur standpoint she played very well. She had facility, a sympathetic touch, and was a fairly good timist. But in music there is a wide gulf between the average amateur and the average professional. The perfect exactitude, the delicate machine-work, requisite for an acceptable accompaniment were lacking. He endured it for a time ; then, with a comical look of despair, he clutched at his hair as if tearing an invisible wig, and swept her from the stool.

"The little public must continue to adorn the proscenium box," he said, "for she is not a success as an orchestra."

"I had thought of practicing," declared Felicia, ruefully. "I had an idea of playing your accompaniments."

"It is not worth while to undertake all that drudgery," he returned.

He was more interested, since it was more definitely in his own line, when she said, some days later, that she contemplated taking up singing. "Only for amusement," she added, quickly. Once she would not have felt thus humbly as to her accomplishments, but she had by this time discovered the wild absurdity embodied in the pleasing delusion indulged in by the show pupils of the fashionable boarding-schools, — the delusion that in point of musical merit their natural voices and their culture would enable them to vie with the lady in white satin and diamonds, charming an audience before the footlights.

He tried her voice and put her through several songs in various styles. He said she had a good soprano, not remarkable for compass; light, but even and pleasant in quality. He added, however, that, to do anything worth mentioning, she must elaborately unlearn all that she had acquired as a "show society pupil" from Signor Biancionelli; she must begin at the beginning, and build up a training from the very foundation-stones. He offered to teach her himself, if she liked; no doubt she would do pretty well, by dint of working hard.

"You see you have not been taught to sing," he explained, lucidly; "you have only learned, after a fashion, some songs."

She said, unconsciously repeating his phrase, that it was hardly worth while to go through so much drudgery.

Often, sitting alone in the box, she took thought of her own position. What was she to do with her life? she asked herself. She could not fully share his, — that was evident. She could not be useful as incentive, as support. He did not need her. He stood alone. She could not absorb herself in his pursuits; she was neither fitted nor schooled. She could not absorb herself in pursuits of her own. In what line was she equipped? In none more definitely than in music; in any she would need preliminary training. "And one does not *begin* at twenty-three," she reflected. "When I was made to study so much, why was I not taught something?" She did not formulate the theory, but she appreciated it as a fact that now, under the influence of strong feeling, groping among foreign conditions for the solution of the serious problems of her life, the heavy and uninteresting details of preparatory drudgery, without the support, as incentive, of an ultimate object and a controlling talent, would be as impossible to her as the aimless and desultory distraction of fancy-work and novel-reading. As to other absorptions which claim the attention of many women, — charities, hospitals, educational movements, — pursuits which might be called community interests, she had heard so vaguely, if at all, of these channels of thought and endeavor that they represented a world as completely removed from her ken as this world of musical life had once been, and they could of necessity offer her no suggestion; it might be doubted, too, if hers was of the natures which find their expression in community interests.

And again, what was she to do with her life,—not that full-pulsed existence of emotion which had absorbed her, but this other imperative individuality which was, day by day, more definitely pushing its demands, — her intentions, her time, her idle energy? Was it possible to live entirely in the contemplation of another's life, which yet she could not share; to relinquish a thoroughly vital entity for a passive acquiescence, for an utter aloofness? This was hardly life at all; it was almost annihilation; it was a sort of self-murder, thus to destroy her identity. "Does it die hard, I wonder, one's identity?" she thought, a little wistful, a little appalled.

And Kennett was very intent that the exacting public should be more than satisfied. What duty was so obvious as that the balancing-pole should be in readiness, the rope stretched tightly? When a man's professional existence is at stake, it behooves him to have his faculties and all the appliances at command. This *allegro* requires a trifle more of fire; there should be a *rallentando* here; and here the sentiment calls for a *tendresse*, which must be given with an "out-breathed effect;" and ah, gracious powers! the brasses *must* be softened in that passage!

Up to this time the callers at the box had been the gentlemen of the troupe. Abbott and Preston had come in frequently; one day Kennett had introduced Whitmarsh, a showy blond Englishman, oppressively friendly with him, and so propitiatory to her that she deduced the fact that he must dislike Hugh very much indeed. Several times the manager of the company had sat with her half an hour or so, and once he had taken her behind the scenes, and explained the mechanism of ropes and pulleys, and the big "sets" and flies. He was as different from her preconceived idea of a theatrical manager as he well could be: a quiet man, with a wife and six children at home. He once showed her their photographs, and was inclined to be homesick when he came to that of the year-old baby, a chubby fellow-citizen, whose portentous frown was the most conspicuous feature of the picture.

One morning she had a new caller, a lady. She glanced up at a sound behind her, and saw, hesitating at the door of the box, the Mrs. Branner who had earlier attracted her attention.

"May I come in and talk to you a little?" asked the stranger.

Felicia's instinct for politeness was the strongest and the most carefully cultivated instinct of her nature.

" I shall be very happy," she said with cordiality, and the visitor entered and seated herself.

Mrs. Branner had a very soft and gentle manner, — so soft and gentle as to suggest the purring of a cat. There was something feline about her face: her mouth was large, and had a tendency to curve upward at the corners; her face was wide and short; her eyes were gray, and she had a habit of narrowing them. Yet she was distinctly a pretty woman: her complexion was delightful in its warm fairness; her nose was straight and delicate; her eyebrows and lashes were dark; she had dense fair hair, and was tall and graceful.

"I am afraid I have taken a liberty, but I want so much to know you," she said, with a manner of much simplicity and candor; her face was very sweet when she smiled. "I hope you are not lonely. I am told that you are far away from your own people, and new to all this. I hope you like it."

It had been so long since Felicia had heard any woman, except an Irish or German hotel chambermaid, speak to her that this tone of sympathy, of fellowship, this sudden reverting to an element which she had supposed she prized but slightly, friendship with her own sex, almost overcame her. Her voice faltered as she replied : —

"Not exactly lonely, but a little — well, strange."

"I can imagine it. Now, as for me, I have known nothing else. Since I can remember I have been on the stage."

"Do you like the life?" asked Felicia.

Mrs. Branner shook her head.

"It is a terrible life. I saw once in a book or

a newspaper that the stage is like a vampire: so much feigning deprives one of one's own nature, as a vampire sucks the blood."

Felicia thought it denoted delicacy of feeling to realize this. She looked attentively at her new acquaintance. It was an odd, intelligent face, she fancied, expressing sensitiveness.

To measure the silent potent influences of circumstances on character and intellect is a feat that can be accomplished only vaguely and clumsily by results. In the last year Felicia had experienced a wide range of emotions: she had sounded the depths of her own heart; she had undergone the strong shock of severing abruptly all the close ties, associations, and traditions she had ever known; she was even yet entangled in the complicated web of thought and sentiment involved in adjusting herself to a new and difficult situation; having been the active and controlling centre of her world, she had become the passive spectator of a world of outside life, in which she had no part, and for which she could discover no substitute; and she was still in the thrall of the most imperative and intense feeling of which she was capable.

Perhaps she was thus an illustration of the theory that the possibilities of the emotional nature are cultivated at the expense of the attributes of the intellect; perhaps the simpler explanation involved in the fact of the loneliness induced by her semi-isolation was the correct explanation. Certainly her judgment was much at fault. A year ago she would have seen, as now, that Mrs. Branner's was an intelligent face, but she would not have credited it with sensitiveness; she would have detected the artificiality lurking beneath the purring manner; she would have known intuitively that the visitor was playing a part, very nicely, very prettily, — the part to which she had become so habituated that it was indeed almost second nature, and the most insidiously attractive she could assume, but still and always playing.

Felicia discovered nothing. She entered with flattering zeal upon the topics that presented themselves, — a wide range, from the plot of the opera, playwriting in general, acting and actors, music, orchestral and lyric, down to fancy - work and even the fashions. This last solecism would have been impossible to her a year before. But with the sudden drifting into the current of feminine interests and feeling, her fastidious taste loosed its hold.

Kennett, looking on from the stage, marveled that she should have become so animated: she was talking vivaciously, eagerly, almost convulsively; she laughed out gleefully, and caught herself like a child at school. When Mrs. Branner had left her, she sat watching the proceedings with smiling eyes. Kennett had little to say when he joined his wife, and they returned to the hotel. "Yes, yes," he admitted, with a shade of impatience in his voice, " Mrs. Branner seems to be very pleasant."

" It is so delightful to meet an agreeable woman," declared Felicia. " I did n't appreciate that there is such a sameness in having only men acquaintances. When I was a girl," she went on, maturely, " I did n't care much for other women. I was interested principally in the adorers."

" And now, having a permanent adorer, it is the other way, I suppose," he remarked, a little absently.

" And was n't it an odd coincidence," cried Felicia, removing her head-gear, and looking at it with an animated smile, " that we should be dressed almost exactly alike ? — she noticed it, too, — black dresses, and black bonnets, and old-gold ribbons. She noticed it, too ! "

" I wish you would not wear that color ! " he exclaimed, impatiently. " I detest it, and it is very unbecoming to you."

She looked at him in surprise. " Well, don't be cross about it," she said, coaxingly. " I will not wear it if you dislike it. It is rather extravagant to throw away this picot ribbon," she added, surveying the garniture of her bonnet. " I wish I had known of your antipathy before I bought it."

" And have this thing re-lined," he resumed, irritably, opening her parasol, looking at it sourly, and giving it a flip that sent it sailing across the room and landed it neatly on the sofa.

Felicia was still contemplating the ribbons. "They need n't be wasted, after all!" she declared, as if making a valuable discovery. "I can use them in a crazy-quilt. How I used to laugh at Amy's crazy-quilt! Did I ever think I should condescend to artistic patchwork! Mrs. Branner promised to show me exactly how to do it. She thinks it *perfectly fascinating!*"

He controlled himself. He did not say "Confound Mrs. Branner!" until after he had shut the door.

Then, as he tramped down the hall, he realized that he was unreasonable. He could not wipe out all the colors of the rainbow, and Mrs. Branner might elect to wear Felicia's favorite gray or violet to-morrow. As to the noble science of crazy-quilting, it would survive his displeasure, and long serve as a tie between the sane and gifted mortals who affect it.

He watched in silent exasperation the acquaintance progress. Mrs. Branner came into the box every morning, to beguile the tedium of the long rehearsals. Twice she called at the hotel. On both occasions Felicia chanced to be out, but she said she intended to return these calls. One afternoon, as Kennett stood in the reading-room, he saw the two coming together down the street. They were talking earnestly, and did not observe him. They parted at the door, and Felicia entered the hotel. He lingered, looking out aimlessly; presently, however, he took his way upstairs.

Felicia had removed her hat and light wrap, and was sitting beside the open window. Spring had come at last, distinctly and definitely, — evidently with the intention of staying. There was a soft relaxation in the air. The golden sunlight sifted down from an infinitely dainty blue sky. The gentle breeze, bringing the pleasant breath of moisture, brought also the odor of cigar-smoke, and the roll of carriages passing swiftly on the way to and from the park, and the cries of boys with the evening papers. Through the foliage, vividly yet delicately green, in the square opposite the hotel, the chattering English sparrows flitted; sometimes the voices of children arose, also chatteringly, from the walks beneath. A big bronze figure looked down, with inscrutable eyes, from its pedestal. Despite the softness, the revivifying influence of the season was asserting itself. The prosaic duty of living was all at once metamorphosed into a privilege, and one's dearest desires assumed the aspect of a friendly possibility. Felicia was under this benignant vernal spell as she gazed out dreamily at the changing pageantry of the street below. She did not turn her head as Kennett entered.

"Come and sit by the window," she said; "it is such a lovely day."

He crossed the room, but instead of taking a chair he stood leaning against the window-frame and looking down at her. He could not have made even an unreasonable objection to the color she was wearing to-day, — a delicate fawn-tinted costume, in several " tones," as the fashion experts say. The fabric, a light woolen goods, fell in soft folds about her; the shade brought out the extreme fairness of her complexion, and deepened the color of her eyes and lips; her cheeks were flushed; she had a bunch of creamy Maréchal Niel rosebuds in her hand, and had fastened others in the bosom of her dress.

" Well? " she said, glancing up as he hesitated.

" Well," he began, " I want to make a suggestion. Were you out with Mrs. Branner this afternoon ? "

" Yes," replied Felicia, vivaciously. " We went shopping. Would n't you like to see what I bought? " with swift generosity.

He detained her with a gesture, as she was about to rise. " No, not now." He had been sufficiently impressed by the fact that the universal dictum as to the extravagance of young ladies of her station is not idle caviling, — if the class must be judged by Felicia. It was not that she spent money from ostentation or because she had many needs, but merely because she could not help it. To buy whatever struck her fancy seemed to her as reasonable as to inhale the breath of her roses, a pleasure which was a matter of course. He had not as yet said anything to check her. He was still much in love, and was weak where she was concerned. He remembered that her lavishness was the habit of her life, and reminded himself of the peculiar difficulties and deprivations of her position. He always wound up his cogitations with the determination that he would " soon " have a serious talk with her, and propose that they should cut down expenses. He felt satisfied that she would prove amenable, but he dreaded her puzzled and pained acquiescence more than resistance and reproaches. For many reasons, he was not now in the humor to sympathetically gloat over her new treasures.

" No," he said, peremptorily. " I want to talk to you."

She sank back, leaving something unfinished about " the loveliest Escurial lace."

" I don't want you to go about with Mrs. Branner," he said.

" I believe you are jealous of Mrs. Branner!" cried Felicia, breaking into joyous laughter. " Dear me! what an opportunity I threw away last summer! I did not once make you jealous. I did not play off any one against you the whole time."

" You could n't play a part," he declared, drifting into the digression. " You would n't know how to dissimulate. I often wonder how a woman trained by Madame Sevier can be so frank."

" I am my father's daughter as well as Madame Sevier's pupil," said Felicia, her eyes filling suddenly, as they always did at the mention of her father.

" Well, *he* is frank," remarked Hugh Kennett, grimly. " I will say that much for him."

After a pause, during which Felicia passed her handkerchief over her eyes, with the furtive gesture of one who attempts to ignore the fact that tears are ready to fall, he resumed : —

"To return to Mrs. Branner. I don't want you to have so much to do with her. I am sorry, as she is the only woman you happen to know; but I can't let you associate with her. I ought to have put a stop to it before this."

"Why?" demanded Felicia, in a startled tone. She had roused herself from her lounging attitude, and was looking at him expectantly.

"Well, she is not a suitable friend for you. There may be no harm in her. I dare say she was only imprudent, but at one time a good deal was said and " —

"And you did not tell me!" exclaimed Felicia, violently, "and you let me talk with her at that theatre, hour after hour! How could you! How could you!"

He was immensely relieved. He had feared that from some quixotism, some championship as of injured innocence, she would espouse Mrs. Branner's cause; he was aware of her underlying willfulness, and he had dreaded to enlist it against him in a contest like this. When he saw how greatly he had been mistaken, he could even afford magnanimity.

"Mrs. Branner was probably only imprudent," he said. "She is stupendously vain, as you see; her husband was very jealous, and " —

"I would not associate familiarly with such a woman for any imaginable consideration," declared Felicia, uncompromisingiy.

"Felicia, you have a pitiless standard," he said, as if in rebuke; and he was inexpressibly glad that this was the case.

"I have common sense," retorted Felicia, dryly.

This episode ended her efforts to take part, even as a sympathetic spectator, in her husband's professional career. She would not attend rehearsals, and risk being again thrown with Mrs. Branner.

"I could not snub her; I would not hurt her; and I will not let her talk to me."

Stage life thus slipped from immediate observation into a retrospect, and she began presently to analyze the chaotic impressions she had received during her constant attendance at rehearsals and performances, and to formulate her experience as a whole. She evolved the theory that she had unconsciously forgiven much, — a certain tone, a Bohemianism of feeling as well as of manner, which would once have been unpardonable in her eyes. Trifles, infinitely minute points indicating character, unnoticed at the time, came back with a new emphasis. To be sure, these people were zealous; they were hard-working; many were talented; doubtless many were faithful in the discharge of duty; they had bitter trials and disappointments even in the midst of their triumphs; to her mind they were much to be pitied. But was she justified in subjecting herself to the influences of stage life merely from idleness and ennui, without the ennobling element of labor and the consecration of an inborn talent?

There was a phrase she had picked up in her association with musical people which seemed to her to be capable of a wider suggestion than its obvious meaning. She often heard them speak of "absolute pitch." The phrase might imply an immovable value other than tone. Was not an exact standard of morals, of worth, of essentials, even of externals, a strict code of habits and manners, which would not fluctuate in the sweep of extraneous influences, a possession intrinsically precious, which it was a duty not to underestimate? She promised herself that if she had the gift of "absolute pitch" in this sense, she would not lightly cast it aside. Better her empty hours and her vague haunting disquiet; and so back to her old loneliness.

It was more endurable now that the season was rapidly drawing to a close, and for the same reason the cessation of intercourse with Mrs. Branner was managed without a seeming estrangement. Plans for the vacation were in order, and absorbed much thought. Kennett proposed to spend the summer abroad, but to his surprise Felicia objected.

"We have been so hurried and harried from place to place," she suggested. "Why not go to some quiet region, far from the army of summer tourists, and have a complete rest? We have seen people enough to last a long time."

He thought this over a moment. "Perhaps that will be pleasant," he acceded, doubtfully; then added, "and certainly cheap."

The place they selected was in a country neighborhood in one of the hilly counties of Kentucky, contiguous to the mountain region. The farmhouse had been recommended to Kennett by an acquaintance, who had once passed a tedious summer of convalescence there. "It is a very plain sort of place," he had said, "but the people are good-natured and sterling, and the accommodations endurable. If you want very quiet summer boarding, you cannot do better."

XII.

So far from the life of cities, of the opera troupe, its associations and traditions, was this landscape of hill and valley that it might seem almost the life of a foreign planet. The rickety "double buggy," which had been sent to meet Kennett and his wife, drew up before the fence of palings which inclosed an old two-story frame house; there was a portico in front, several hickory and sycamore trees grew in the yard, and a big vegetable garden lay at one side. The cows were coming home; the mellow clanking of their bells resounded on the air. Across the tasseled blue grass several turkeys were making their way in single file, evidently with the intention of joining their companions already gone to roost in the branches of an oak-tree; the yellow sunset gilded their feathers to a more marked uniformity with those of their untamed relatives in the woods. In the background were visible a rail pen, a few feet high, where young turkeys were kept, and a henhouse, which hens and cocks entered and emerged from at intervals, apparently finding it very difficult to persuade themselves that bedtime had really come. The house was situated on the slope of a high hill, which, in the background, rose into imposing proportions, heavily wooded save at the top, where a clearing had been made, from which a crop of wheat had been taken. This bare space, so incongruous in the midst of the thick umbrageous forests, gave the elevation a curiously bald-headed look. The windows commanded a long perspective of valley, which, subdivided by jutting spurs, seemed many valleys; the purple hills grew amethystine in the distance, then more and more faint of tint, until the dainty landscape close to the horizon was sketched in lines of sunlight. Over all was a rosy glow, for the day was slowly waning. The cicadas ceaselessly droned; the odor of thyme and clover blossoms was on the fresh, dry air. Kennett looked, with the disparagement of the city-bred man, at the arrangements of the "company room."

"It *is* very 'plain,' I must say," he remarked.

Felicia turned her flushed cheeks and bright eyes from the window, and critically surveyed the faded ingrain carpet; the four-post walnut bedstead, surmounted with a red canopy and ornamented by a "log-cabin" patchwork quilt; the heavy stoneware furnishing on the wash-stand; the rush-bottomed chairs; the plaster-of-paris dog, and very green parrot, and very yellow canary decorating the high, narrow wooden mantelpiece; the several works of pictorial art on the walls,— an engraving of Stonewall Jackson, one of Samuel at his devotions, a colored print representing a young man in buff trousers and a blue coat, and a young woman in a red dress and with black ringlets, reading from the same big book, obeying as well, perhaps, as the circumstances permitted the legend "Search the Scriptures." Everything seemed very clean, very bare, very primitive. Then she looked at Kennett's serious face, and broke into a peal of joyous laughter.

"How you are going to miss my ' properties,' " she cried, "my poor, dear 'properties,' that you scorned! Yet *you* don't care for the artificialities, — oh, no, indeed ; you have such simple tastes. For my part, I think it is all very nice, and the air is exhilaration itself."

"If you are pleased, I am delighted," he returned, ruefully.

He left her presently to see about the baggage, and she watched him as he joined their host and hostess at the gate. The farmer had just driven up with a light wagon, in which were the trunks, and was in the act of handing out to his wife the shawls, satchels, and lunch basket. Felicia said to herself that she could not make a mistake in *this* woman's face. She had a firm chin, delicate lips, and the transparent complexion usual among the dwellers in high regions. Her hair, brown, scanty, lustreless, and sprinkled with gray, was brushed back from her sunken temples, revealing her features in full relief, and her expression was more than serious, — it was almost austere. She wore a dark calico dress, which fell in scant folds about her; her white linen collar was held by a pin containing a badly executed likeness of her husband. He was grave of face, slow of movement, and sparing of speech, with meditative blue eyes, brown hair and beard cut in defiance of city standards, and he was dressed in a much-worn suit of cheap, shop-made clothes. Felicia looked at them both long and attentively, and then looked back into the room. She drew a deep breath.

"Yes," she said aloud, "very plain — intensely plain — and *so* respectable."

They entered next day upon a life new to both, — entirely so to Kennett, although Felicia had vague reminiscences of something similar when, in her childhood, her father had had the whim to take her with him through the rural regions of his circuit. Kennett, the man of cities and of artificialities, found a certain difficulty in adjusting himself to such unprecedented conditions. He could lounge systematically enough during his vacations, under ordinary circumstances; but now, without boating, driving, billiards, acquaintances, he was at a loss. For the first few days he said at least a hundred times, "Felicia, I shall die of *ennui* in this place." It seemed to him almost perversity that she should be so genuinely contented. "If we had been obliged to come here because it is cheap, you would have thought it a calamity," he declared, reproachfully. She laughed at this, and said he was hard to please: he was always insinuating that she liked to spend money; now that she was helping to save it he was not satisfied. After this he drifted into what he called the yawning stage. It came upon him uncontrollably, ungraciously, persistently, regularly. " It must be malaria," he would say, bringing his jaws together by a mighty effort and with his eyes full of tears.

• " It is the relaxation from a tension," returned Felicia, learnedly. " You have been strung up to concert pitch for so long. It shows that you need a complete rest."

" If it were any one else, I should say it shows complete laziness."

The lazy phase came a little later. Then he could not even summon the energy to yawn. For hours he would lie motionless on the grass, or swinging in the hammock which they had brought, and which impressed their rural entertainers as a most felicitous contrivance. Sometimes Felicia read aloud ; often she " condescended to talk," as he laughingly phrased it. Apparently she had dismissed her anxieties ; her joyousness and spontaneity suggested the happy days of last summer ; when her mood was graver, she evinced a depth of thought and feeling at variance with her other self. She had often appeared to him many-sided ; never so much as now. There was an unexpectedness about her which lent a certain piquancy to her companionship. " I never know exactly what you are going to think or say on any subject," he remarked one day.

"It is just the reverse with me," she replied. "I know what you are going to think or say before you do yourself."

The time seemed to pass blithely enough for her. She amused herself about the house and yard like a child. Occasionally she undertook light household tasks, under the direction of Mrs. Wright, — shelling peas, stoning cherries, capping strawberries, and the like. He could hear rising on the soft, warm morning air her voice and infectious laughter, as the two women sat together in the shade of the vines that covered the portico. Once she made a "lady cake," all by herself, except baking it, she declared, exultantly; and Mrs. Wright slyly smiled superior, and did not expound the *summum bonum* of the cake-making art. "I believe I have a talent for cooking," said Felicia, complacently. "I should have been a famous housekeeper, if I had had half a chance."

To the elder woman, looking out from her meagre, colorless life, the bright young creature, with her quick wits and warm heart, was in some sort a revelation. They drew close together in these summer days. Sometimes their talk was serious and retrospective. She told Felicia of the two children she had lost, and showed her their faded daguerreotypes and some of their little clothes. "The girl would have been twenty-three next fall, if she had lived. Jest your age," said the mother, looking wistfully into the dewy violet eyes, and vaguely bridging that terrible gulf of empty years with an elusive airy structure of what might have been. "Ah," she said, with a long-drawn sigh, " God knows best. His will be done."

Her sunken eyes turned to the shimmering landscape close to the soft horizon; her sinewy, worn hands dropped upon the faded garments on her knee. The sunshine lay on the floor; the wind wafted in at the window the purple banners of the " maiden's bower; " the wing of a bird flashed past. " God's will be done," she repeated.

Felicia, imperious, intolerant, rebellious, shrank appalled from the hypothesis that every life holds the elements of bitter woes, like in degree, differing only in kind. She resolutely reverted to lighter themes; she shut out the thought of grief. She promised herself that she would have happiness, — that was what she craved. She would not be balked of her lightness of heart.

Perhaps her theory of the relaxation of a severe tension in Kennett's case had been correct. At any rate, by degrees something of his former methodical energy asserted itself. He assigned to himself the duty of going to town for the mail; occasionally he procured horses and took his wife riding; sometimes he went on a shooting excursion with the hobbledehoy son of the house, returning with a few birds or a rabbit as a trophy. Once he bought from a mountaineer a deer just killed, — game laws are a dead letter in that region, — and brought it home on his horse in true rural sportsman fashion, greatly enjoying Felicia's delight in his supposed skill, when he drew rein before the portico and called her to the window. "You think this better than an encore for 'When the bugle sounds'?" he asked.

"Oh, much, much better!" cried Felicia; and she added that, in her opinion, killing a deer was more appropriate to a big six-foot man than an absorbing interest in costumes and wigs and feathers, and infinitely small points about *pianissimo* and *con fuoco* and intonation.

June had passed. July, rich, luscious, brilliant with color, redolent of sweet odors, languorous with sunshine, was glowing into August. Through the soft bloom on the big peaches the warm red deepened day by day. The grapes were purpling. The mellow, perfumed apples dropped heavily on the grass, and the busy "yellow-jackets" rioted among them. Where bearded ears of millet had waved in the wind the shocks were piled, and already the encroaching crab grass was overcrowding the prickly stubble. The call of quail vibrated on the air. The forests were densely green. The streams flowed languidly, for the showers, sudden and profusely punctuated by peals of thunder and flashes of lightning, were short, and but little rain fell. On these perfect afternoons, the very acme and culmination of summer and light and vivid life, Felicia loved to

stroll up the steep slopes, not stopping till a certain " blue spring," near the summit, was reached.
A jutting spur of the range cut off all extended
outlook ; no house or clearing was visible; the
valley was walled in on every side ; a sea of foliage below the crag sent up a monotonous murmur.

" It is as lonely here as if we were on a desert
island," remarked Kennett, one day, — not, however, in discontent; having once adjusted himself
to the eventless existence, he found the simple
routine endurable enough. He was lying at
length on the cliff. His appearance gave token
of the rural life he had been leading: he was sunburned ; his hair and mustache, under the manipulation of the village barber, were longer than
formerly, and their luxuriance gave the depth of
coloring his face had lacked in his close-clipped
trim ; he had taken on flesh, and his raiment suggested careless wear. He was more picturesque
than formerly, but not point-device.

" Some of these days," he went on, with the
deliberate manner of one to whom time is no object, " when the resources of the country are developed, this place will be a summer resort ; half
a dozen mineral springs in a stone's throw, a railway only three miles distant, healthiest air in the
world, no mosquitoes, — what more can the heart
of the summer sojourner desire ! "

" You are as eloquent as an advertisement," responded Felicia.

"The hotel would be on that level stretch, and the bowling-alley there to the right," he continued, raising himself on one elbow, and looking about with the serious attention sometimes characteristic of the very idle in contemplating a far-away possibility.

"There would be an 'observatory' just here," said Felicia, entering into his mood, "where the band would play the stage-coach up the mountain; and people would flirt on the piazzas, and women would talk gossip, and men would smoke and play euchre. On the whole, I like it far better as a desert island."

She fixed her eyes on the vast slant of motionless foliage across the basin of the valley. A haze was thickening in the sunshine; an ominous stillness was in the air; athwart a mass of black cloud that was imperceptibly stealing up from the west quivered a slow pale flash; the roll of thunder, indistinct yet sinister, sounded beneath the horizon.

Felicia spoke suddenly, with the ring of intense feeling in her voice.

"I wish this were a desert island!" she exclaimed. "I wish we could never see any more people, or hotels, or Pullman cars, or theatres. I like this life."

"You would soon be tired of it," he rejoined.

"*You* seem to like it," she said.

He had thrown himself down again at full length. "Yes," he replied, after a long pause,

"I like it. It has been extremely pleasant. It is very gentle and peaceful, and very aimless. I am glad to be rid of the turmoil, and tension, and effort."

" Why not be rid of them permanently ? " asked Felicia, in sudden sharp agitation.

"It is not what is pleasant, it is what a man is fit for, that he must consider." He roused himself from his recumbent attitude, and leaned against the bole of a huge oak that projected over the rock on which they sat. " Then," he said, "there's this."

He inclined his head slightly, as if he were listening, and, with a half smile, clapped his hands softly together.

"It is not merely the applause," he added, after a moment's reflection. " I will do myself the justice to say that. Half the time the public does n't know why it applauds. It is the consciousness that the applause is deserved."

Then both were silent. An acorn detached itself from among the leaves above them, dropped with a resonant thud on the crag, and, rebounding sharply, fell into the valley below. A blue jay chattered antagonistically and vivaciously somewhere in the foliage. An imperceptible current of air brought to them the fresh odors of fern and mint from the banks of the spring branch near by ; they could hear the water drip over the cool mossy stones. From the black clouds, ever rising higher above the western mountains, came again a peal of thunder, muffled, but definite at last. The wind was rising.

All at once Kennett began to sing.

The volume of sound — smooth, melodious, rich, resonant, permeated through and through, from its gentlest tone to the full capacity of its compass, with that mastering, constraining intensity which for the lack of a better phrase is called the sympathetic quality — rose and fell with a certain majesty of effect. Perhaps it was because of the long rest, perhaps because of the strangely perfect serenity of the last six weeks, perhaps because she had become trained to discriminate, — certainly that voice had never seemed to her so valuable merely as an organ.

Once she had asked him if it were not possible that he and his friends overrated his gift; if a man of thirty-three, thoroughly trained, has not attained, or at least approximated, his best possibility. Was it likely that he could after that become a great singer, instead of merely an excellent one?

He had the anxious vanity of the musician; the question hurt him, but he replied as dispassionately as he could. In all candor, he said, he was of opinion that neither he nor his friends overrated him. "No man of sense deliberately determines that he will be a supremely great dramatic singer, any more than a playwright of set purpose sits down to rival Shakespeare." He added that he would admit that he was not so

well known or so fairly appreciated as he deserved
to be, but he had been constrained by the circumstances in his case. He had been compelled to
take whatever engagements offered ; he could not
choose or wait for better opportunities. He could
not say that he hoped ever to become one of the
few supremely great singers ; but there were
many degrees, and he fully expected to stand far
higher than he had yet done.

Felicia had also a theory that in vividness of
imagination he was not preëminent. He was always appropriate, controlled, but to her he seemed
to lack the sudden flame of inspiration. She
thought him too well trained ; he was limited by
traditions, precedents, reasons. The fine fire of
his capacity burned steadily, with too even a glow.
To-day she retracted this judgment, as, with the
precision of an instrument in perfect tune, with
the adroit management of an accomplished musician, with the subtle enthusiasms of a sensitive
soul, he sent the pathos and the passion of Lohengrin's Farewell pulsating across the uninhabited
sea of verdure at their feet.

"No, no," he said, as the last sound wave died
away, and he rose, extending his hand to assist
her. "I am dedicated to ' *Mein lieber Schwan*,'
whose other name might be called Melpomene.
That is what I was born for."

And she, — she said nothing. In her soul she
knew he spoke the truth. What was there for
her but — to say nothing ?

Before they reached the house, the black cloud, suddenly in swift motion, had overspread the whole sky. They barely escaped the storm ; the first heavy drops were falling as they shut the gate and ran up the pavement; in a moment more the whitening sheets of rain were dashing against the window panes, the lightnings were playing over the landscape, and the thunder pealed.

They found their host and hostess in what was called the "settin'-room," a square, sparsely furnished apartment, opposite the parlor. Mrs. Wright looked up, with her slow smile, from the peaches she was paring for supper. Her husband, tilted against the wall in a split-bottomed chair, took his pipe from his mouth as Kennett entered.

"You was singin' up thar ter the blue spring, warn't ye?" he demanded, with a trifle of vivacity. "I thought it must be you. Well, ye're a good singer, shore."

"You ought to go to meetings Sundays, and lead the hymns," said Mrs. Wright. She had not yet been able to fully comprehend the mental and moral attitude of people who do not desire to go to church. "Mr. Wright says you're a choir all by yourself."

Felicia glanced at Kennett. Obviously he was pleased. Ah, the insatiate vanity of the musician, — flattered by such a tribute as this!

"Bob's been to the post office," said Mr.

Wright, suddenly. "There's a letter fur ye on the table."

Kennett took it with the alacrity with which people in the country receive their mail, read and re-read it, then slowly placed it in his pocket.

"It is a matter of business," he said, meeting Felicia's eye.

The next morning, however, he showed it to her.

"Do you know what this means?" he demanded, with exultation. "This means grand opera another season, under the most auspicious circumstances."

"It is only an offer for a concert tour with the Asterisk Quartette, at the fashionable watering-places, as a substitute for their tenor, who is obliged to resign on account of ill health," said Felicia, her eyes still on the letter.

She had heard of the organization, which was in many respects exceptional. A notable manager had induced certain superior artists to give up their usual vacations for the discomforts of a professional season, plausibly arguing that a rich harvest might be reaped if the leisure class — bent especially on enjoyment and on spending money — be offered first-class attractions. So far he had been very successful, both as to the material secured and the practical result.

"This is just the opportunity I want," said Kennett, walking about the room in unwonted excitement. "This is the best organization in the country. To take Stuart's place gives prestige by itself. If I can hold my own, — and I can, — this means rapid advancement."

"But you have already signed with Mr. Hallet."

"Only for the next season. After that I will choose."

Felicia sank down on one of the straight-backed chairs, and gazed absently at the floor, the letter still in her hand.

"Well, Hugh," she said at last, looking up at him, "I want you to decline this."

He stared at her.

"I am going into town in the next half hour to reply by telegram, as they desired," he returned. "I shall most certainly accept it."

"You show great consideration for my wishes!" she exclaimed, bitterly.

"You are unreasonable," he rejoined.

"Because I am happy here, living in this quiet, simple, inexpensive way, you want to give it up."

"I have been happy, too; but if an idle, purposeless existence is pleasant, must a man jeopardize his future?"

"Oh, you *promised* — you *promised* to stay another month, and now you are going to drag me back to that tawdry falseness! It would be different if the season had opened; then it would be necessary; but this is so gratuitous."

"This is so beneficent," he corrected. "It is an opportunity that may never occur again."

She burst into tears. He attempted coaxing, but she interpreted this as a sign of relenting, and grew more insistent. He tried argument, and was met by the positive declaration that what is wisest is not comparable to what is happiest. Now that she had at last relaxed her hold on her will she was as unreasonable and as persistent as a spoiled child. At last he too lost his temper.

"This is intolerable," he said, angrily, rising and turning to the door.

She sprang before him, and stood, one hand on the bolt and the other on his arm, as if to push him back, her body thrown forward in the poise of suddenly arrested motion, and an intent expression on her beautiful face.

"Oh, Hugh," she cried, "I beg — I insist that we don't go yet! Let me be happy a little longer!"

He looked at her coldly.

"*You* may have mistaken your vocation," he said. "You have a good pose — a very good pose — at this moment. There's nothing like a pronounced success in domestic melodrama," he added, with a laugh.

His sarcasm stung her like a lash. She slowly withdrew her hand from the bolt, her eyes full on his; she slowly crossed the room.

He regretted his words; already his anger was melting.

"Forgive me," he entreated.

She stood silent a moment, and looked at him with hard eyes.

"Send your telegram," she said.

He left the house without another word. When he returned from town, he found her in her traveling attire, the rooms bare of their effects, and the trunks packed. He walked about restlessly for a few moments; he looked at her in anxious indecision.

"You are not angry?" he asked, in deprecation.

"Oh, no," she replied, with a certain metallic clearness in her laugh. "I am only obedient."

XIII.

THE next six weeks, outwardly brilliant, were a prolonged trial of skill, in which Kennett, instead of merely preserving his rank as *facile princeps*, as in Hallet's troupe, found it necessary to hold his own among singers more nearly his equals. He threw himself heart and mind into the effort to do his capacity full justice, and in this' protracted crisis his professional interests absorbed him more than ever to the exclusion of his personal interests.

Perhaps no man fully interprets that subtle and obscure scripture, a woman's nature, least of all the nature of a woman like Felicia, supersensitive, proud, intolerant; in a certain complicated sense insistently conscientious: susceptible to definite yet delicate influences which might not affect a differently organized individuality. Kennett did not realize all she felt, and he dared not allow himself to dwell upon the possibility that she was suffering. It was a positive and practical necessity that he should eschew any cause of agitation and disquiet; that he should live in a simple, normal, prosaic emotional atmosphere. There had been a reconciliation between them, — tears, regrets, self-reproaches, — and each had

promised to remember no more the other's hasty
words. Kennett had made this promise in all
good faith, and had dismissed the episode but for
the recurrent suspicion, which he sought to ignore, that it still remained with her.

She had no deep absorption to lighten gradually the intensity of her contending feelings.
Her pride, her wounded self-esteem, her love, made
the thought intolerable to her, yet she brooded
for hours on that crucial interview. That he
should have looked at her with those cruel eyes, —
that he should have spoken those sneering words!
She would remind herself that she had promised
to forget it, but she would recur to it with a sort
of willfulness despite the pain; a certain obdu-
racy was aroused in her; it was strange to her
that her heart should be at once so sore and so
hard.

Is there not a trifle of ambiguity in our exposi-
tion of moral values? Those sweeping phrases,
generosity, selfishness, for example, — in certain
jugglery of forces, do they not become sometimes
interchangeable? The soul that can invest itself
in what one may call a state of slippered ease;
that can acquiesce, concede, constrain its own
approval, shut out the turmoil of endeavor, the
exactions of a definite ideal, the embittering processes of contention with the antagonistic forces of
other ideals, is in a certain sense a fortunate soul.
And generous? We usually say so. But this
suggestion is submitted : to forego is an easy
process.

Felicia's standards, artificial, perhaps, — perhaps, unworthy, — were imperative. It would have been comfortable to compromise; with her, compromise was impossible. What she deemed due to herself was always a potent force with her; she was still more exacting when her feelings were deeply involved. The life, too, brought its peculiar elements of trial. There was much in this abnormal, showy, brilliant midsummer "season" against which, loyal to her estimate of the becoming, she revolted. Last winter's seclusion was now impossible. Then the contact with the public had been slight enough, confined principally to the hotel dining-rooms and railway trains; now, in these sojourns at the crowded resorts, life was all out-of-doors, — on piazzas, at the spring, on the beach. Felicia, accustomed from her earliest childhood to be regarded by strangers with respectful admiration, was stung by the eyes which rested upon her with curiosity, admixed perhaps with a little wonder that, being what she evidently was, she should be placed as she was. Infinitely more bitter it was to her whenever it chanced that Kennett's striking appearance attracted the attention of certain notable men, as they lounged about, watching the kaleidoscopic pageantry on the esplanade. She would see their glances follow him, and would divine, as they turned to some well-informed *habitué*, that they asked who he was. They were for the most part portly, red-faced fathers of families, — judges, like her own father, bank presidents, railroad magnates. These, last winter, had been merely a portion of the great, unindividualized public; now they were separate personalities, easily differentiated. Sometimes it almost seemed to her that she had been endowed with a sixth sense denied to happier people, — a sense of intuitive mental vision, by which she knew, as well as divined, the process through which the curiosity of these gentlemen was transmuted, as their inquiry was answered, into a surprised comprehension, too slighting in its quality to be even contempt. It was intolerable that this valuable element of society should esteem her husband " a singing fellow," as if he were of another order of beings. It does not come easily to such a woman as Felicia to say, concerning the man she loves, "nevertheless," to make allowances, to overlook, to palliate. She would fain have exulted in him. She realized poignantly how proud she could be of him, had he attained a measure of success in what her father and brother called " the sane walks of life " equal to that which he had achieved in this vocation of his. She said to herself, fierily, piteously, helplessly, that it was his right, his due, that he should have a place among estimable and successful men of position, — and ah, how many of these there were in the world! —a place as an equal, even a superior; for who can say how far force may carry when exerted in the right direction! She craved this for him; and yet she too held almost religiously her father's and her brother's views as to the sane walks of life. Her heart ached for him that he should be deprived of the solid values of existence; she was almost enraged against him that he could not understand his deprivation.

So grievous was this chagrin that it even dwarfed what she felt when she met the amused contempt in the faces of the women who knew her own story; for not unfrequently they encountered women who knew her story. It seemed a very perverse fate that this should happen now, yet the previous summer, when she would have been glad to meet any of her old schoolmates or acquaintances, she saw only strangers.

In the first episode of this kind a deeper sentiment was involved than amused contempt. The incident occurred at one of the notable seaside hotels. Kennett and Felicia had just finished their late breakfast, and were walking down the long piazza. A trio of ladies, presumably last night's arrivals, was advancing toward them. Suddenly Felicia quickened her steps, with an exclamation; her lips were parted in such a smile of pleasure as they had not known for many a day. The trio faltered; indeed, the eldest, a large, well-preserved, well-dressed woman of fifty, almost came to a standstill; then she swept onward, detaching an eyeglass from its catch and adjusting it composedly.

"How do you do?" she said, bowing and smiling graciously. "Glad to see you here." And she would fain have proceeded.

It was an awkward moment, — doubly awkward because of spectators; a number of persons,
sitting and standing about, were looking on with
the intense interest of the desperately idle.   Felicia had been so evidently pleased, her acceleration
of pace and her exclamation were so noticeable,
that to pass now without pausing would be very
marked.   With an *aplomb* hardly to be expected
in so young a woman, she halted unflinchingly in
front of the elder lady, and extended her hand.
Mrs. Morris's condescension, it must be admitted,
was distanced in the spirited half minute's dash
that ensued.

"So pleased to see you," said Felicia, with composed ceremoniousness of manner.   "Let me introduce my husband.   You will have the pleasure
of hearing him sing.   Shall be glad to send you
tickets.   Your daughters are quite well?"   She
smiled and beamed on the hesitating young ladies.   Her tone was that of a woman advanced
beyond them in some way, — much older and long
ago married.

She held the fort; she was the centre and
mainspring of the situation. She had never
looked more beautiful. She was in brilliant
health; the long hours she had spent in the open
air, this summer, had suffused her delicate skin
with a rich glow which was very becoming to her.
About her slim, elegant figure floated the folds of
one of her effective costumes, at once simple and
elaborate, gray of tint with elusive suggestions of

faint green. Her pose, as Kennett might have said, was good, — very good; her head was erect, but not held haughtily; her attitude had a certain alertness, as of a bird about to fly; her eyes were very bright, and dark, and smiling; her teeth gleamed through her parted red lips; she was airily self-possessed.

"I hope you will be here for some time," she said, with suavity. "*Good*-morning. Au revoir."

She swept away, with Kennett beside her. The Morris girls glanced over their shoulders at her tall, impressive, well-dressed blond husband. They thought Felicia's fate romantic, and said to each other that she was more beautiful than ever.

"Why did you snub the old lady?" demanded Kennett, selecting chairs where they could look out upon the drive as well as at the palpitating blue sea.

"Didn't you understand? She attempted to snub *me*. She doesn't consider me as important as she once did."

"Oh," he returned, enlightened, "was that it!"

"And Mabel Morris and I were like sisters once!" cried Felicia, with a sharp pain in her voice. "I used to go to their home as familiarly as they themselves. And papa could never pet them enough, because they were fond of me. And when he was in New York, it was one continual round of opera, and theatre, and driving, and presents, and lovely times for us three. And

Mrs. Morris was fond of me, too; and now she does not want Mabel to speak to me. I am an awful example and a dangerous acquaintance."

He thought she was on the verge of tears, but she pulled herself together by a violent effort, and gave a bitter little laugh instead. He saw how keenly she was hurt.

"I would n't care for her," he said, soothingly.

"I don't care for her; I care for myself," said Felicia, dryly.

Mrs. Morris's fears as to a renewal of the old intimacy were groundless. Somehow, whenever she or her daughters chanced to be thrown into Felicia's vicinity, something particularly interesting was on hand. "That great three-masted vessel an English ship with a cargo of jute? Jute! How interesting!" Or, "Only see, Hugh, how those sail-boats are tossing on this choppy sea; they seem to be courtesying to each other." Or she had just been told that the strange commotion in the water was occasioned by the passing of porpoises, and she was absorbed in watching for a glimpse above the waves of the ungainly creatures, only aroused to a consciousness of the existence of her friends when Kennett gravely bowed as he raised his hat. Then she would look up suddenly and also bow, and smile the society smile, which means many things or nothing at all. At first Mrs. Morris was relieved to discover that that bland "Au revoir" had been merely a figure of speech, but later she was angered.

" Felicia Hamilton poses as if she were still Felicia Hamilton ! " the astute lady declared, in irritation.

" She seems very happy," said the elder daughter pensively, looking at the couple as they strolled down the beach. He was opening her parasol ; he had her light wrap over his arm ; he bent his head as he talked to her.

" And he is very handsome," added Mabel.

Mrs. Morris glanced sharply from one to the other.

Later in the day, Mabel remarked, apropos of nothing, that the basso, Mr. Dallon, was also very handsome ; and it was within an hour that Mrs. Morris was smitten with a dreadful pain in her eyes, which she said must be due to the intense glare of the sun on the water. She felt sure that she had better take the first train for New York and consult an oculist, and thence proceed to some place where shade was possible, — the Adirondacks, perhaps. Trunks were hastily packed, and before sunset the party was off, — a handkerchief binding the eyes of the suffering lady.

Felicia did not again make the mistake of manifesting pleasure upon meeting old acquaintances. A bow, a smile, sometimes a few words when the advances came from the other side, constituted her social experience during the summer. Her sensitive pride, thoroughly on the alert, defended her against a second peril of discomfiture.

One of these chance meetings was an encounter

with the Graftons. It occurred in the dining-room of the hotel at which the Hamilton party had sojourned while at the seaside the previous summer. She and Kennett were entering; the Graftons were going out. Little Mrs. Grafton peered at Felicia with startled, beadlike eyes, her pointed mouse-like head inquiringly askew, her diminutive nostrils quivering. Then she glanced affrightedly up and down the long floor, as if in search of a hole to run into; then she said, "How do you do?" in a very high, thin voice, much as she might have said, "Squeak, squeak," and walked on with the air of scuttling. Nellie stared with her hard, round black eyes, — Felicia thought Madame Sevier was not doing much for Nellie. Alfred bowed frigidly. "How he must gloat over my ill-regulated mind!" meditated Felicia, bitterly.

Meeting him here brought back last summer very vividly to her recollection. By an odd coincidence, the room assigned to her was the one she had then occupied. She softened a little the first evening of her arrival, her eyes on the chair by the window where she used to sit and look out, as well as she could for her tears, at the shining track of molten silver light, as the moon sailed over the sea. "How unhappy I was!" she thought, commiserating that other self, and losing in the recollection of the old grief some of the poignancy of the new. She had half resolved to tell Kennett, when he should come back from the concert, the history of that little chair, — how she used to sit there, night after night, with her head on the window-sill, and weep her heart away because he had not answered her note. Perhaps he would be interested; perhaps the constraint of feeling that had infused itself into their relations would disappear, and life would become more endurable.

He returned in a bad humor, however; something had gone wrong with the accompaniment, and he commented bitterly, — a rare thing with him, for control of his temper was a part of his professional system. " When a damned idiot," he said fiercely between his set teeth, " who pretends to know nothing *but* music, can't see a *rallentando* when it is marked plainer than print, what *is* he fit for ! "

Once Felicia might have suggested " treason, stratagems, and spoils; " but pleasantries did not come to her readily nowadays, and she only looked at him in silence as he kicked the historic chair, that happened to stand in his way, and instituted a tense and vivacious search for his slippers, and demanded of her if she thought it was beneficial to a neuralgic headache to sit before an open window. Obviously it was no occasion for sentiment, and before he recovered his equanimity the impulse had passed.

He was not altogether satisfied with his work during the summer engagement. To be sure, he had been praised, he had made reputation; he was persuaded that he would receive such offers as he desired for another season. But he realized that not once had he done himself full justice; not once had he sung as he could sing, — as he sang that afternoon to the empty woods, and the coming storm, and the tender heart of his wife. It was a very subtle difference, but very strong, — the difference between excellence and exaltation. From time to time, as the weeks wore on, he canvassed within himself the policy of saying something of this to Felicia. Such a course — a direct appeal to her generosity — might have been wise policy. But a man of pride is likely to find a certain difficulty in submitting to his wife, who somewhat ungraciously protests against his vocation, a plea for her smiles as a factor of his success in that vocation. Caution, too, withheld him. There was no predicting how she might, with her strong feeling upon the subject, receive the suggestion. It might be applying fire to the fuse. With his professional existence dependent in a great measure on serenity, it would not do for him to risk explosions.

Little had been said between them, of late, as to his professional work, but that little had served to deepen his realization of her objections. To him her attitude was even more illogical than heretofore. There was some talk, about the beginning of the regular season in September, of substituting, during the coming winter, for Prince Roderic, which, although still drawing well, was now a trifle familiar to a change-loving public, a new work, — one of those that belong to what might be called the romantic-grotesque school, which, through music more or less meritorious and costumes always effective, sometimes gorgeous, has reopened fairyland to people who have forgotten the fairyland of youth.

When Felicia heard this suggestion she openly rebelled, little though it availed her, as she knew. Since she had come to understand something of her husband's professional life, and had realized the gap between his estimate of his capacity and his opportunity, between his exacting and elevated musical and dramatic sense and the slightness of the compositions to which he must devote himself, she had experienced an extreme irritation for his sake. Intensely as she deprecated his career, she resented as intensely that he did not at least have the place in it which he coveted. His acceptance of whatever task was set before him, as a step upward, as means to an end; his respect for his own work, in however distasteful a guise; his careful and conscientious rendition of rôles unworthy of him, almost dismayed her; she thought his patience tragical. She had constrained herself to say as little of this as she might, and he did not divine that even so questionable a sympathy as this sort of partisanship was involved in her disapprobation of his calling.

In regard to the proposed addition to his *répertoire*, however, she suddenly abandoned her bitter neutrality. She was deeply agitated when she entreated him to refuse such a rôle. To his amazement, the objection she urged was that the opera was amusing. He could not appreciate her distinctions when she seriously declared that it was more endurable to sing in such an opera as Prince Roderic, because it was a romantic opera; that the character of Prince Roderic was digni- fied, and even noble. She insisted that there is an immense difference between wit and fun, — that one is a brilliant, and the other mere paste; that it is admirable to be witty, and odious to be funny; that even in genteel comedy, while the author and the work may have the quality of wit, the delineator upon the stage does not share its dignity; he is only funny, is only comical.

All the world knows more or less of that strange contradiction which almost suggests the idea of a dual set of mental qualifications apper- taining to the histrionic artist, by which the medi- ocre mind suddenly becomes endowed with a for- eign intellectuality, the trifler conceives heroism, the jester tragedy, the small soul invests itself in majesty. Thus Kennett, the gravest and most sedate of men, held as an instrument the strings of mirth, and played airily upon them at his will, with the delicate touch of the born comedian, with irresistible drollery, with incomparable hu- mor. Felicia had often meditated on this phase of his talent, so strangely at variance with his na- ture, and with that massive, heroic histrionism which he arrogated to himself. Had he truly the two developments of the dramatic gift? she wondered; or did he mistake himself, — would his rendition of those exalted rôles, to which he was so sure he could give new and worthy interpretations, prove only clever unconscious imitations?

With her contradictory ambitions for him, — all at war with her sense of fitness, — she, too, would fain have lifted her eyes to the great heights of the profession. And so the lesser gift was unendurable to her, — that a turn of his head, a lift of his eyebrows, should send ripples of laughter over the house, rising into peals when he chose. When she further reflected on the possible make-up in the rôles of the unknown opera which was presently to be put in rehearsal, — it was rumored already a marvel of melody and grotesqueness, — she looked at him piteously through her infrequent tears, declaring that it would be like death to her if she should see him make himself ridiculous. Surely, she insisted, he must feel sufficiently strong in his position to stipulate that he should have only serious and noble characters like Prince Roderic.

He could think of no rational reply, except that he could not in prudence attempt to dictate to the management as to the cast. With his lifelong habit of looking at such matters from the purely professional standpoint, he could only consider these views of hers absurd.

"It does not seem to me a very fine thing to

sing the rôles of Assad or Lohengrin, as you hope some time to do. But this! This is advancing backward. Yet you think you are ambitious!"

He winced; his color rose; he bent upon her a sparkling eye.

"Do you mean that as a taunt," he demanded, sharply, "because I get on slowly?"

She made no reply; she had turned aside her face; he could see the tears slipping through her fingers.

Mindful as he always was of the dictates of policy, these might not have restrained him now, so intensely was he irritated. But there was something in her attitude so piteous, expressing a grief which was almost desolation, that he experienced a revulsion of feeling; his anger vanished. He took her cold hand in his; he kissed her averted cheek; he attempted to argue the matter. She only turned her head and looked at him. He saw how far too deep for coaxing or reasons was her chagrin, and in sheer futility his words died on his lips.

The recollection of this scene did not offer any inducement to attempt to establish more sympathetic relations as to his professional work. Further considerations added their weight, — not perhaps distinctly acknowledged to himself, but vaguely appreciated. He was beginning to feel that for other reasons the divergence between them was widening. In a matter of importance to them both, the matter of economy, it seemed impossible that they should act in accord. He had, with reluctance and misgivings, broached the subject of his financial condition. At first he was greatly relieved that she received the communication with composure and philosophy, and promised readily that she would spend as little money as possible. It was only by degrees that he learned that economy, like other sciences, is not to be picked up in a day. In order to cut off superfluities it is necessary to recognize them as superfluities. It seemed to him unaccountable that her ideas should be so vague. Expenses which, in his opinion, the merest common sense should have suggested the propriety of curtailing were allowed to continue, while others, which were as plainly necessary, she proposed eliminating. Her lavishness was not so much an expression of self-indulgence as an expression of taste, and this fact added another complication to the puzzle of her attitude. He could not understand why she so often unreasonably and spasmodically indulged her whims, when she was evidently capable of relinquishing them lightly and without regret. The explanation was the simplest and most prosaic possible. To arrange expenditure so judiciously as to reduce self-denial to the minimum is only to be learned through practice. Felicia had had no such practice. To her economy meant deprivation. She could endure, when she happened to remember his injunctions, to give up what she liked; she did not know how to arrange to attain what she most liked.

She had no realization that she was inconsistent and thoughtless; on the contrary, it was evident that she was in good faith disposed to take to herself credit for moderation. She showed him one day, for example, a wrap which she had just bought, and seemed to expect him to be gratified that it cost fifteen dollars less than another which she had preferred. "The one at sixty-five had much more *chic*," she remarked, contemplatively, as she held it up, "but this will have to do."

"That little affair cost fifty dollars!" he exclaimed, aghast. "Surely, Felicia, you don't need so expensive a wrap. Why can't you wear the one you bought last spring until it is cold enough for your cloak?"

"I wore that all the spring, and the trimming on this is much prettier; indeed, it is quite a new idea. I had to get something to wear with my dark silk dresses," she had replied, looking at him with clear, convincing eyes. "A severely plain walking costume isn't always suitable, you know. And fifty dollars is very reasonable for such a dolman as this."

He could not argue the matter. He too was subject to heavy demands from the tyranny of fashion. It was part of his stock in trade to be always exceptionally well dressed and prosperous looking, off as well as on the stage. He could not estimate her needs, but he experienced much irritation when, after a long silence, in which she was evidently thinking deeply, she rose, opened the wardrobe, and placed beside the new wrap the one he had mentioned.

"After all," she said, meditatively, "there is very little difference in style. I wish I had not bought this. It did not occur to me at the time, but I *could* have managed without it."

"You should have considered that earlier, now that you understand our circumstances," he said.

He thought her carelessness culpable; she thought his look and tone of cold reproof unwarrantably severe.

Such episodes did not tend to reëstablish harmony between them. She felt that he did not appreciate the efforts she made to meet his views, and it might have been well if her chagrin because of this had expressed itself in tears and reproaches. He could not gauge her intention; her constraint of manner impressed him as insensibility; it seemed to him that her acquiescence had been merely a matter of form, and that her course argued an extreme indifference to his wishes. This was the more bitter as he had become far more harassed than she supposed, — what involved man ever tells his wife all his affairs! Kennett had said he was afraid of getting into debt, and he was in debt; not very deeply as yet, it is true, but these things are relative. His resources were slight, and under these circumstances a small debt is a large one. The money he had made in that unexpected prosperous summer "season" was already gone, — how, he could hardly say.   He felt that it might be wise policy to go over the whole ground with Felicia, and tell her frankly how he stood; but, with the illogical perversity of the man who is the prey of financial anxiety, he upbraided her severely in his thoughts, because of her indifference to those troubles of his which she did not know, as well as her supposed insensibility to those of which he had told her. He shrank from further talk on the subject, and put it off from day to day.   It appeared to him now that he had made a serious mistake in not securing her hearty coöperation in this matter of economy in the early time of their marriage, when, as he believed, his influence was much stronger than now.

It seemed to him that even mentally she had become strangely at variance with her former self. He remembered the interest she had felt in the drama of life as it was enacted before her; its slightest episode gave her food for thought, for comparisons, conjectures, conclusions.   No human beings were too insignificant to attract from her a certain contemplative attention, as being results of that great experiment, Circumstance, and as carrying within them, however superior, or commonplace, or sordid their environment, the burning fire of regret or aspiration, the ache of disappointment, the bloom of joy or of hope. Now she saw no dramas; she interpreted no more lives.   She had lost her unconsciously semi-philosophic attitude.   If, by chance, seeking to rouse her interest, he directed her attention to some incident denoting character, which she would in that former time have found suggestive, she gave it a perfunctory notice, soon displaced by her own absorbing personal musings. She even seemed antagonistic to those human sympathies. Once she said to him with bitterness that it would have been appropriate, considering how very tiresome it is to see so many strangers, that a plague of Faces should have been sent upon the Egyptians in addition to the plagues of locusts and frogs. He did not fully apprehend the significance of .this development of her character. Strange that he, so thoroughly accustomed to the dramatic world, should not have realized so obvious a matter as the difference between the standpoint, the outlook, of spectator and of actor.

In his augmented anxieties he was denied the relief of irritability, which, bitter though it may be, is in some sort a safety valve. It had long been his creed that serenity is of the first importance to a singer. The habit of self-control stood him in good stead in one sense : he did not have to contend against the exhausting effect upon the nerves of outbreaks of temper. But the strenuous restraint involved also a sense of effort, and he began to suffer from a depression which became more and more paralyzing. Under its influence he saw only the dark side of his affairs, and he vaguely presaged calamity : that his work would become mechanical ; that his voice would lose its magnetism, his acting its spontaneity; that his popularity would wane or his health would fail.

He made the best fight he could against his increasing morbidness, but in those days heavy cares beset him, and he grew very taciturn and thoughtful.

That year the autumn came on early, with long cold rains and leaden clouds which the sun did not penetrate for weeks. The continuous dripping, dripping, of the rain seemed to extinguish by degrees all the fire in Felicia's nature. As a last resort for occupation she had addicted herself to fancy-work, and the endless plying of a crochet or an embroidery needle dulled without soothing her. The work was as spiritless as that of a tread-mill, for she had little interest in the results, which were in truth of doubtful value, — this was another art in which she was not proficient. When she had completed a miraculous tidy or "banner," she would listlessly push it away, reassort her materials, and languidly begin another. Often as not she left these trophies of her skill at the hotel, upon her departure, and the admiring chambermaid regarded them as a godsend.

They continued *habitués* of the first-class hotels. Kennett, however, still casting about for means of cutting down expenses, had fallen into the habit of engaging rooms in the upper stories of those caravansaries which made desirability of location a matter of price. While comfortable, these rooms were not so luxurious as those on the

lower floors, and somehow their elevation added
to their dismalness. When the dense clouds
rested on the cornices of the roofs opposite, and
the street lamps were merely a yellow blur in the
thick-falling rain, and the wind swept around the
corner with a dreary moan, the sense of isolation
was complete. Then Felicia, sitting alone, would
let her hands and party-colored worsteds fall
upon her lap and wonder piteously at the strange
sarcasm of her fate. She would say to herself
bitterly that she had no mother, no sister; her
father had cast her off; her brother hated — no,
scorned her; she had not a friend to whom she
could go for comfort or companionship; her place
in the world was, in her estimation, uncouthly incongruous. Once she had hoped that God would
send her children. Now she told herself that it
would be well if this should never fall to her lot.
Every blessing proved for her a bane. He had
given her beauty, wealth, health, friends, love, —
to what end? To have tears as comrades and
bitter thoughts as her part in life; to be as distinctly alone in this busy, throbbing, eager world
as if she were indeed cast away on a desert island,
in the midst of a lonely sea. So her griefs asserted themselves and took possession of her.
The gas flared, and the rain trickled down the
window-panes, and the wind moaned about the
room perched up so close against the black cloud;
while Kennett, half a dozen squares away, with
a light heart or a heavy, it mattered not which,

splendid and glittering in crimson and stage jewels, posed before the footlights, and sang of love
or revenge, and stabbed himself or his rival, as
circumstances required, with propriety, precision,
and a stage dagger.

About this time she became conscious of a bitter experience, — she became conscious that she
had relinquished a standpoint which once she
had esteemed of worth. The worldly-mindedness
which her father had deplored in her nature had
so far expressed itself in a definite appreciation
of the insignia of worldly values, — environment,
high-breeding, luxury, culture. Now it seemed
to her that she went further than this; she felt
that money was in itself a fine thing; that it was
a first necessity to be rich and highly placed.
Once she would have said it was well to be at
ease in regard to money; that appropriate surroundings, beautiful dress, and associates of elevated social station were the charming incidents
of a fortunate position in life, but to care inordi-
nately for these things was vulgar; they should
be a matter of course if one had them, a matter
of slight consequence if one had them not; they
were accessories. She had arrogated to herself
some credit that she could thus regard the matter.
Once she had been capable of the resolve to look
upon the men and women about her as human
beings, apart from their station; now she disdainfully refused to make such effort; she was conscious only of their solecisms, their professional

and other slang, their Bohemianism, — even their shabbiness of dress in the dishevelment of railway trains and hasty appearances at hotel tables. Contradictorily, this angered her against herself, and she would upbraid herself as a snob. She would ask herself how it was that she, who was of this stratum of society, should ally herself in thought and feeling with the class who would scornfully reject her could they suspect such presumption ; that she, who had no position, should so vividly appreciate the position of fortunate people ; that she, who was a wanderer and homeless, should look with wistful eyes at the showy, spacious city mansions, the big comfortable suburban villas, of magnates like her father and brother, her social superiors, and picture to herself the life encompassed by those imposing and solid walls.

It was a many-faceted emotional experience she was undergoing with such stolidity of demeanor as she could command. Kennett did not apprehend it in its entirety ; he might only realize the phase immediately presented. His deductions, sufficiently bitter and in one sense correct, did not put him fully in possession of her troublous heart and mind. Yet, so far as he could judge, her whole state of feeling was revealed to him one night when, in their progress through the South, they entered the city to which the little town of Blankburg, her former home, was contiguous and tributary. There had been a railway accident, — a freight train in front of them had been wrecked, — and they did not arrive till after midnight. As they drove from the depot to the hotel, her consciousness was impressed with the strong sentiment of place, so indefinable, yet so tyrannous. How was it that even the obscurity of night, which might seem the full expression of nullity, was so distinctly imbued with the flavor of locality! The taste of the soft, bland air as she inhaled it, the drawling intonation of voices on the street, even the sights and sounds common to all railroad termini, were as if inalienably characteristic of this place only among so many similar places, and suggested vividly to her, with inexpressible melancholy and remoteness, another life out of which she seemed to have died.

It chanced that they were detained in the press of vehicles in front of a dwelling which was lighted from garret to cellar, evidently the scene of festivity. During the stoppage the window of their carriage gave a full view of the occupants of another carriage close by. So close were they that every feature of two young girls within it was distinctly visible in the yellow light from the street lamp. They were dressed in fleecy fabrics, with much airy effect of laces and suggestive bloom of flowers. They had gentle, candid eyes and fair hair ; their voices had a soft, suave quality and a distinct drawl, as they spoke to the sleek, dapper young fellows with downy mustaches, and very point-device as to dress, who

were lingering with adieux and last words at the
carriage door. They all laughed appreciatively
at mutual witticisms, and were evidently enjoying
with all the capacity of their natures every moment of the occasion. Other ladies and gentlemen in festal attire were descending the steps;
adieux, and laughter, and the confusion of coach-
men's voices, and conflicting orders, were on the
air; evidently the moment of dispersion had
arrived, although the music of a band was still
audible through the open windows.

Felicia felt acutely that she was looking on
with some of the spirit animating the loafers
about the sidewalk, standing agape as the fine
folks filed down the steps, — a sense of utter
exclusion, of admiration, of distance; and were
these also admixed with envy and bitterness?

The jam was over; the carriages were moving
slowly apart; the eyes of the young girls met hers
with a long, friendly look. She could see that
they were about her own age, and how old she
felt! · Somehow, that moment of fellowship with
them was sweet to her. She glanced back over
her shoulder at them, a half smile on her lips.

"How happy they are!" she said.

"And how frivolous!" added Kennett, as the
buoyant laughter of the callow beaux split the air.

The carriage rolled on into the darkness. The
sound of music and the murmur of voices died
away.

"After all," said Kennett, sharply, "the flesh-
pots of Egypt are precious to you yet!"

She too spoke sharply. " Especially as the supply of manna is rather meagre in my instance," she said.

Tears had rushed to her eyes, but he did not see them. He looked gloomily out of the window at the distant gas jets jeweling the darkness, stretching in two long lines across the bridge, and disappearing on the opposite shore. He could credit her only with the most obvious and primary sentiment implied by her words and manner, — that she realized acutely all she had renounced ; especially, it seemed to him, its more trivial and least worthy values. He did not remember that to her these trivial values had extraneous worth as exponents of a status. He had conceived the idea of exile, in a sense. He could give the character of expatriated prince a professional " reading ; " but the real thing is a development only to be fairly apprehended by actual trial. It is a unique experience, not to be compassed at second hand. Kennett was breathing his native air; he could not fully interpret banishment.

The troupe had gone South from the Eastern cities by way of Washington, and as the route took them from New Orleans northward they experienced rapid climatic changes. It had been something of a trial to Felicia, the previous season, to spend two weeks in Chilounatti. The estrangement from her brother and his children had then been a great grief to her, bitterly as she had resented his opposition to her marriage. Now it was far worse. The realization of their close proximity came upon her sore heart with a new, heavy weight. She would stand at her window, when Kennett had gone to the theatre, looking from her great height, and attempt to single out one roof in the sunshine in the sea of roofs, or one yellow spark in the darkness among the great constellation of yellow gleams. She often had a tyrannous impulse to walk in that direction, with a shrinking hope that she might, unseen, see her brother, or his wife, or the children; then she would recoil from the half-formed intention, in terror lest she should be recognized and ignored. She pictured to herself their routine, — dull, perhaps, but constantly widening since the days when she made a part of it; simple and seemly, with its recognized duties, and appropriate pleasures, and the passing zest of its incidents.

Her experience of life was not such as to suggest the sardonic consolation that matters were no worse, and that her lot had even certain prosaic alleviations. In the long segregation, during those years at Sevier Institute, from the atmosphere of domestic existence, the married state had been presented but slightly to her contemplation. She had speculated vaguely upon that foreign land seen through the haze of preliminary romance, and even her observation of domestic life in John Hamilton's household had failed to dispel certain rose-tinted illusions. It was barely possible, however, that Sophie was conscious that the matrimonial yoke could gain a galling quality in the good-natured tyranny of a headstrong husband. In other happy women, a certain deftness in conciliating might have suggested the idea that this suave influence is of value in a life in which masculine temper, not being repressed in deference to a stringent professional system, may become a distinctly assertive element. It did not occur to Felicia to congratulate herself that her husband regarded her *au grand sérieux,* — not merely as a dear soul, and in some sort humorously; or that he controlled his temper; or that his qualities of mind and heart were not, as in cousin Robert's case, only adjuncts, in fastidious estimation, to personal peculiarities and eccentricities. Unluckily, she too took herself *au grand sérieux;* and for the rest, she had not thought to compare her husband with other men. Perhaps it would have been better if her attitude had not been so lofty. Such a comparison is a prosaic process, but it has uses. She realized no palliations; to her the conditions were intolerable. She was very unhappy.

Her case suggests a puzzle. Have we one set of theories in principle, and another set for practice? Is it our expressed creed that the inmost self, which is made of emotions, principles, sentiments, that complex essence which we may call Soul, should in all right thinking and in all right action rise superior to Circumstance; and, in prosaic truth, is Circumstance lord of Soul?

XIV.

THE monotony of a long November rain, dripping, dripping down the window, was broken at last, and one night the darkness was pervaded by indefinable murmurs, a vague sense of continuous movement, a soft, semi-metallic clicking as of crystal faintly responsive to crystal; and when morning broke the ground was deeply covered with the first snow of the season.

Its advent was most welcome, to judge from the number of sleighs seen early on the streets. Toward noon these were even more frequent, and sleighing parties were rapidly organized, — on the principle, perhaps, of making hay while the sun shines. For so deep a " dry snow " was rare, and in this capricious climate the length of its continuance on the ground was a matter of the wildest conjecture.

On Kennett's return from rehearsal he brought suggestions of festivity. A certain Mr. Foxley, well known in social circles, ambitious to be considered particularly *au fait* in matters pertaining to music and the drama, and well up in worldly affairs in general, had invited the more notable members of the troupe to join him in a sleigh-ride and a subsequent refection, pledging himself to get them back to the theatre in time for the evening performance. Kennett had accepted the invitation, and hurried off before lunch.

Felicia consoled herself bitterly with the reflection that a few lonely hours more or less were of little consequence, in a life made up of gradations of unhappiness.

After her solitary meal, as she stood at her window looking down at the street, she realized the tempting quality of the brilliant clear sunshine and the cheerful aspect of the thoroughfare. She glanced in indecision at the worsteds on the table, debating in her mind the value of fancy-work as a resource, this afternoon, in comparison with a stroll. Finally she put on her hat and wraps, and set out. Depressed as she was, the exhilaration of the air and the vivacity of the scene, the passing groups and swift vehicles, had their tonic effect. Her mood lightened; she looked about with interest; she walked more briskly. The air was balmy, almost warm, although a thaw had not yet set in. The sky was intensely blue. Long shafts of yellow sunshine struck adown the street. The light clouds about the west were slowly growing crimson, and were flecked here and there with brilliant golden flakes. Much of this afternoon radiance, falling in a broad sheet upon the plate-glass windows, was reflected back in dazzling sheen; and as Felicia passed the establishment of a well-known dealer in pictures, she was only indefinitely conscious of something vaguely familiar in the look and attitude of a man who lounged against the nickel-plated railing and gazed at the engravings displayed within.

He turned suddenly, and as his eyes fell upon her he addressed her abruptly, making a somewhat negligent pretense of lifting his hat.

"You going to give me the cut, too?" he asked.

It was her natural kindly impulse to remove any discomfort he might experience because she had not recognized him. It was her grace of breeding that unluckily caused her apology to do this so efficiently and so cordially that Abbott, entirely placated, was moved to stroll along the sidewalk with her.

She found a certain hardship in thus accepting his escort. She had always been fastidious as to her choice of associates. Under no circumstances would she have patiently endured his companionship, — to-day least of all; yet she was sensible of an excessive humiliation that she should experience so intense a panic lest her brother or his wife, or any of her few acquaintances in Chilounatti, should chance to meet her walking with her husband's most intimate friend. He was shabby, — shabbier than usual. His shoes were unblacked, his hat unbrushed. He had been drinking ; his eyes were bloodshot. He was evidently in the state in which a man is both captious and plaintive.

"I'll tell you what it is," he declared, thrusting his hands into his overcoat pockets, — "I 'll tell you what it is : if a man has got no money, he'd better die. Prussic acid don't cost much, and the outlay for a coffin is a permanent investment. He don't have to be paying that every week, like the butcher's bill. There is no place in this world for a poor man. It's a pretty big world, but there's no room in it for the fellow with the empty purse. Look at that chap Foxley, for instance. What in the name of sense would he be without his money? And he knows it. He values himself for nothing but his money. He don't respect anything but money. What does he care for Kennett or Preston, do you suppose? But Preston is one by himself, and what he has he can afford to spend on himself, and wear good clothes, and cut a dash. And Kennett has married rich, and always looks about right. And Hallet is the manager, and makes money. That's all Foxley cares for. He pretends to know something about music. He don't. He's got no use for anything but money. And if a man's got no money he may go hang, for all Mr. Henry Foxley cares."

Felicia understood his pitiful grievance. He had been neglected in the invitation to the afternoon festivity. It was hard for her to bear a part in a conversation like this. She attempted to evolve some commonplace to the effect that we have good authority for the belief that the love of money is the root of all evil. But he interrupted her, evidently valuing more the opportunity to air his woes than her consolation.

"I guess you don't know much about it," he said, sourly. "You 've had nothing but the soft side of life so far, — the roses, and the lilies, and all that sort of thing. It 's easy enough to be contented and smiling when you 've got everything heart can wish. But how do you suppose a man feels when he knows he 's looked down on and sat on by his inferiors? Oh, I tell you a man had better be dead than carry a flat pocket-book!"

He laughed, and scowled, and took out his purse, which was indeed rather flat, tossing it up and down and catching it with deftness as he walked.

"Bless you," he added, "sometimes I am actually minus a nickel for street-car fare."

She wondered if he were ever minus a nickel for a "schooner" of beer; she thought not, judging from the puffy appearance of his eyelids and cheeks, indicative of devotion to that sort of liquid consolation for the woes of life. She scorned herself that her heart should flutter as it did a moment later. She felt her breath come fast; her limbs trembled; her voice was unsteady.

"This is the library," she said, suddenly. "I am going in here." She turned sharply, and began to ascend the stairs. She had not intended to make a visit to the library an incident of the afternoon's excursion; but advancing toward her was one of the solid and stolid old gentlemen she had met at her brother's house. She felt almost sure that he would not remember her. She felt perfectly sure that she could not risk the possibility. To her chagrin, Abbott accompanied her into the building, and as they ascended the stairs together he remarked that he did n't know that strangers could go to this swell library. Apparently he considered the privilege very valuable, and seemed to felicitate himself on the accidental opportunity.

Felicia reflected in increased annoyance that it was more probable she would be recognized by the librarian or some of his assistants, as she had once been an *habitué* of the institution, than by the absent-minded old gentleman she had so anxiously avoided. Had it not come to a strange pass, she asked herself in extreme impatience, that she should skulk about; that she should seek to hide from the people she had once known, as if she had indeed something of which to be ashamed, — as if she merited the contempt that she feared?

She did not go into the reading-room, realizing that it would probably be difficult to induce Abbott to comply with the regulations requiring silence. She threw herself into a seat in an alcove, and Abbott took the place beside her.

"Won't you catch cold here?" he asked. "Shall I close the window?"

The room had been overheated, and several of the windows had been put up, among them the one by which they sat. She replied that she preferred the air, reflecting that perhaps, on account of his voice, he would be alarmed by the possibility of taking cold himself, and leave her. He seemed, however, to have no such fear, as he lounged in his place and resumed his talk. It was much in the same vein as before, and she settled herself to endure it with what fortitude she might. Her absent eyes rested now on the silent, motionless figures, seen through the vistas of open doors, in the reading-room; now on the softly moving officials coming and going; now on the pictures and groups of statuary near at hand; now on the wall of the building across the street. In this building there was a window on a level with the one by which she was sitting, and its sash also was thrown up. Felicia listened mechanically when a few keys were struck on a piano, very audible across the street and through the open windows. There ensued some rapid and showy phrasing, a few resolving chords, the restful, determining effect of a tonic chord, and then a man's voice arose, — a rich, sonorous, impressive voice, under masterly control. In another moment a mezzo-soprano, which she also recognized, full, sweet, and brilliant, took up the complement of the melody, and a duet that was new to her pulsated on the air.

Abbott stopped abruptly in what he was saying, and looked at Felicia in surprise.

"How did Kennett happen to give up the sleigh-ride?" he asked.

In the sharp confusion which suddenly seized upon her she had but one distinct idea, — that she should preserve her self-command. She summoned all her faculties ; she controlled her voice ; she met his inquiring look with a casual, unflinching glance.

"He said something about going," she replied, "but I suppose he changed his mind. I have n't seen him since luncheon."

Abbott accepted the answer. She had played her part so well that he merely turned his eyes speculatively upon the window opposite, and remarked reflectively that he supposed old .Verney — who was the musical director — had decided to substitute that duet, after all, and they had to go to work to get it up at the last minute.

"I suppose so," she said.

"Just like him," rejoined Abbott, sourly ; "changing his mind, and making singers take the risk of a new number without a rehearsal with the orchestra."

In a certain way Felicia was scrupulous. Under ordinary circumstances she would have taken herself to task. She would have asked herself if she, who esteemed herself highly, had by implication told a falsehood to this man whom she esteemed so slightly. In her moral problems the difference in valuation would have been an element of consideration. Certainly she had created a false impression. Now she was only glad that the false impression was so complete.

It was well for her that Abbott, absorbed in his grievance, took no thought of her manner. He did not notice that she offered no observation, and responded rarely and at haphazard to his remarks. She rose to go presently, saying, with a shiver, that she was cold, after all, and that the open windows were making the room very chilly.

"Don't you want to get a book or something?" asked Abbott, in surprise.

No, she said; she did not care for anything to read. She only came up here sometimes to rest when she was out walking.

"Want to hear Kennett practicing his pretty little songs with Mrs. Branner, hey?"

He broke into a disagreeable laugh, wrinkling the corners of his eyes satirically as he bent them upon her. Surely she was becoming well versed in the intricacies of a world of thought and feeling heretofore far enough from her ken. Once it would have seemed strange to contemplate the possibility of meeting and baffling such an adversary as this on his own ground.

"Mrs. Branner is very handsome," she said, easily. "Are those pleasant rooms she has? I have never been to see her here."

He had noticed at the time the cessation of her intercourse with Mrs. Branner, and had explained it to his own satisfaction by the theory that Kennett's wife was too "stuck up" to associate even with the "*bon ton*" of the troupe. Such as himself and his wife, he would say, with his bitter

parade of humility, did n't expect any of her society, but Mrs. Branner ought to be "tony"
enough for her. Men of his peculiar temperament, however, have no past and no future ; his
life had no perspectives, and the whole matter
had slipped from his recollection along with many
episodes, great and small. Thus it was that Felicia's management of a commonplace again effected
the work of a prevarication. He only remembered that there had been an acquaintance, forgot
that it had abruptly ceased, inferred that visits
were often exchanged in other places besides
" here," and relinquished as " no go " his vague
idea of exciting a jealous distrust on Mrs. Branner's account.

" Well, moderately nice rooms," he observed,
diverted to another train of thought. " They
would n't seem anything to you, you know, stopping at all the fine hotels as you do, but they are
pretty well for Mrs. Branner ; and, my Lord !
they 'd be gorgeous to my wife and me."

In his curious aptness in being disagreeable,
which almost amounted to a genius, was a certain
capacity to make the possession of advantages
and superior opportunities a lash for the lucky, —
a sort of lash of two thongs ; for he could lay on
alternately his own deprivations and his friends'
good fortune with such discrimination and acri-
mony that Kennett was often lost in doubt as to
whether these friends would be more comfortable
if less well off themselves, or if Abbott were more

generously endowed with whatever he might esteem desirable.

He had drifted again into the wide current of
worldly differences, — a felicitous subject enough,
requiring little in the way of comment or reply.
Thus Felicia was enabled to give almost her un-
divided mind to the consideration of the strange
thing which had happened. In the very com-
mencement of this episode of her life she had the
strong support of a quality which, in her nature,
took upon itself much of the high function of
principle. To her intense pride of character she
owed it that she was able to see and reason with
a certain degree of fairness and composure.
When she had collected her faculties sufficiently
for consecutive thinking, she asked herself if it
were possible that a man who possessed qualities
which could secure and hold her heart was capable
of trifling with her, deceiving her even in so slight
a matter as this question of an afternoon engagement. Could *her* husband palm off an excuse
upon her in order to conceal the fact that he desired to spend two or three leisure hours this afternoon in the society of another woman? Had
she mistaken him like that? Did he care for her
so little as that? She declared she owed it first
to herself, then to him, to admit such a possibility
only on the most irrefragable testimony; and the
proof in this case was very flimsy. He had probably heard, after he left the hotel, that a new duet
was to be substituted in the opera for a familiar

one, or introduced, and felt compelled to relinquish the sleigh-ride in order to practice it. Nothing, she argued, could be more probable than this.

She had lost much, she said to herself, in worldly position, in opportunity, in peace of soul, but she was sure — and she dwelt on the stipulation with a sort of eager insistence — of her husband's good faith in every emergency, great and small ; and she was sure of herself, — she could not harbor jealousy and suspicion on inadequate grounds. And a moment later she was torn with humiliation, with unspeakable bitterness, that she should thus seek to reassure herself.

The attention she accorded Abbott became more and more perfunctory, but she could not get rid of him until she reached the ladies' entrance of the hotel. He seemed to wish to be asked in, and was disposed to linger at the door and make conversation about small matters. She found it necessary to infuse into her formal " Good-afternoon " something of the spirit of a dismissal, which he accepted rather sulkily, and with another negligent pretense of lifting his hat he slowly dawdled down the sidewalk.

She found her room suffused with the red glow of the sunset, and along the golden shaft which slanted through the half-open blind the yellow motes were drifting and dancing. The sound of a canary bird's shrilling in the next room rose and fell unintermittingly, and the jingle of sleigh-

bells came up from the street. Still in her hat
and wraps, she sank upon a chair, and attempted
to quiet the tumult at her heart, — a tumult
which was a question, a protest, and an intolerable pain. She could only go over the ground
again by exactly the processes she had followed
before. She could only say it was impossible
that her husband could deceive her in any matter,
great or small, that no doubt he would of his own
accord explain, when he should return, the circumstances that had caused the change in his plans.

He did nothing of the sort. The sunlight
faded. Twilight came on, and filled the still
room with vague violet shadows. Presently the
electric light outside cast a lividly white similitude of the window on the dark wall. A star
looked in.

Kennett came at last; not hurriedly, — he
never hurried, — but absorbed and inclined to
silence. And yet, more absorbed, more silent
than usual? — she demanded of herself, holding
desperately to the theory she deemed endurable,
and resolved to make every phase of circumstance
conform to it. He was naturally serious and composed of manner; of late his gravity had increased. As to his making no mention of his
afternoon engagement, she reminded herself,
fighting her growing dismay, that little was ever
said, nowadays, touching his professional life, —
as little as in the early time of their marriage,
when she had persistently kept from herself all

knowledge of its every detail. It was natural that he should not speak of the duet, of the sudden necessity to practice it, of the possibility of its pleasing at the evening performance — when had he spoken of duets, or rehearsals, or performances ? — that he should talk instead, in their usual desultory dinner-time *tête-à-tête*, on any casual subject which might arise, the great cattle convention, for instance, the value of some of the badges worn by the delegates, the large number of people coming in on every train, the gigantic growth of the cattle interest, the immense fortunes sometimes achieved. This subject exhausted, they drifted into a slight discussion of some changes that had been made in the lighting of the dining-room since they were here last, and compared the house with others at which they had sojourned. They even spoke of the weather, and he remarked that the thaw had not yet set in. Their talk was very languid, and was broken by long silences.

After their meal Kennett left her at the elevator, saying that he had more than usual on hand, and was pressed for time.

And so back into her own room, to review word by word all that had been said, to speculate on what had not been said and why he was silent, to reiterate her assurances, to alternately rebel and wince because she found those assurances of less and less avail, — thus she passed the next three hours. Sometimes she felt that it was an inex-

pressible cruelty that she could not have had further speech with him, and saved herself this ordeal
of pain ; she might at least have asked him about
the sleigh-ride, and have judged if he had intentionally misled her. Then she pulled herself up
sharply. Ask her husband in effect if he had
told her a lie? Ah, life was hard at best, but
what an intolerable burden it would be when *that*
should become a possibility !

Again she strung her will to its utmost tension.
She forced herself to believe that she was glad
she had not mentioned the matter. She might
have lost her self-control. She might have made
a scene, with tears and reproaches, and have
earned with her own self-contempt his bitter contempt. She could never forgive herself if she had
asked him a question which would imply even to
herself a moment's doubt of him.

Yet ten minutes after his return from the
theatre she asked this question, — carefully, judi-
cially, coolly. With a sort of impersonal amazement, she heard herself speak the words she had
resolved not to speak. Her will seemed as totally
out of her own control as if it appertained to another entity.

"You did n't tell me about the sleigh-ride,
Hugh," she said.

"I did not go with them," he replied.

It seemed to her that he spoke simply, naturally, without hesitation or reserve. But — he
could act. She knew how well he could act.

"Old Verney flew into a rage this morning," continued Kennett, "because the trio in the finale did not go to suit him, and declared he intended to substitute a duo by Neukomm; it is rather rare and new here. Nobody believed him, but just as I was about to start with Foxley's crowd a messenger came, on a dead run, with the score, and I had to go to Mrs. Branner and get it up."

How simple, how reasonable, how perfectly credible! Her heart was growing light again.

"Was n't it dangerous to attempt it without a rehearsal with the orchestra?" she asked.

"Well, yes, rather risky. It is a difficult, crabbed piece of instrumentation. The flutes came very near getting into the woods several times. The whole thing would have been a fiasco with any soprano I know except Mrs. Branner. She fairly controlled those fools in the orchestra with her eye and her voice. Old Verney himself was scared."

There was a pause. Kennett had risen, and was standing looking down into the fire. He had a sort of retrospective contemplation on his face.

"Intelligence is a wonderful force," he said suddenly, with something like enthusiasm, "and what a voice she has! A lovely voice, — a very rare voice."

He seldom criticised any of his associates; it was still more seldom, actuated perhaps by professional jealousy, perhaps by the high standard' of excellence of the artist, that he accorded praise.

Felicia said nothing. As he glanced down at her, he was struck by something in her face. Not an expression so much as an absence of expression, — a certain blankness; from intense feeling, or lack of feeling? from repression, or emotion, or indifference, or objection? He did not understand it.

"I beg pardon for talking shop," he said, in deference to its possible meaning. "I know you don't like shop."

What was this new torture which beset her, this piercing, sudden pang that had resolved itself into a heavy pain, and would not relax its hold?

It seemed to her now that her terror of this afternoon, that he had willfully deceived her, was a small grief in comparison with what she felt when she remembered how his face had lighted as he spoke of that woman and praised her intelligence and her voice.

This was jealousy. On its indefinite, malevolent power she had speculated vaguely and pitifully as on some far-away calamity, in the nature of things infinitely removed from her lot, — as a pestilence, a fatal tidal-wave, an earthquake in a foreign land, wreaking woe. Vaguely and pitifully, but an infusion of contempt had been admixed in her contemplation of that convulsion of the human soul. And now it was upon her with its terrors, its sense of irremediability, of inevitability, its intolerable pain, its humiliation, its despair.

Being what she was, she could not offer herself explanations, reasons, questions, now. The fact, the one insuperable, undeniable fact, remained, how his face had lighted when he spoke of that woman and of her voice, — a fact seemingly vast enough, predominant enough, to fill a universe; to exclude all other thought, all other care, all other considerations. Yet, vast as it was, there came to be presently room enough in her consciousness, being what she was, for an added realization to slip in, — the realization that they were all three of the operatic world, a shabby world from the standpoint of her previous existence; excluded, set apart from ordinary rules and traditions. It was perhaps meet, she said bitterly to herself, that in this alien world his wife should see his face light up at the name of this woman, — of such a woman!

This was the position in which she was placed, — she who had once been Felicia Hamilton, a cherished daughter, a loved sister, an admired heiress; so fortunately endowed as to be out of the reach of detraction or envy, out of the possibility of slight or supersedure. This was what it had all come to, — this absurd calamity, this most contemptible tragedy.

In the anguish of her wounded love and her writhing pride, in this first bitter experience of the torture of jealousy, she could still see the matter in its worldly aspect.

XV.

In the allotment of complex and delicate forces which constitute an intellectual entity, are the functions of certain faculties capable of only a fixed amount of work, or perhaps of work only in certain directions, precluding activity in other than accustomed channels? For instance, when an appeal was made to Kennett's carefully cultivated artistic sensibilities, they responded readily enough. Given a dramatic situation, elements of rage, despair, love, revenge, remorse, his consciousness was instantly imbued with an adequate realization of those emotions; alert to assume them as a habit; adroit to fix upon them the medium of word, look, and action appropriate for vivid portrayal. In this sense of a keen artistic susceptibility he did not lack imagination. From another point of view he did. In the simple and prosaic machinery of his life off the stage he was not quick to interpret complications of feelings; he was clumsy in the analysis of shades of manner. His experience had been of simple natures, — of soul developments that lay close to the surface, easily accessible.

In these days he misinterpreted Felicia in contradictory ways: sometimes he thought her cold;

sometimes he thought her sullen; sometimes he was vaguely impressed with the idea that she was deeply and secretly unhappy, — a theory he rejected when her composed eyes met his, and her mechanically cheerful voice fell on the air. If it had been on the stage, he might have recognized it as bad acting; as it was, he did not recognize it as feigning at all.

Thus it was that the next morning, as he was about to start for rehearsal, he hesitated at the door, and turned back into the room in uncertainty.

"You don't have fresh air enough, Felicia," he said, abruptly. "I know you dislike dictation, but I think I ought to insist that you should be more in the open air. Keeping so closely in these hot rooms is enough to kill you. You look anything but well to-day."

"I have a headache," she said.

Her heart was thumping heavily; she was fighting with the emotion that strove to express itself in her voice, and so her voice seemed measured and cold.

"You would n't like to walk with me around to the theatre?" he asked, doubtfully, repulsed by her tone. "You need n't go in, you know, unless you choose."

"If you can wait a few moments," she replied, unexpectedly.

He came back into the room, threw himself into an armchair, still wearing his hat and overcoat, and resumed the morning paper.

She said to herself in scorn that it had come to a strange pass that a wife should be shaken, affected, agitated almost beyond control, if her husband condescends to notice that she is pale and asks her to walk with him ; for as she adjusted her wraps her fingers were trembling with haste and eagerness.

An almost perfect physical organization, with its strong and subtle elasticity, its alert susceptibility to external conditions, has also intense endowments of hope and courage. It was strange to her that, under the influence of the sunshine, the air, and the motion, her heavy heart should grow lighter. She felt a sense of reassurance in the few words Kennett spoke ; his very silence was all at once restful, so unstudied and natural did it seem. Her thoughts were slipping the leash of the subject which had held them in thrall. She was half unconsciously noticing the circumstances about her, — the passing people, the vociferous English sparrows, the crisp sound of the crunching snow under foot, the filmy lines of cirrus clouds drawing an almost imperceptible veil over the sky.

After she was seated in the semi-obscurity of the proscenium box, her thoughts went back to the efforts she had made six months before to share her husband's professional life. How hard she had tried ! How completely she had failed ! Was it her fault ? In this unexpected lightening of her mood, she could review the stretch of time since she first sat looking on at a rehearsal with the determination to endure, to withstand, to concede. Was she right then? Was it a mistake to give up that resolve through fear of some ill to her precious ideals? Was not her happiness — and his — of more value than her standards? And if she could have done this, life would have been, perhaps, an easier thing; she would have been a happier woman. She could have taken her environment less tragically. She would have kept her hope, her spirit, her influence. In that case she might have met whatever charm was arrayed against her with conscious effort; with an intention to regain, to retain; with the potent countercharm of her own undismayed individuality. She looked across the stage at Mrs. Branner. She asked herself, Was a wife proposing the possible feasibility of entering the lists against another woman for the prize of her husband's heart, — of summoning the fascination of the coquette against another coquette? Under any circumstances, could she have so developed that that would be possible? Would it be well for her if she could? She said to herself, No. Love is a blessing or a curse, as fate wills; not a bauble to be auctioned off to the highest bidder. Never could she have come to such a pass as to truckle, to scheme, to bribe, to cajole.

Those members of the troupe whom she knew best came into the box, in the course of the rehearsal. Felicia noticed a certain change in their manner since the early days of her marriage, when she first visited the theatre. Then there had been a marked deference, even an evident awe, too sincere to be concealed. But she had become a familiar presence, and then had withdrawn herself. Perhaps something of resentment was expressed in the sort of cavalier assertion she detected in them. Perhaps in her earlier acquaintance she had been too gentle, too conciliatory. She knew much of human nature through intuition, but she had not yet learned that the grace of concession is subject to misinterpretation. She had felt that she condescended in meeting them as on equal ground; they may have received her complaisance as admission of equality. Possibly it elicited in them, not appreciation, but self-aggrandizement; perhaps it had not lifted them, but had placed her on a lower plane in their estimation. *Après vous* is endurable only among social equals.

It may have been this feeling of resentment that influenced Mrs. Branner's manner when she too entered the box, with greetings and welcome. She in especial had been taken up on trial, as it were, in an effort to find her endurable, and dropped, — not an experience to be received patiently by a woman of pronounced vanity. The spark in her eyes, the ring in her voice, were not, however, so definite as to be distinctly discernible to normal sensibilities, but the delicate antennæ of Felicia's instincts, intensely on the alert, apprehended an antagonistic sentiment.

More vivacious than usual was Mrs. Branner; she had a fine color, and after the first few sentences of salutation she talked with fluency and eagerness, with frequent lifting of her eyebrows and gestures of her ungloved hands, — large, soft, white, well-shaped, and delicately tended hands, that expressed some sort of supremacy and strength in their possessor, making merely pretty hands seem weak and ineffective.

A few moments after her entrance the conversation drifted from Felicia, and she found herself excluded, as she had no knowledge of the circumstances of which they spoke. She gathered that Mrs. Branner, having some time before received a small legacy, had invested it injudiciously, and was now disposed to sell out precipitately at a considerable loss. The others expostulated with varying degrees of earnestness. Once Felicia heard her husband quoted in Mrs. Branner's replies. She looked up quickly. Their eyes met. In that moment, replete with meaning, with the subtle forces of recognized and half-recognized emotions and antagonisms, whatever was the unexpressed thought that flashed from one to the other, it induced a sudden silence. The singer hesitated. Then, with a heightened flush and a quick change of expression, — a sort of indefinite lightening of look, — she went on: " Mr. Kennett says," and once, " Hugh thinks I had better sell now and take what I can get when I can get it."

Her lips were smiling, but there was taunt in her eyes. The wife felt herself growing white; her eyes burned as they met that mocking glance. She rose slowly, saying nothing. To control her face; to make no sign which Abbott and Preston and Whitmarsh — all keen men, and alert by training to interpret minutiæ of manner as expressive of feeling — might detect; to remove herself from this plausible, mocking creature, with the smile upon her lips and cruelty in her eyes, — this was her one thought.

Rehearsal was over. The singers on the stage, invested with wraps and hats, lingered in groups, chatting or discussing the morning's work. The members of the orchestra were dispersing. Kennett was entering the box.

"You are ready to go?" he said to Felicia.

"Oh, Mr. Kennett, by the way!" cried Mrs. Branner, suddenly. "*Did* you stop at Cranlett's yesterday afternoon and get my photographs, as you promised? Of *course* you forgot. I *am* so sorry."

He thrust his hand into the breast pocket of his coat as if in sudden recollection.

"Of course I did not forget," he said. "Here they are."

He handed her the package, with a smile and a bow of exaggerated ceremoniousness. In the pleasantry was suggested much of the ease which characterizes two widely different states of feeling, — the superficial friendliness induced by a habit of constant and not disagreeable association, as well as the cordiality resulting from the more serious elements of congeniality.

Mrs. Branner was tall; her eyes were almost on a level with his. She looked straight at him with her own artless, dulcet smile.

"Oh, you dear boy!" she cried, vivaciously. "You never forget anything that *I* ask you."

He looked surprised. He moved away; he laughed constrainedly. As Mrs. Branner opened the package of photographs, he said again to Felicia, "You are ready to go? I am at your command."

"Wait one moment, only one moment," exclaimed Mrs. Branner, "and see my pictures. Oh, how hideous!"

She distributed a number of cabinet photographs among the group, remarking that it was a shame to be so caricatured.

"What are you giving us?" said Abbott, scanning one of them. "It's perfectly dandy. You know you don't think they are hideous. You think they are particularly swell."

"Why didn't you get yourself taken in costume?" objected Preston. "You look like any other blonde woman in a black lace dress."

Felicia made no comment. Kennett observed that the likeness was good.

"I'll forgive you, Mr. Kennett," cried Mrs. Branner, coquettishly, as he was leaving the box, "if you have kept one of them! I don't intend to count them."

She tossed them gayly from one hand to the other.

"That's very good of you," declared Kennett, lightly.

Felicia looked over her shoulder as she went out. She it was who stealthily attempted to count them as they were shuffled by those smooth, shapely hands of Mrs. Branner's. How many did she hold? Preston had one; Whitmarsh held two, which he was comparing, each to each; Abbott had one; and had a dozen been taken, or half a dozen? Had Kennett one in his pocket? And the wife had caught herself trying to count them that she might know! The humiliation of it!

Added to those elements which had made her torture last night there had come to her now an ecstasy of anger that held her dumb. She might not speak lest she break all bounds of self-control.

As she and her husband retraced the way traversed only two hours ago with such different feelings, — with the dawning of hope, the possibility of courage, of endurance, of dispassionate reflection, — Felicia was perceiving vaguely that the most terrible phase of the passion which possessed her was its sharp alternations.

Kennett broke the silence as they neared the hotel.

"Did you notice," he said, with a reminiscent laugh, "how kittenish Mrs. Branner is to-day? Quite flirtatious."

He looked at her with smiling eyes, and she looked at him. Even her lips were white.

"I do not choose to talk about that woman," she said, icily.

He seemed at a loss. His smile faded, and his face wore an expression of surprise.

"Ah, well," he said, with a sudden depression of manner, "if you don't want to talk of her, I am sorry I mentioned her."

It was now Felicia's chief care to preserve her self-command. She looked forward with dread to the afternoon alone with Kennett. With her inflexible sense of what she deemed due to herself, what she felt that life and others owed her, she shrank with inexpressible repugnance from the thought that she might lose her hold upon herself and betray the torment of jealousy which she was enduring. Justifiable or unjustifiable, she felt that nothing could lighten the degradation that she should go through such an experience, and that he should know it.

Chance intervened to spare her the ordeal of an afternoon's *tête-à-tête.* Kennett asked, just after luncheon, if she would not make a call on Abbott's wife, who was ill and " blue."

" He told me he wished you would come. His family live here, you know. You won't mind it if it is a little distasteful to you? They live rather shabbily, I believe. Their expenses are pretty heavy. He says they are as poor as Job's turkey this year."

His tone was apologetic and a trifle anxious. He looked at her in uncertainty.

" It will give me pleasure to go," she replied, gravely. "He did not mention it to me, either to-day or yesterday afternoon. I had a long talk with him yesterday. I am sorry I did not know before that his wife is ill."

Then she said to herself in much bitterness of spirit: " Hugh thinks I am a most consummate snob, and perhaps I am; but it seems to me that I don't object to Mr. Abbott's poverty as to pocket, but as to soul."

She rose, and took from the wardrobe her cloak and bonnet.

" If you will order a carriage," she said, " I will go at once."

He looked at her, with strong impatience in his face. He spoke sharply. He so seldom let go his self-control that that which in another man might have seemed only irritability seemed in him extreme anger.

" Felicia, do you *desire* to be so extravagant?" he asked. " Is it through perversity that you spend money so foolishly? I have remonstrated again and again. You know how I am situated. We can't afford carriages for casual afternoon outings and shopping. The livery bill is already unreasonably high. Why not go in the horse-cars, like other people? "

She returned his look fixedly. There was something in her face, difficult of interpretation, which made him sorry he had spoken so abruptly. Yet she did not seem hurt, and in her expres-

sion came a sort of indulgence; a dawning softness contended with the underlying pain.

"I will go in the horse-cars," she replied, quietly. "I did n't remember the expense of a carriage."

He walked about the room in perturbation.
Apologies did not come very easily to him. He
was used to being in the right. Still he made an
effort.

"I don't intend to be cross," he said, penitently,
"but you seem very thoughtless, and I am worried to death about money."

She made no reply for a moment; then, as she
tied her bonnet-strings under her chin, she gave a
bitter little laugh.

"How happy a human being must be," she
said, "to have for a *bête noire* only — money!"

He accompanied her downstairs, hailed a car,
assisted her into it, and gave the conductor directions where she was to stop and change cars. The
vehicle trundled on drearily through the murky
streets; for the clouded and dense air, permeated
with the thick smoke from the bituminous coal of
many factories, was almost a tangible medium;
though still early in the afternoon, twilight seemed
already close at hand.

A sort of lethargy had succeeded the vividness
of Felicia's emotions; her thoughts dwelt with
the heaviness and inelasticity of a fatigued mind
on the subject which absorbed her. She was only
indefinitely conscious that her feet were cold; that

she shivered in the biting draught, as the door
was opened for the admission or exit of passengers; that the straw in the bottom of the dingy
car was spotted with tobacco juice; that her companions were for the most part old women with
market baskets, and middle-aged men who dif-
fused the odor of garlic as they animatedly con-
versed in guttural tones, with many an "ach"
and "Gott," and the wild gesticulation of unbri-
dled argument.

When the car stopped, and the conductor
opened the door and signified that she had reached
her destination, she descended into a region unfamiliar to her.

"Your car 'll be along torec'ly, lady," he said,
as he gave the driver the signal to proceed.
When he reached the next corner, he suddenly
thumped the rail of the platform with his big
glove in recollection. "Bless the Lord, if I did-
n't put her out on the wrong street!" he exclaimed. "The cars go *down* that street and *up*
the next."

He laughed a little at the thought of her discomfiture, and stopped the car for a fat Irishwo-
man with a basket, — clothes, this time.

Felicia stood for some minutes on the corner,
waiting for a car. Several passed going down,
none going up. So little were sundry practical
phases of life familiar to her that she did not notice that the track was a single one, and that of
necessity no car could go in the direction she

wished to take. The wind whistled around the corner on which she stood. She shivered as it struck her, and finally began to walk up the street, pausing now and then, and looking over her shoulder, in the hope of being overtaken by the big, lumbering vehicle. Her thoughts had been diverted into a new channel, and she became, as she walked, more and more alertly conscious of the unaccustomed phases of life suddenly presented to her view.

It was no doubt a serious misfortune to her that whatever she deemed objectionable angered as well as repelled her. She could not endure with indifference that people should be stupid or ill-natured, boorish, foolish, overdressed or inappropriately dressed; that they should not know what to say, and when and how to say it; that they should not move with ease and have good manners. Her respect for the proprieties, the decorous and seemly in life, had been cultivated until it was almost a religion. With all her mental scope and avidity of imagination, she had not enough of the poetic gift to see anything picturesque in poverty through its repulsiveness. She had known so little of lowly lives and their surroundings that she had slight sympathetic insight or appreciation of their woes, their heroism, their struggles; she saw only the grotesque exterior. To-day she was brought into closer contact with those sorry conditions than she had ever been before. Her own deep absorptions gave way to the contemplation of this unlovely status. Her route took her through one of the humbler retail arteries of the city, which, while respectablé, were in their shabbiness far removed from the well-to-do, fashionable pathways. She saw frowzy, anxious, peevish women; noisy, neglected children; whistling, quarreling boys; coarse-faced men; shabby tenement houses, — all repeated *ad infinitum* along the vistas of the side streets. It was a positive offense to her that the shop windows should be filled with tawdry finery, — absurdly imitating the fashions, — placarded with figures far above their value, but indicative of marvelous cheapness; that forlorn feminine gulls should chaffer over the counters attaining these bargains, or covetously gaze at them from without; that in front of the huckster shops crates of vegetables and coops containing restless live chickens and ducks should impede her way; that she should pass saloons with rough men lounging about. The din was deafening; great wagons laden with iron bars clanged by in continuous succession; the air was now and again pierced with the shrill tones of fruit-venders, the still more dissonant notes of the knife-grinder's bell, and the doleful cry of " Rags! rags! rags! "

By degrees she entered a quieter region. The shops were fewer and dwelling-houses were more numerous. A series of vacant lots, with piles of ashes and tin cans, gave nevertheless a welcome sense of space and air, and in this vicinity she found the address that had been furnished her. It was a small brick dwelling, placed considerably back from the street, and with a ragged front yard. The bell wire was broken, and it was only after a persistent knocking, which left her knuckles sore, that Felicia heard first a shrill voice calling peremptorily, then the sound of steps. They were strange, rattling, thumping, irregular steps, rising above a mingled chorus of loud exclamations, as of fright or anger, and convulsive laughter. After a few moments of fumbling at the bolt the door suddenly flew open, and revealed a tall, slim girl of twelve, wearing a dark calico dress and a white apron; she had a shock of curly brown hair, and was uncertainly -balanced on a pair of roller skates. Two or three younger children, following her, had apparently impeded her progress. All were panting and flushed as if from a recent struggle.

"Mrs. Abbott?" she repeated, in answer to Felicia's inquiry, looking at her with a hard stare, at once curious and indifferent, from under her tousled bangs, and vigorously working her jaws upon an exceedingly obdurate piece of chewing-gum. "Come in," she added, shortly. Then she thrust her head into a door close at hand, and calling out, "Sister Jenny — lady wants to see you!" skated off, eluding the suddenly outstretched hands of her companions, balancing herself with her swaying arms, — she was evidently a novice, — and laughing wildly.

The sordidness, the shabby disarray, deepened Felicia's intense depression, as she stood hesitating in the dusty, unkempt hall, and she was not reassured when Mr. Abbott appeared at the open door. He was in his shirt-sleeves; his waistcoat and trowsers were profusely and freshly wrinkled; his hair was tumbled, and his eyes were bloodshot and swollen. He was plainly just awake, and when, still somewhat dazed, he invited her in, she was sorry she had come. There was so evidently no preparation for the reception of visitors that, as she took the offered chair near the fire, she felt painfully that her call was an intrusion.

The woman in a faded calico wrapper, sitting in an easy-chair, supported by pillows and half enveloped in a blanket, wore on her sharp, thin features so many expressions that it was hard to say which predominated, — melancholy, physical suffering, discontent. The room was sparsely furnished, but in great disorder, the scattered articles giving it an overcrowded appearance.

Mr. Abbott did not have to be awake long to achieve his unreasoning perversity. With that sharp insight of hers, Felicia divined that he was pleased because she had come, and that, contradictory as usual, he resented it as patronage.

"You must take us as you find us," he said. "It's not a very elegant way to live; but every man can't put up at the swell hotels, like Kennett. All of us were not so lucky as to marry heiresses."

He smiled with an air of amiable inadvertence, and reflected that this stroke would cut both Felicia and his wife, who was gazing at the visitor with a face of blank amaze.

Felicia realized that he had spoken to Kennett of the illness in his family in such a way as to make her husband feel that she had been remiss in not coming before, but without the slightest desire that she should come at all. She usually had herself under good control, but now she was cruelly embarrassed. She had colored deeply; her voice faltered as she spoke to the wife. "I am sorry you are ill," she said.

"I never am well," returned Mrs. Abbott. "This is the meanest climate in the world."

"The climate is very changeable," said Felicia, sympathetically.

"Say! you're always putting it on something!" exclaimed Abbott to his wife, with sour jocoseness. "Yesterday 't was because the kids worried your life out."

"Well, they *are* a bother," retorted Mrs. Abbott.

"And none of them are worth the powder and lead 't would take to kill them, are you, Tom?" added Abbott, addressing a stout youngster of three years, who had come in from the back room and planted himself before Felicia, at whom he was gazing with sharp gray eyes. As his father spoke, he turned upon him for a moment his irregular, preternaturally intelligent features; then shaking off the half-caressing, half-teasing paternal hand from his head, which he had crowned with the remnants of an old blonde wig, that gave him an inexpressibly elfish and comical appearance, he again gravely addressed himself to staring at the visitor.

Felicia took the little boy's pudgy hand in hers and asked him his name, to which he vouchsafed no reply; then, as his attention was attracted to her muff, he passed his other hand along the fur, and looked up at her with a dawning smile.

"Are you going to take the rôle of Ludovic," said Felicia, "with your long lovelocks, like your papa?"

"No," said the child, promptly, "he sings ugly; he's mean; I hate him."

Abbott burst out laughing. "That plucky little rascal ain't afraid of man or beast," he declared, pridefully. "Sometimes he is great friends with me. I don't know what ails him to-day."

He rose and went into the other room. "He's got to have his snack," said his wife; "he always eats something when he wakes up. Nelly fixes it for him since I been sick so much."

Through the open door Felicia could see a young woman moving about; there was something vaguely familiar in her appearance, which presently was recognizable as the recollection of the chorus singer whom the manager had mimicked, on the occasion of that first attendance at rehearsal.

"Nelly's my sister," said Mrs. Abbott, who seemed pleased with a new acquaintance, and glad of an opportunity to talk. "She stays with me when the troupe is here, and helps me a deal about my young ones. She's in the chorus now, but she'll get her chance some day. She's quick an' smart, an' she's understudied ever so many parts. I tell her to keep clear of marryin', if she knows what's good for her."

The subdued roar of a gasoline stove was on the air, and presently the aroma of coffee arose, mingled with the odor of the burning gasoline and of broiling meat. The mantelpiece in the adjoining room, seen through the open door, was ornamented with a large assortment of tin tomato and fruit cans and some wooden butter-boats; a section of a table covered with a red lunch-cloth, and holding several plates, cups, and saucers, was also in full view. Soon there was heard the clatter of a knife and fork, above which was the sound of voices in subdued altercation. Suddenly, Abbott, tilted back in his chair, became visible in the doorway.

"Nelly wants me to ask you to have something. Come in, if you think you can stand such snide cooking as hers," he said with a grin, "but I don't promise you much."

Nelly also appeared in the doorway, all trace of her pertness gone, flushed and confused.

"I can bring you something, — you needn't move," she said, diffidently.

There is some merit in Madame Sevier's system, after all, — or perhaps it was only inborn instinct that prompted Felicia. " I have just had dinner," she said, — she realized that Abbott would consider it " frills " if she called the meal luncheon, — " but I should be glad of a cup of coffee."

They were all pleased that she should take it, and Mrs. Abbott was perhaps pleased as well that it should be taken here, and that the dishevelment of the other room was not also fully on exhibition. The coffee was very bad and very badly made, but Felicia drank it heroically; and it is possible that her assertion that she enjoyed it will, on the day of final reckoning, meet with leniency, in view of extenuating circumstances.

Nelly had placed a plate on the floor beside two little girls, who addressed to her not one word, but mechanically and absently devoured their meal, while they did not cease to carry their respective dolls through the various episodes that presented themselves to apparently redundant imaginations. The half-grown sister, still on skates, walked noisily through the room, and seated herself at the table in the inner apartment. The boy climbed up to his chair beside her, and calmly disposed of whatever pleased him, feeding himself unceremoniously with his chubby fingers.

It was evident that this was the usual family life in the queer home. Was it necessarily, she wondered, so forlorn a home? Did it require all their time, and thought, and effort merely to live, to the exclusion of neatness, of beauty, of comfort, of the becoming and appropriate? At any rate, a little gentleness and tender consideration might inhabit it with them, instead of the husband's jeering pleasantries, and the wife's weak complainings, and Nelly's pettish temper, aroused more than once by Abbott's mocking sallies.

Felicia brought the visit to a close as soon as possible, without making merely a duty call. This was, however, the manner in which Abbott chose to regard the incident.

"I'm glad Kennett sent you," he said, as he accompanied her to the front door. "Jenny don't have many pleasures. Why," he broke off, in simulated surprise, looking down the street, "where's your carriage? You came in the street-cars? I should n't suppose you'd condescend to ride in them, like any ordinary person. Is Kennett getting stingy to you? Ah, well, love's young dream is not what it's cracked up to be, is it?" His face was deeply wrinkled with his mocking smile, particularly intense at this moment.

Bearing away this last sarcasm as a sort of flavor, giving a biting character to her other troublous emotions, Felicia left the house and walked up the street. What mistaken impulse controlled her that, in this mood, she should, instead of signaling the car going down-town, turn her face in the direction of her brother's house!

XVI.

FELICIA walked rapidly, as if with definite purpose. By degrees she entered a region that gave evidence of more prosperity and comfort. Still going westward, she came at last into a fashionable neighborhood of showy dwellings, ambitious in architecture and finish, the abodes of the wealthy class of the city.

The quick-coming winter twilight was already at hand. Snow was again falling, sifting delicately down, incidentally as it were. Lights had sprung into many windows; the round dimpled faces of children looked out sometimes. In front of one of the large houses a florist's wagon had drawn up to the curb, giving suggestions of impending festivity. Before a great stone church stood a number of carriages; and presently there was a stir among the expectant groups on the sidewalk, as a bridal party emerged from the arched doorway. And at the next corner was a procession returning from the cemetery: a hearse with sombre plumes, and vehicles containing black-robed figures with chilled, grief-marked faces. The muffled drivers urged their tired horses. Darkness was gathering fast. The still, snow-covered city of the dead lay miles away in the dusk.

She had no sympathies, no reflections, no deductions, half acquiescent, half philosophical; no "*bonheur, malheur, tout passe*," as a mental comment. In certain states of feeling one's own grief dwarfs the universe, annihilates joy and sorrow, save as factors in one's own fate.

She had reached that very desirable corner and the big new double house. She paused suddenly. The window shades had not been drawn, but the gas was lighted. She seemed to have stood thus in front of the building many times, and looked in at the glowing room, so vividly had she imagined the situation. It was all exactly as she had pictured it, — the chandeliers, the paintings, the upholstery. And here was John; just in from dinner, no doubt, for he threw himself into an easy-chair, and caught up the paper with his own inimitable, long, visible, post-prandial sigh. And here was Sophie, sinking into her rocking-chair, with the baby in her arms. The baby — no, another baby. Ah, changes of which she was never apprised came in their family life, from which she was excluded. The old baby, the superseded baby, her namesake, little Felicia, was walking sturdily across the floor in her dainty white dress, with her soft fair hair about her brow, holding out her dimpled hands toward — Oh, why had she come, — why had she come! Suddenly she saw her father, unchanged, save perhaps that his hair had a more silvery gleam. He stooped and took the child in his arms; he kissed the delicate cheek. Did he call her "little daughter"? Did he say in his old, tender, peremptory tone, "Felicia"? Did he never remember another Felicia, whose heart was breaking?

She got back to the hotel as best she could. She was so white, so rigid, with the effort at self-command that, as she met Kennett in the hall, near their room, he looked at her in alarm.

"Has anything happened?" he exclaimed.

She entered the room, and he followed her. Then, as she closed the door, she confronted him with haggard eyes.

"Can I endure it longer?" she cried, wildly. "Can I live like this? Live! Am I living? And yet I am not dead. I could not suffer so if I were dead."

He saw it at last. She was suffering poignantly. He attempted to soothe her.

"Don't try to comfort me!" she said. "Don't tell me it does n't matter. We must face it; we must meet it."

"Now be calm, Felicia," he said, in that reasonable voice of his which could once control her, but which now, in some moods, irritated her beyond endurance. "Tell me what you mean. I promise beforehand to do anything possible that you desire."

She tried to control herself, to subdue her heavy panting and the strong trembling that had seized upon her, to steady her shaking fingers as they convulsively unfastened her wrap and removed her gloves. One of her rings was accidentally drawn off and fell upon the floor. As her husband bent to recover it she stopped him.

"What does it matter!" she cried. "It is only a bauble. But when our happiness, our priceless happiness, slips away from us, you make not the slightest effort to get it back. You never see it. You never stoop for it. You don't even know it has gone. You never miss it."

Her slim fingers tightened on his arm. Her agitation communicated itself to him. There was a responsive tremor in his voice.

"Are you reproaching me?" he asked.

"No, no!" she exclaimed. "I will not reproach you."

Again she put a strong constraint upon herself. She removed her hands from his arms, and crossed the room. She laid aside her wrap and bonnet, and as she came back she stooped, picked up the ring, and placed it on her shaking finger. With marked deliberation of gesture she seated herself, and when she looked up he saw how much her forced calm was costing her; her strength was spent.

"Don't be angry," she said, piteously.

"I am only distressed," he replied, gently.

"I want to be reasonable," she went on, more firmly, "and I will try not to distress you."

"What is it?" he asked, as he seated himself.

"Hugh, it is the life we live. It is a terrible fate to be excluded from everything of value, from all the world, from all appropriate surroundings; cut off, exiled, interdicted, denied, yet tantalized with the sight of it, so close to it! Is there nothing — is there nothing we can do?"

He looked at her in silence.

"It is such a false position," she went on passionately, her meagre stock of calmness already giving way, "that you, with your nature and your talents, should have for your best friend that — that — venomous man! He is your equal in station, and yet he is *not* your equal any more than a drunken tramp; and his wife is not my equal."

"I ought not to have asked you to go there," he said. "Yet what does it matter to us? Why do you care for Abbott's manner? He can be very disagreeable, but he has some good qualities. At any rate, he is nothing to us."

"Oh, facts are — facts! He and his wife are our friends, our circle, — the only circle we have. Think of it! That is the only woman with whom I have exchanged a dozen words since — since Mrs. Morris was so kind and polite, last summer."

She broke into a bitter laugh that ended with a gush of tears. She brushed them away hastily.

"And such a home! so ignoble, so grotesque! such rudeness, such unkindness, such loutish indifference! too stupid to be even unhappiness. It is not the poverty; it is the dreadful, dreadful tone; it is almost disreputable. And there are other homes so different. I see them through the windows as I go along the streets. Homes .where husbands respect their wives, and children

love their parents; where I see serenity, and
security, and tenderness, and veneration. Oh,
Hugh, Hugh, I passed John's, and — oh me —
papa — papa!"

Her voice broke into cries; her figure was
shaken by convulsive sobs; the tears trickled
through her fingers. He could only look at her
miserably, forlornly, helplessly.

By degrees the violence of her emotion ex-
pended itself, and she leaned back in her chair,
holding her handkerchief to her eyes. He took
her other hand, cold and nerveless, in his, but he
said nothing.

"I did not intend to tell you that," she went
on, after a long pause. "I only wanted to tell
you what I was thinking on my way back. I
went over the whole ground. I reasoned it out
calmly. I feel that we must get out of this false
position, away from this odious association with
unendurable people. If we would, we could take
the place we ought to have in the world, — a
solid, valuable place. We would not be rich,
perhaps not more than comfortable; but we
could live, we could be very happy, and very —
very " —

He stared at her in such unfeigned amazement
that she faltered. Was she seriously proposing
that he should relinquish his career because Mr.
Abbott was ill-natured, and lived shabbily, and
had a commonplace family, and because she had
given up, as she had expected to do, the associations of her girlhood?

"It seems to me that you are talking very wildly," he said, with coldness.

"Hear me out, Hugh!" she cried, placing her other hand on his with a firm grasp, and looking at him with earnest eyes. "You would n't mind it after a little. You were satisfied last summer. We were very happy. We could be everything to each other; could we not, Hugh? Once we were. Oh, you know we were once! As it is, I do not share your life. I have none of my own. I merely exist, like a parasite, — a poor, useless, insignificant appendage. And you, — are you not worthy of a better niche than that which Mr. Abbott and Mr. Preston aspire to fill? You could get into something intrinsically valuable. A man of your capacities can do anything."

He marveled that she could be at once so quick and so dense.

"Capacities count for nothing in any line," he said, "without special training. I have had training in only one direction."

She looked at him vaguely. "Is n't there *something?*" she asked.

"If I should give up the stage," he went on, — "the mere idea is preposterous, — how could we live? Do you think it would be well for me to devote my life and talents to giving music lessons because you consider that more genteel?"

"Are you going to be sarcastic to me — *again?*" she cried, with a sharp ring of pain in her voice.

His sense of irritation had been asserting itself over his dismayed surprise. Now it received a check. He resolved that, say what she might, he would speak no words that could rankle as those words which he once spoke in his wrath had rankled.

"My only opportunities lie in the line of music," he continued. "I might do something in the way of composing songs, but in my case that would be too precarious to be considered. A man could not rely for a living on lucky inspirations which would sell. They might not present themselves."

Was this all? Could life hold out to him, with his mind and his character, no other fate than such a meagre uncertainty as writing songs, or the ill-paid drudgery of music lessons, or the opportunity of singing in tights and with a painted face for the well-to-do, well-placed people who held themselves immeasurably his superiors?

She spoke suddenly, with a new firmness.

"You *can* give up the stage," she declared. "We can live perfectly well on my property that my mother's father left me. You remember, when I finally decided to be married, my brother sent a lawyer with settlements for you to sign, and you signed them, and the income is to be put aside for me. Why can't we live on that property? Why need you do anything? How can two people who love each other say about money,

'This is yours,' or 'This is mine'? Will you weigh my happiness against your pride?"

He made no reply, but his face expressed strong displeasure. She broke again into entreaties. Her loss of self-control was rare. With perfect health and strong will, she was intolerant of nerves, and tears, and weakness. The utter relinquishment of her wonted composure added to his difficulties.

"It is not that I am a snob," she persisted. "I don't want you to misunderstand me. I don't value the opinion of rich and great people. I don't care for their money or their approval. I don't care for poverty; that is not what I fear. I don't want a fine house, and carriages, and horses, and *carte blanche* to spend as I choose. Once I thought I did, but I know myself better now. I did myself injustice. That is not what I value."

He looked at her vaguely. "Then what is it you value?" he asked.

"My pride, — my sacred pride."

He said nothing.

"It is stabbed every day, — every hour. My portion in life is humiliation. It is not because the people who have a valuable position think ours an unendurable position; it is because I myself think it unendurable. And so I want to give up this life which offers nothing that is truly of worth, — nothing but the praise of your singing from a foolish public which does not know any-

thing about singing. I want to go to the plantation, and live there unostentatiously, and quietly,
and suitably. Promise me, Hugh. We could
have a home. It would not be fine, but it would
be our own home." She glanced at her little be-
longings, that so vainly simulated that altar before
which every woman's heart prostrates itself, sooner
or later. "We could live for each other there.
We should not need to have those odious misunderstandings as part of our lives. Promise me,
Hugh."

There was a long pause while she sat clasping
his hands, her eloquent eyes on his face.

"The thing is impossible," he said at last,
"even if I were to consent, which nothing would
induce me to do."

"Why is it impossible?"

Again he hesitated. "I prefer not to tell
you."

"But I insist, — I insist."

"I hope you will not force this upon me," he
said, rising and walking in indecision about the
room.

"I do force it. I will know."

"Why, Felicia, you evidently don't understand
that the income of that property would not support us in even the plainest style. The property
is at present utterly unsalable. Much of the
land is heavily wooded ; much of it has been de-
nuded of trees, and is covered with cypress
stumps, and beside is cut up by bayous and is

under water nearly half the year, — it is unfit for cultivation. The rents of the small portion that has been cleared are not enough, I should judge, after the taxes are paid, to do more than compass your dressmaker's bills. The property may have a future, when it is cleared, or when railroads are built and the country is developed, but at present it is unavailable from many points of view. I would not live as you propose if it were possible; as it is not possible, you had better dismiss the idea from consideration."

She looked at him blankly.

"I never was there, but I thought it was a fine plantation. I thought we might go there and live quietly, — as happily as we did last summer."

"It is not a fine plantation. Besides, there is no house on the place except a few negro cabins; and if there were a house we should die of malaria. Neither of us is acclimated to the swamp. And there is practically no income."

A long pause ensued.

"But I have always been called an heiress," she said, piteously.

"You have been called an heiress more on account of your expectations from your father than because of what you actually possess," he replied.

She was bitterly disappointed; in surprise he saw that she was bitterly humiliated. She had sunk in her own estimation.

It was not, perhaps, to his credit that he stood on higher ground in certain regards than she.

He owed it rather to his Bohemian method of living than to any innate nobility, that he cared for money because of what it would buy. While she did not sufficiently prize, in one sense, money, she definitely prized wealth, its subtler as well as its practical values. Her fortune, her consequence, her expensive social training and education, and her position, had all been a part of herself; she had adequately, perhaps unconsciously, appreciated them; she had appreciated herself much because of them.

She lifted her dismayed eyes to his. All at once she held out both hands with an expressive gesture of despair.

"If I am not rich," she said, in a tense, low voice, "what am I? I have no talents, no occupation, no hopes, no friends, no home. And no money as well? I am indeed a poor thing, — a parasite, mean and insignificant."

In some respects hers was the stronger nature; under her influence he saw her sorrows with her eyes. It might have occurred to a different man to suggest that she was, instead of this, a wife who held in trust her husband's happiness as well as her own.

Suddenly she cried out sharply: —

"And we have no choice? You are sure? We must live on this way, in this repulsive atmosphere, — with these men we know, and these — these women? Can't you see that it is killing me? I am dying by inches! I am torn to pieces!

I am broken on the rack! To breathe the same air that she — that they do! To see you — to see you look as you did last night when — when — you spoke of — Oh, what am I saying! And she calls you — calls you ' Hugh '! She dares to call you by your name! And last night — when you spoke of her you looked — you looked — Oh, how can I remember it and live! " She rose and walked wildly about the room, striking her hands frantically together. He sat motionless, staring at her, the amazement in his face canceling all other expressions. For the moment he was possessed by the idea that she had lost her senses. Then there flashed into his mind the thought that there was something deeper than the grievance of their mode of life, — something more bitter than merely external conditions, bitter though he knew they were to her. In his surprise and agitation he had hardly followed what she was saying.

" I — I don't understand you " — he began.

In a moment there came to him a vague realization of her full meaning. He rose and confronted her. " Tell me," he said, catching both her hands in his, and bringing her irregular progress to a stop, — " tell me what it is you mean."

She stood panting, and looking at him with dilated, terrified eyes. For all at once she was afraid of him. That latent ferocity which was so seldom called to his face expressed itself now in the stern eyes, the strong lower jaw brought heavily forward, the set teeth, the intent frown. She shrank away from him. "I don't know what I meant!" she cried, piteously. "It is all folly. I am ill. I am nervous. I don't mean anything!"

"What did you mean by what you said?" he persisted. "Look at me, Felicia. Tell me what you meant."

His deep gray eyes, lit by that unwonted fire, constrained her. In what broken words she could command she told him what had been in her thoughts for the last twenty-four hours. She interrupted herself sometimes by cries and hysterical sobs, and more than once declared wildly that she had been nervous and ill; she had not been herself; she had been frantic with a delusion. In her agitation she did not see that she had taken all the blame to herself; she only saw that he was intensely angry, and her arraignment seemed to her now strangely inadequate.

He heard her through without a word of reply. When she had concluded, he stood motionless a moment; then he threw her hands from him. It might have been a sarcastic commentary upon the habit of mind which had, through years of training, come to be his second nature, that, at this moment of supreme earnestness, the gesture was one suggestive of finished feigning, — the accepted stage expression of renunciation. He caught up his overcoat, tossed it over his arm, and looked about for his hat, still ominously silent.

"Oh, Hugh, Hugh," she cried, catching at his hand, "you are not going without a word to me?"

"Such discussions do no good," he said. His voice was cold, but it trembled; his hands were shaking.

"You are angry with me! You will say nothing — give me no assurance" —

"You want your husband to assure you that he is not a scoundrel? I cannot find words for that."

He opened the door and made his way along the hall, striving to quiet his nerves and master his agitation. He walked downstairs instead of ringing for the elevator. As he passed through the office, the current of his thoughts was sharply altered. His eyes chanced to fall upon the big clock. He took out his watch, and hurriedly compared the two timepieces. There was no mistake.

These complicated domestic discussions require time. It was past eight o'clock.

He encountered a messenger in red-hot haste, as he neared the theatre. When he arrived, he met black looks, and swift reproaches, and eager injunctions. He heeded nothing. He absorbed himself, mind and body, in the feat of changing his clothes in the least possible time, and, without an instant's intermission, he who had so ordered his life that for ten years he had not permitted himself to be hurried, or agitated, or derelict,

who accounted serenity of soul and mastery of the
physique the first elements of artistic excellence,
walked upon the stage into the presence of a large
and critical audience, dazed, panting, breathless,
dinnerless, — prosaic consideration, but of primal
importance to a singer, — his limbs trembling,
his nerves shattered, his memory and his voice
at the mercy of the accidents of the evening.

It seemed as if the long anguish of that performance would never drag to its conclusion.
His previous habit of self-command was as if it
had never existed; it had prepared him for no
such emergency, no such tumult of feeling, as this.
During the waits he struggled frantically for composure. "You 're all right now, dear old boy,"
Abbott said to him again and again; and was
that the voice so often heard in bitter satires, and
in taunts that stung like the lash of a whip?
Venom? It was so gentle and mellifluous, so
fraternal and cordial, that Kennett found himself
relying on it as he had never before relied on any
power outside of his own control. While he was
on the stage, he would without warrant or prece-
dent change his place, that he might feel the
strong support of a friendly proximity; a sympathetic hand laid on his shoulder when it might
be; a few words in an undertone; the glance of
eyes that he had often known as mocking, often
quizzical, but now kind — kind.

This influence helped him to regain in some
degree his tranquillity. To the general public

there was as yet nothing unusual. To those versed in the minutiæ of theatrical matters a hurry was perceptible, an eagerness: a lack of the polish, assurance, control, that usually characterized him. Perhaps his modicum of self-possession came to him a little too early, bringing with it a relaxation of the intense strain that had served him in lieu of his wonted calm equipoise.

In the last scene of the last act he had a solo, through which ran, as an accompaniment, a series of *pianissimo* phrases by a chorus of female voices, — a nice effect and very popular. It occurred at an important moment, — the culmination of the act, and indeed of the whole work. What was the matter with it? Was the orchestra to blame, the chorus? In another instant the fact was evident. The voice of the soloist was not only faulty of intonation, but false, — glaringly, grotesquely false; by turns flat and sharp, completely out of tune. The most unmusical auditor could not fail to notice it; it was an affliction to connoisseurs. The volume and robustness of tone only intensified the discord; the anguish on the singer's face pointed the disaster.

"This is the beginning of the end," said Abbott to Preston, off at the right wing.

"Fee, fo, fi, fum,
I smell the blood of an American man,"

returned Preston, smothering his laugh.

The English tenor also smelt the blood of an American man; he kept, with what decency he might, his elation out of his face, but his eyes were gleaming.

Kennett was calm enough at last; the worst had happened. He dashed aside the icy drops that had started upon his brow; he moved with ease; his voice was itself once more. There was little after this for him to do. He did it smoothly and mechanically enough. As he took his way to his dressing-room, he passed, near one of the wings, the manager, who did not look toward him, and whose face wore a certain absolute neutrality more expressive of intense anger than the most indignant glance.

"Go and get drunk, Kennett," said Abbott, bitterly, — "go and get drunk. That's the only thing for you now."

He made no reply. He composedly changed his clothes, and took his way to the hotel.

He hardly looked at Felicia. In his preoccupation, he did not notice, as he entered the room, that she was coming toward him with outstretched hands, — that her face was eager, her eyes appealing. She stopped abruptly as he spoke.

"Does it never occur to you," he said, crossing his arms on the back of a large easy-chair and leaning on them, "that you undertake a serious responsibility when you use your influence on a man to frustrate his ambition and nullify his talents?"

"What has happened?" she asked, tremulously.

"I made a bad failure to-night, for the first time in my life." After a pause, he added, with a short laugh, "A few more such unnerving scenes as we had this evening, and it will not be a question of *relinquishing* the stage."

He had intended to say much in reproach; he did not relent, but suddenly all the fire of his indignation seemed spent. He was leaning heavily on the chair, his tired eyes on the floor, his listless hands hanging before him.

She took one of them in hers: it lay unresponsive in her clasp for a moment; then he withdrew it.

"I must get into the air!" he exclaimed, abruptly.

He went out without another word.

He walked far that night, — at first irregularly, spasmodically; his heavy feet hardly dragging along in obedience to his languid will; his deadly fatigue a trifle less potent than the torture of restlessness that had taken possession of him. Gradually the reserve force of his splendid physique began to assert itself; his step grew more firm and rapid; he made his way doggedly through the thickly falling snow, which stung cruelly as it fell, for a blizzard was blowing. And from the vague haze of his mental processes consecutive thought came to him, — dreary thinking. He went back over many years of toilsome endeavor and patient purpose. It had been hard to compass his present place; he had expected to go much further; he had felt that the end justified every labor and relinquishment. If it were indeed ungenteel, according to superficial standards, what did that matter? Little points of spurious worldly value were not to be considered. It was his calling, for which he was fitted by the gift of nature and half a lifetime of effort, — a possession of intrinsic value, æsthetically and practically.

And now, what of the result, — what of his future?

That he should retrace lost ground, bitterly won; retrieve his prestige; recapture the favor of the exacting public, easy to offend, hard to propitiate; overcome the eager and insidious disparagement which follows so close upon failure or partial failure, and fatally difficult to confute when the point at issue is anything so intangible as purity of tone, pitch, quality, — this was his immediate future. And for the rest, — his ultimate future? In one brief moment to-night he had been grieved by his wife's grief; his heart had been more cruelly stabbed by the affront of her jealousy. Now these considerations were in the background; already they had taken their place only as an element affecting the development of his ambition and his capacities. So it was that he asked himself what, if hampered by the influence of an unhappy domestic life, was to be his future. It was to enter into a race handicapped; to essay to soar with clipped wings; to drag down to the plane of mechanical, unlighted drudgery the delicate and ethereal achievements of inspiration and talent, and a most artistic school. It was to convert his life's ambitions into a life's failure, — not tame, inconspicuous failure, but public, absolute, ludicrous, pitiable, egregious.

XVII.

One of the distinctive qualities of a woman's grief is its possibility of duality. During Kennett's absence at the theatre, Felicia, reviewing the scene between them, feeling vicariously all that he had felt, the pain, the repulsion, the amazement, the shocked realization, was also acutely conscious that he had not uttered one word of vindication, of denial. She endured for him as well as for herself: the poignancy of his wounded pride and affection as a humiliated and insulted man; her doubts and despair as a wretched and jealous woman.

And when he returned, instead of the reproaches she feared, the reconciliation she hoped, he told her of his failure. That seemed a minor matter until she noted the change in his face. The expressions he had formerly worn were as foreign to it now as if that other happier, more fortunate entity he once was had been the inhabitant of another planet. Sharp care had registered itself in strong, definite lines between his brows and about his mouth; the muscles of his face seemed to have relaxed; it was strangely heavy, inert; beneath his eyes was that indescribable yet unmistakable imprint left by a stupendous nervous shock. His expression was as if he had received a mortal blow.

She heard, with a sort of anguished incredulity, slowly resolving itself into dismayed realization, those bitter words of his which imputed to her the responsibility of his failure. And she had done this thing? Was it through her that this calamity had come upon him?

It was like murder, she said to herself, in her terror and abasement and tumult of anxiety, to interfere with a man's life-work, to obliterate his ambitions, to frustrate his achievement, to be the cause, direct or remote, which brought him to a crisis affecting him like this.

And when he again left her suddenly, declaring that he must get out into the air, she had these thoughts for company. Her grievances, her disappointments, even her doubts of him, were far from her now. Had she done a cruel thing? Was it irreparable? Had the elements which had been at work in her character during the last year — since, in fact, she had, with her eyes open and aware of her peril, dared the conventionalities and married him — been in insidious and deadly conflict with the only possibilities which made life of value to him? She had been afraid of her marriage for her own sake, — what if it had ruined him? She had attempted to conserve all that she deemed of value, — what if she had wrested from him all that he deemed of value? Their ideals were as far asunder as the poles.

Had she arrogated to herself the office of judge as to which should survive?

As to that other responsibility which she had assumed toward this art of his, her thoughts lingered vaguely about the theory which was to him so real a fact, — that the development of certain tendencies in art is a great power in intellectual growth. Had she interfered to rob the world of some subtle, far-reaching possibility of achievement which might have ennobled and sanctified other minds and ambitions in a sordid age, sorely in need of eyes that lift themselves to the stars? The world? Well, with her limitations, it was hardly within her horizon to comprehend what is meant in saying that the world should be robbed. But since it was he who so tensely held his eager ambition to bestow upon it his " great future," she might seek to realize what throes were his in relinquishment, what desolation for love of the thing itself.

And now the woman whose heart ached for him must endure with what fortitude she might the knowledge that in his hour of disaster it was his impulse to escape from her, and be alone with the winter wind and his griefs.

The wind was high. She could see through the window that it was sweeping across the sky vast masses of black clouds that held cavernous depths, defined sometimes by illusive pallid gleams and mysterious swirls and rifts; strange of contour, suggesting the volcanoes and mountains and gigantic remnants of continents that appertain to some burnt-out world, still obeying the great uncomprehended law which set it in motion and sent it revolving through space. The snow had ceased to fall. Once was visible for a moment a dim, veiled moon, with a yellow aureola about it. The chaos of black vapor was bathed in a pale radiance; and suddenly it had vanished, save for fugitive flecks of white light that gleamed a moment longer, then one by one were gone. And ever the strong wind, with its sense of resistless motion, and the inexplicable suggestion of impending calamity which comes with the implacable rising and falling of that mighty voice, swept along the sky, and over the vast plains of the prairies, and through the corridor-like streets of the city.

Kennett came at last, with a heavy tread. There was deadly fatigue in his face. He spoke in a stern voice.

"If you want to ruin me, now is your chance," he said. "It is necessary that I sleep; so only talk to me with excitement, and the game is up."

It is one of the tragic elements of intense feeling that it can make no compact with policy. The faculty to cajole, to palliate, to deplore, to predict good fortune for next week, for to-morrow; assuming the guise of partisanship, to resent calamity as an affront, — this adroit management in arrogating the office and functions of ally is a most potent factor in the art of consolation.

Perhaps it is too much to assert that this is possible only when sympathy is lukewarm, but certainly the heart that feels another's disaster as a supreme calamity prompts few pat phrases. And these same pat phrases, — how welcome, how healing, how indispensable! Kennett, strong as he thought himself, expected them, longed for them, felt that he could not exist without them. He glanced wistfully — his inconsistent bitter words still vibrating on the air — at her face; white it was, and tense. In the utter collapse of his powers, he could only feel indefinitely that it held deep meanings; he could not now comprehend the expression in her eyes, as she lifted them mutely to him.

He sighed heavily as he walked across the room. "I don't want to be waked till the last moment before rehearsal, to-morrow," he said.

For all her alertness of interpretation in the trivial crises of life, she did not understand the feeling underlying his words and his stern, almost cruel tone; she, who had so many tactful devices at command when nothing was at stake, was helpless now, her faculties paralyzed in the realization that a calamity had through her come upon him, and in the thought of his anger. Long after he had fallen into a sleep so profound that he seemed to have passed into the vague border lands that lie between life and death, she still sat motionless, staring with a white face out of the window at the dark, tempestuous night.

striving to definitely realize what had happened in all its relations to his life and to hers.   ·

By degrees the wind sank; the clouds broke slowly apart; stars looked through the rifts, icy and aloof; the pale gibbous moon stole into view, sending long shafts of spectral light into the room.

After all, does much of our woe come about because we have no mental system of appraisement? If we had such a formula, — simplest of processes, — if, for instance, we should definitely consider as a set-off against possible bliss, valued, let us say, at 90, the joy actually in possession, should we not write against it also 90, even 100? In its deep subconsciousness, overswept by the turbulent, superficial emotions of daily life, does the soul distinctly realize its possession, while lighter values drift along lighter currents, or gleam prismatic on the surface? And is it these which, in our careless habit of thought and speech, we call precious?

She had often said to herself in the past year that life was worthless without appropriateness, dignity, embellishment. It had not occurred to her to weigh against these potent forces that strong element which had come to be a part of her very existence, until she feared that its possession was threatened. Now, so distinctly did it assert itself in this vigil of hers that all artificialities were as if annihilated, and the terror of losing her hold upon her husband's heart was even of more moment than the terror of menace to him.

The theory that she was losing her hold upon his heart received, apparently, the next morning, the fatal corroboration of accident. He came back from rehearsal gloomy, absorbed, with no words of greeting for her as he entered. He stood silent before the fire for some moments, then suddenly crossed the room and seated himself at the piano.

She summoned her composure. She made a strong effort to overcome the timidity and anxiety that had taken possession of her. She too crossed the room, and stood beside him. She placed her hand on his shoulder. But her hand was trembling; her face was pale; tears were in her eyes.

He glanced up, with a palpable shrinking. He feared her, she said to herself, — that was evident. He thought she was on the verge of another scene; he deemed her a weak, hysterical, jealous creature, ready for wild criminations and ecstatic reconciliations, which would tear his nerves and exhaust his strength when he most needed the full mastery of his faculties. Yes, it was evident. He feared her.

The thought controlled her. She stood motionless for some moments; then, after a few casual words when she could trust her voice, she turned away. His face expressed relief, — she could not mistake it, — and she could only say to herself again and again that he feared her; he could hardly look at her; he dreaded that she should even speak to him.

As the long day wore on she became an adept in self-torture. She believed that her reproaches and exactions had borne fruit in his indifference, even his aversion. Her sense of justice was paralyzed; she no longer recollected that she too had been severely tried; she only saw the years stretching before her in which she would slip further and further out of his life, and become, indeed, only its unlucky incident, with which it might well have dispensed. In her despair she humbly kept in the background, that she might not in an unguarded moment say something which would agitate him and again place him at a disadvantage.

He was silent and absorbed throughout the afternoon. His manner was evidently unstudied, unintentional; it was not designed as punishment, to mark his displeasure because of that ill-timed outbreak of hers; it was not the luxury of wreaking on another something of his own suffering. He gave her little thought, — that was the simple explanation. With his somewhat blunt perception of actual in contrast with imaginary emotion, he did not compass the tumult of feeling in which she was involved. He considered her not at all; he remembered only his own troubles, that this was a determining crisis in his career.

But as he was about to leave the room for the theatre he turned back suddenly. It was only an impulse. He had noticed nothing of the white despair in her face, so absorbed was he, and so still a presence had she beoome. He took her in his arms and looked into her eyes. His own were still anxious and haggard. His very soul seemed to gaze from them. Under that long, tender look her heart began to beat heavily; the slow tears welled up. He kissed her as he turned away. "Good-by, dear," he said.

It was only an impulse. It was not because he forgave her; he had forgotten that he had something to forgive, — he loved her much. It was not a plea that she should forgive his reproaches last night; these too he had forgotten, — he knew she loved him much.

For her it was a benignant impulse; it gave her back, as it were, to life. The throbbing of her heart and her tumultuous rising tears seemed to pulverize and wash away the heavy, numbing, poignant pain she had endured.

As he opened the door and started out of the room, he turned again and closed it.

"Surely, surely," he said, in the insistent tone of one who would fain constrain what he desires to believe, " my voice *must* be all right now."

He drew himself up, inflated his lungs, and began to sing. The opening phrases of the unlucky solo which had come to grief rose in smooth, mellow resonance, — delicately accurate in pitch and modulation, indescribably rich and effective in quality. The anxiety and intentness on his face faded; he drew a long sigh of relief, looked at her with a half smile, and was gone.

He loved much, too, what he called his art.

"Art" is a word of elastic significations. Just now all its vast systems of science and presentation, its potentialities, its ramifications, its possibilities, were merged into the personation that night of Prince Roderic.

His Highness was her rival, with his powder, and his paint, and his curls; with his attitudinizing and his triumphs of facial expression; with his robust metrical defiances and his languishing love ditties, — he and such as he.

And her only rival?

She was sure of that now, because, she said to herself with conviction, his eyes could not look into hers with truth in them while his heart held a lie. Her doubts had not been very logical; perhaps her reasoning now was as inconsequent, but to her it was certainty, and it sufficed.

As she sat alone that night, she had no prevision of the fate coming so fast. Her reaching thought, that would fain have pierced the future and foreseen its promise, and in anticipating its menaces annulled them, lifted no fold of the veil which hid the next hour. When she roused herself, it was with the realization of an unusual commotion on the street. Then a heavy rattling invaded the air, and the sharp strokes of a gong rang out peremptorily. She drew up the shade, opened the window, and looked out.

A strong wind was blowing; the night was bitterly cold. The stars glinted frostily above the snow-covered roofs. There was a deep red glow against the horizon, extending to the zenith ; it was strong enough to pale the lamps, and cast a roseate light along the façade of the buildings that lined the street. A number of men on the pavement below were hurrying in that direction ; several had stopped, and were speaking excitedly to others.

It was a strange thing for her to do, — she was not consciously alarmed, a fire was such a usual incident, — but, obeying some imperative inward demand, she leaned out of the window and called to them.

" Where is the fire ? " she asked.

They looked up as her silvery tones split the air suddenly. Then the answer floated to her : —

" The Opera House is burning."

For one instant they thought she was about to throw herself from the window, she swayed so violently forward. The next moment she was running along the dimly lighted hall, down the stairs, and out into the street.

Strangely enough, she was not conscious of terror, — she was only unnaturally conscious of the external conditions : that more snow had fallen ; that the pavements were covered ; that the hurrying crowd of excited men was constantly increasing ; that the sullen red glare was intensified ; that another engine, and then a hose carriage, sharply turned a corner as she was about to cross the street. She was caught by strong hands and held in a firm grasp, as she would have dashed in front of the madly plunging horses; the driver's loud, hoarse cries of warning and anger resounded above the unceasing clamor of the gong. Then they had passed, and she wrested her arm from the detaining hands and hurried on. And now in the crowd were gentlemen, with wild eyes and white faces, hatless, their gala attire crushed and torn. And soon she was meeting women as well, frantically agitated, many screaming piteously. And always the crowd was denser, until it was difficult, even with all her faculties preternaturally alert, to edge her way through it. When at last she turned a certain corner, the scene revealed might have been Pandemonium.

From the roof and windows of the great building flames were shooting, — red and deeply orange, sometimes veined with purple gleams, and again shading into amethystine banners that waved fantastically. Where streams of water were thrown, columns of steam and of black smoke ascended, and through them played fiery jets of sparks, that floated high into the air, and traveled far on the wings of the wind. That bitter north wind had already done strange, effective work. Gigantic icicles, growing momently more massive under its arctic influence, hung, glittering and splendid, from every projection on which the streams of water chanced to fall. The firemen were encased in gleaming icy mail that rattled with a loud sound.

As they appeared for an instant within the glassy arches surrounding the windows, or moved about on the roof, the red light, falling upon their sparkling vesture and their ice-covered hair and beards, was reflected back with prismatic gleams. Suddenly, a loud, peremptory command rang out, and a moment later, above the roar of the flames, and the heavy panting of the engines, and the continuous swash of the water, there arose a long, loud, hideous crash, as a portion of the eastern wall gave way.

Felicia was swept with the retreating crowd out of the rain of cinders that drifted downward. Mechanically she dashed the burning fragments from her hair, her hands, her face; then, as she looked up, she stood as if turned to stone.

Many other eyes were fixed on Kennett. Never had drama more effective stage-setting; never had actor more intent audience. In the background, high above the high roofs of the building, rolled dense clouds of black smoke, permeated through and through with upward-drifting sparks, and elusive scarlet and orange plumes of flame that capriciously waved, and shot swiftly out, and vanished, to flare anew on a higher level of the cloud.

When he had sprung suddenly upon the roof, it was as if he had emerged from that chaos of fire and smoke. He stood for a moment gazing about him; then he walked to the edge of the building. At that great height he seemed to move with con-

summate grace and lightness. He was dressed in
the costume he wore in the last act of Prince Roderic. The blue and silver vividly accented his
figure against the darkly rolling clouds. He
stood motionless, looking at the sea of upturned
faces; at the building across the alley; at the
fiery gulf into which the eastern wall had fallen;
at the firemen on the lower roofs of the building,
separated from him by that maelstrom of flames;
at those other flames, each moment fiercer, more
implacable, more assertive, shooting out of the
windows below him; then he looked again at
the mass of human beings on the streets. There
rose to him incoherent murmurs, breaking into
frantic exclamations. The intense terror, inherent in human nature, of that most frightful
fate, death by fire, manifested itself in quick, wild
cries, uttered by men ordinarily sane enough, of
insistence that he should jump. Then in a breath
came counter cries, — " Wait ! " " Wait ! " —
then loud calls for the hook and ladder com-
panies, then assertions that there was no time to
wait; and again desperate injunctions to jump
rose into a loud chorus inexpressibly shattering to
the nerves in its quality of uncontrollable terror.

Presently he turned slowly, and retraced his
steps toward the scuttle. Already the space along
the flat roof was greatly lessened; fire and smoke
were bursting out in many places.

There was a pause of uncertainty and speculation. Would he try to go down the stairs, in the

hope of finding egress through some door or window not yet essayed? Such an effort was manifestly futile.

In another moment it was apparent that his intention was to leap across the alley and reach the opposite building, an achievement barely within the limits of possibility.

He stooped and tightened the straps that bound his light sandals about his feet. Then he placed his hands upon his hips, and ran so swiftly, so lightly, so elastically, that the effect was as if he were miraculously destitute of weight. It was an infinitesimal interval of time before he reached the edge of the roof. He threw his hands in front of him as he leaped and launched himself into mid-air. For one second the swift figure — a gleam of white and blue and silver — was visible in transit across the sheer space between the two buildings; and for that wild instant the realization of the deadly danger was annulled in the exultant sense of the stupendous achievement. How high he was, how light, how strong! Inexorable physical laws, — how airily he waved them away! And did he leap or fly!

In one second more a huge dun-colored cloud of smoke, with its fiery embroidery of sparks, drifted down and hid him from view. There had been tense silence until this instant; now arose a clamor of ejaculations and eager questions. Had he made it? Had he missed it? Had he fallen? And " Ah, God help him! " cried many.

A moment later they saw what had happened.

At the foot of the wall lay a mass of blue and silver, blood-stained and contorted, and a face and figure mutilated past recognition. There was a quiver of unrealized agonies, and then — problems solved? ideals attained in higher fruition than the paltry human mind conceives? values estimated with the clear cognition of the immortals? What strange, wise presence, set free in one tremendous moment, went forth into the darkness!

The events of that night wrought radical changes where Kennett had been closely concerned. Judge Hamilton discovered he held the opinion that a tragedy can dignify even an absurd situation, and that, under the circumstances, it was not unseemly for him to forgive his daughter. He took her home with him shortly, and thus she was restored to the appropriateness, the dignities, the embellishments, of life. These were not of so much worth to her as once they had been.

Does it take the mighty problems of life and death to elucidate the lesser problems of relative values? Can we discriminate fairly as to relative values when vast and complicated forces, extraneous conditions in unnumbered combinations, inherited tendencies, the tyranny of tradition, the tyranny of training, the implacable, exacting human heart, are elements of the problem?

Is the artificial entity which we labor to endow with strong and subtle qualities, which we ambitiously call Character, and which we bestow on our inmost selves, saying, "Soul, this is thy twin. Walk hand in hand through life," — is it, after all, the stronger, more subtle, more uncontrollable, of the two? May it not prove even antagonistic, and in the end destroy its dedicated companion?

This chronicler is no Œdipus to solve these riddles.